SEA KING'S MALICE

AUTHOR: Alex Kammer

DEVELOPERS: Jeff Harkness and Edwin Nagy

PRODUCER: Bill Webb & Zach Glazar

PROJECT MANAGER: Edwin Nagy

EDITOR: Jeff Harkness

PROOFREADERS Kelly Laishes and Pat Laubach

ART DIRECTOR: Casey Christofferson

LAYOUT AND TYPESETTING: Charles A. Wright

COVER ART: Alayna Lemmer-Danner

INTERIOR ART: Julio De Carvahlo, Adrian Landeros, Santa Norvaisaite, Terry Pavlet, Hector Rodriguez, Josh Stewart, Michael Syrigos

FRONT & BACK COVER DESIGN: Charles A. Wright

CARTOGRAPHY: Robert Altbauer and Alyssa Faden

PLAYTESTERS: Huzzah Playtesters! — Andrew Hitchcock, Sean Riley, Eric Engbloom, Royce Thigpen, Josh Hoyt, Ryan Quint, Jason Knutson, John Tetzlaff, Jonathan Robb, Michael Hantsch, Michael Mossbarger, Quinten Sharpe, Walter Jaehnig, Scott Brand, Caleb Brand, Garrett Brand, Mark Greenberg, James Lewis, Dustin Short, Ryan Vondross, Raymond Holding, Keith Hershey Jr., Deana Young, Steve Zap, Michael Jones, Robert C Korb, Robert R Korb, Andrew Armstrong, Milton Oberlechner, Nathan Oberlechner, Jeff Imrie, Albert Ramirez, Kevin Hogan, Scott McKinley, Ryan Simm, Skeeter Green, James Redmon, Curt Gould, Ian McGarty, Corwin Getty

SEA KING'S MALICE STREAMING PLAYTESTERS: Satine Phoenix, Cynthia Marie, Kyle Vogt, Jason Charles Miller, John Ladarola

DEDICATION: This book is dedicated to the amazing fans and backers. You all made it happen!

FROG GOD GAMES

5TH EDITION RULES,
1ST EDITION FEEL

ISBN: 978-1-62283-729-8

Special Thanks

I would like to thank a number of additional people for their invaluable assistance on this book. First of all, thank you to the Frogs for asking me to write it in the first place and especially to Zach, Edwin, and Casey for putting up with so many questions and comments. Thank you to Scott Fitzgerald Grey for the developmental read and all the fantastic input. Thank you to Skeeter Green for the early read and helpful suggestions. Thank you to Steve Marsh for creating the Sahuagin in the late 1970s as well as to Skip Williams for his excellent supplement, The Sea Devils, which was a true inspiration on this project. Next, I have to thank the lovely country of Costa Rica which directly inspired several elements in the book. Finally, I must thank my wife Kelly for her constant support and encouragement and my two kids, Vivian and Jove, for their numerous suggestions of things that should be in the book, two of which were as follows:

Finally, I expressly and fully disclaim any responsibility for any and all aquaphobia, selachophobia, ostraconophobia, thalassophobia, fear of tridents, or general concerns about jellyfish that may result from reading this book.

—Alex Kammer

Table of Contents

Introduction 4
  Using This Book 4
  Running the Adventure 6

Chapter One: Bridgeport 8
  The Festival of Blooms 8
  Meeting Jaxon Brand 10
  Joshua Cree 13
  The Discovery 13

Chapter Two: Departure 15
  Stowaway 16
  Dinner with the Captain 16
  Castaways 18

Chapter Three: The Open Sea 19
  Dragon Turtle 19
  Doldrums 21
  Storm 21
  Adrift Reserch Ship: The Discovery 23
  Mutiny on the Bounty 28

Chapter Four: Crocodile Island 29
  To Shore 34
  Unwitting Allies 37
  Dangerous Flora 37
  The High Moor 38

Pass 38
Captain Garth Blackbeard's Cavern Complex 38
The Sulking Giant 40
Dangerous Pet 41
Mud Slide 42
The Hidden Valley 42
The Craniform 43
The Craniform Colony 46
The Ritual 48
Kzanto's Story 51

Chapter Five: Into The Depths 53
  The Tooth 57
  Conclusion 78

Appendix A: Gazetteer 79
Appendix B: Glossary of Magic Items 81
Appendix C: Nautical Terms 83
Appendix D: Sea King's Malice Bestiary 84
Appendix E: The Ship Registry 117
Player Handouts 120
Player Maps 127
Legal Appendix 142

Introduction

Due north of the Strait of Praeis, on the east coast of the Crescent Sea, lies the bustling anchorage of Bridgeport, a commercial hub serving as the primary port for the Free City of Brookmere, Mose, and many other cities inland. Since the shoreline stretching from the Falconmere Peninsula up to the Worntooth Peaks is either too low and swampy or too high and rocky to support good moorage for the large vessels that ply the Crescent Sea and the Sinnar Ocean, Bridgeport is the closest safe port for large merchant vessels arriving through the Strait of Praeis and is the last safe port before departing the Crescent Sea. These geographical factors bring Bridgeport much in the way of heavy shipping and merchant traffic that the city does its best to support and encourage. The favorable anchorage is the very reason why initial settlers picked this spot. What began a millennium ago as a humble village clinging to the eastern shore of the Crescent Sea, Bridgeport has since slowly grown over the ages to become the bustling seaport that it is today.

Bridgeport is an ancient city. While it is a busy place humming in tune to the harmony of commerce and business, it pays open homage to its past with a robust Oldtown and its slightly archaic or stilted ways. Travelers find Bridgeporters to be unrelentingly friendly and cheerful, but also a bit provincial in dress and manner. Transactions are all done in person, and a deal is not considered a deal until consummated with a handshake all the while maintaining direct eye contact.

Using This Book

To run this adventure, you need the SRD for the fifth edition of the world's most popular roleplaying game. Everything needed is contained therein, but feel free to use the multitude of add-on materials available.

> Text that appears in a box like this is meant to be read aloud or paraphrased for the players when their characters first arrive at a location or under a specific circumstance, as described in the text.

A creature's or NPC's type is shown in **bold** the first time it is mentioned in a given encounter. If there is no footnote, a stat block for that type can be found in the Fifth Edition SRD. Creatures with a footnote can be found in **Appendix D**. Magic items and spells are italicized, and the same goes for them. If there is a footnote, its description is in the appendix; otherwise, it is part of the Fifth Edition SRD.

Naturally, adventuring parties vary in numbers, strength, and style of play. Adjust this adventure to suit the capabilities and play style of your group.

Characters start this adventure as seasoned adventurers of 3rd level. They should already know that the adventuring life is for them and be confident in their abilities. They can be of any conceivable class with any possible background. If you are not campaigning in the Lost Lands, "Bridgeport," a medium-sized coastal town, can be placed in any setting in a semi-tropical region.

The Days of the Week in the Lost Lands

Solsdag	(Day of Solanus – Goddess of the Sun)
Ardsdag	(Day of Arden – God of Life [now a dead god])
Djinsdag	(Day of Da-Jin – God of Death)
Mootsdag	(Day of Market – day of Man's commerce)
Manesdag	(Day of Manes – day of Man's souls)
Sistersdag	(Day of Narrah and Sybil – Goddesses of the Moons)
Thingsdag	(Day of the Heldring assembly [the Thing] – day of Man's government)

"Dag" is the Heldring word for day and reveals the influence of that language upon the common tongue of Westerling. It is often pronounced with the "g" silent, giving it the more traditional "day" pronunciation, though some purists insist on using a hard "g."

The Commonly Used Calendar of the Lost Lands

Common Name	Hyberborean Name	Named For
Oeros	Firstmonth	Oeros, first Imperator of Hyperborea
Foeros	Secondmonth	Foere, House of Overking Macobert
Freyrmond	Thirdmonth	Freyja (Freya), Goddess of Spring
Eostre	Fourthmonth	Eostre (Muir), Goddess of Virtue
Tiwemond	Fifthmonth	Tyr (Thyr), God of Justice
Daan	Sixthmonth	Daan, Hero of Akados
Haymond	Seventhmonth	Haymaking month
Hummidos	Eighthmonth	Battle of Hummaemidon for Hyperborean independence
Mithrond	Ninthmonth	Mithras, God of War, to mark the final month of military campaigns
Blótmond	Tenthmonth	Annual sacrifices (blóts) of the Heldring
Winterfyll	Eleventhmonth	First full moon of winter
Yule	Twelfthmonth	The Feast Month, Yuletide and Hogmanay

Each month has 30 days (consisting of four seven-day weeks, plus two festival days in the month) and there are an additional four High Holy Days, one on each equinox and solstice, for a total of 364 days in a year.

The Green Realm
The Great Akadonian Forest
Cresent Sea
Syldryll Vale
Sydryl River
South Pacstel Woodes
Verdent Plain
Northern Tongue
Kothan
Linn Syldryll
Emerald Mountains
(Green Warenith)
Satanna Vierta
Gold Wine River
Solis Alvaris
Linn Merku
Forest Coast
Bitter Island
Tandril Island
Trinidar
Kamba Mountains
Foot
Ilber Nole
Chindelanga Mountains
Ajiak Telek
Linn Yark
The High Barrens
Treachery Bay
Mud Coast
Talanos Peninsula
Braku
Barren Coast
Vilik Strad
Port Ruin
Kamis
Borsa
Dragon's Heights
Lost Token
East Token
The Mouth of Akados
Narilis Isle
Mandible Isle
Falconere Peninsula
Tremont Bay
Crownsreach
Strait of Procis
Southern Reach
Stoneborough
Ravenscar
Broken Mountains
Hornik Forest
Kindler's Bell
Bridgeport
Bottomborough
Oakfall
Overlook
Loaquater
Splind Vale
Corumcorth Reach
Eldevere Forest
Neumine
The Dale
Niad River
The Long County
Briarwitch
Free City of Brookmere
Sylvabus
Cailin Lee
Tourne
Eben
Tarry
City-State of Castorhage
The Brine
Meath
Kingdom of Vast
Seilo Ford
Streech Ferry
Plains of Eauxe
Poinetre
Principality of Oldavai
Mose
Westfort
Genev Gap
The Grimm Fortress
Blackrock Mountains
Barony of Baile
Dundland
Mains River
Arbo
Novgorod
Turin's Crossing
Freevak Wood
Darkhollow
Manwood Forest
Corvusroost
Ems
Gilded River
Denz
Cloud Hills
The Mean Shore
Barrier Islands
OCEAN

Running the Adventure

If you are a player, stop reading! The rest of this adventure is for GMs only!

Wherever the characters are from and by whatever means they arrived, Bridgeport proper is where this adventure starts. The tale begins during the Festival of Blooms, Bridgeport's annual spring festival.

> "And on that moon when the tides glisten with blood, the Hunger will awaken and woe to the world of the sun. Their sands, mountains, and green lands will all drown in their own blood."
> — *Translated excerpt from a sahuagin shell carving "liturgy of the tides."*

And as adventure hooks go, any that you prefer are fine, but most likely these adventurers will be looking for work. And they find it in the person of Jaxon Brand.

Adventure Hooks

Hungry for Work: At 3rd level, the characters are looking for real adventuring work. While asking around virtually anywhere in town nets the characters the usual sort of advice — that many of the farms are hiring farmhands and that the Galley's Hands (the Rowers and Seafarers Guild) are always looking for some stout oarsmen — they quickly learn of a rumor around town that Jaxon Brand of Zephyr Assimilated is looking to put together an expedition to search for a lost ship.

A Better Offer: The characters are hired as short-term bodyguards for Daniel Kruse, a merchant from Mose who has come to Bridgeport to explore a persisting contract or relationship with one of the major mercantile houses. After arriving in Bridgeport, Kruse sends the characters to inquire of Jaxon Brand of Zephyr Assimilated concerning his potential interest in an introduction to Kruse. The characters find Jaxon greatly distracted. As they endeavor to explain why they are there, Jaxon interrupts them and pointedly offers to hire them, as he is "looking for capable adventurers" and will pay double whatever they are getting paid currently.

After a meeting with Jaxon Brand, the owner of Zephyr Assimilated, a well-known and respected trading company, the characters learn that Mr. Brand has a serious problem. His daughter, Elisa Brand, the best sea captain of his fleet, is missing along with her ship. Captain Elisa Brand and her ship are several months overdue, and Jaxon Brand has no certain information about her or her ship's whereabouts.

Not content to sit and wait any longer for news concerning his missing daughter and ship, Jaxon Brand informs the characters that he is mounting an expedition to search for them. In just a few days, the *Z.A. Bounty* under the command of Jaxon's oldest son, Timothy, will depart heading east toward Warsley, the city of last contact with Elisa and the *Z.A. Zephyr*. Master Brand very much hopes that the characters join that expedition and help find his daughter.

After learning what they can about the fate of the *Zephyr* from sources in and around Bridgeport, the characters depart on the *Bounty*, headed east toward Warsley.

Adventure Timeline

Winterfyll (November) 15th: The *Zephyr* (Captain Elisa Brand) departs from Bridgeport.

Yule (December) 8th: The *Zephyr* arrives at Warsley.

Yule (December) 11th: The *Zephyr* departs from Warsley.

Oeros (January) 17th: The *Zephyr* experiences major damage to the rudder that necessitates extensive on-water repairs.

Late Foeros (February): Jaxon Brand becomes concerned about the lack of news concerning the *Zephyr*.

Freyrmond (March): Bridgeport's Festival of Blooms occurs, and characters are retained by Jaxon Brand; shortly thereafter, the *Bounty*, bearing the characters, departs Bridgeport.

Freyrmond (March) 16th: The *Zephyr* encounters the *Discovery* on the open water of the Sinnar Ocean.

Eostre (April) 4th: The *Zephyr* arrives at Crocodile Island; the characters, on board the *Bounty*, arrive at Crocodile Island some weeks later.

Character Advancement

This adventure is designed for four to six characters starting at 3rd level and takes them to 10th level. This adventure uses a story-based character advancement mechanic. Of course, if you want to tally experience points to advance characters, have at it. Please note though that the encounters in this adventure have not been weighted with exact experience point math in mind. So if you find that your party has gotten to a "level up" signpost and the characters do not have enough experience points to level up, consider awarding some additional experience points based on story accomplishments so that the characters are capable of facing the challenges of that section.

Characters are likely to attain 6th level after surviving the **Open Sea** section and before arriving at Crocodile Island. They should attain 8th level by the end of the **Crocodile Island** section. Finally, the characters should be at least 9th level before confronting King Bachzarisaa the Insatiable in his lair deep in the sahuagin city of Tzar'Grandula.

Cast of Characters

- **Baron Goron Ulien**, the Baron of Bridgeport
- **Jaxon Brand**, owner of Zephyr Assimilated
- **Elisa Brand**, Jaxon Brand's eldest child, Captain of the *Zephyr*
- **Bram Zander**, owner of Judicious Passage out of Brookmere
- **Joshua Cree**, former sailor who unexpectedly has information regarding Elisa Brand
- **Timothy Brand**, Jaxon Brand's eldest son, Captain of the *Bounty*
- **Jace Westhoff**, first mate on the *Bounty*
- **Gar Turnbull**, stowaway on the *Bounty*, a doppelganger
- **Jasper Cronks**, sea captain who tells Elisa Brand about Crocodile Island
- **Zeb Quindal (Deceased)**, captain of the *Discovery*
- **Halen Drand** and **Sylros Clearsky**, surviving crewmembers of the *Discovery*
- **Jyrcyx**, **Zogren**, and **Tati**, craniform priestesses
- **Kzanto**, craniform youth who is an escaped slave of the sahuagin
- **Petruska**, prisoner in the Tooth in the sahuagin city of Tzar'Grandula
- **Gamaa the Brackish**, a sequana genie emissary from The Palace of Prisms, the seat of rulership for the Great Durbar of the Sequana from the Elemental Plane of Water
- **Enzu**, high priestess of Dajobas, and wife and consort of King Bachzarisaa
- **King Bachzarisaa the Insatiable**, king of the sahuagin city of Tzar'Grandula (City of Feasts), located to the south of Crocodile Island

Once on the open water, the characters, now sailors on the *Bounty*, brave a number of encounters, the most important being locating the *Discovery*, an adrift research ship out of Brookmere. On this ship, for the first time, the party confront the terrible sahuagin and unearth some important clues about the *Zephyr* and Elisa Brand that point the characters to a small, uncharted island.

After arriving at Crocodile Island, the characters find the missing *Zephyr* at anchor and completely empty of life. They discover signs of a combat on the ship that likely involved sahuagin but find no sign of the missing crew or Captain Elisa Brand. However, they do find that Elisa mounted an away team to explore the island.

Having no other leads at this point, the characters go ashore and find the trail of the *Zephyr's* away team. The party has a series of encounters on this dangerous and tropical island while following Elisa Brand's trail, including an odd talk with a volcano giant and the possibility of locating a now long-dead marooned sailor's lair.

> "Anon comes the Slaughter! The Red Feast signals the gorging on the infidel! The consumed apostates will fail to sate the Hunger and time itself will be devoured!"
> — ***Translated ravings from a sahuagin priestess***

The characters eventually discover a saltwater lagoon nestled in a valley in the middle of the island. They learn that a band of sahuagin ambushed the *Zephyr's* away team and that the few survivors, likely including Elisa Brand, were taken under the waves as prisoners. Taking prisoners is an unusual practice for the sahuagin.

At this point, the characters meet a peculiar group of humanoids: the craniform. These friendly but very strange creatures welcome the characters as saviors from the terrible sahuagin and offer help in the form of information and a ritual that allows the characters to safely and comfortably exist underwater.

After successfully completing the bizarre ritual, the characters are provided a guide to lead them to Tzar'Grandula, the City of Feasts, where the cruel King Bachzarisaa the Insatiable reigns and where the captured crew of the *Zephyr* were taken. The characters may learn that Elisa Brand and members of her crew were taken alive in order to be sacrificed in a profane ritual to Dojabas, The Devourer, the cruel shark god of the sahuagin.

Fortunately, the characters' guide shows the party a secret way into the heart of the dangerous sahuagin city and directly to the king's "palace" — a long dormant submerged caldera, the most likely location where Elisa Brand and the survivors from the *Zephyr* were taken.

After braving a series of difficult encounters in the sahuagin stronghold, the characters may get a chance to confront the terrible sahuagin king and his evil high priestess consort and free the imprisoned sea captain.

CHAPTER ONE: BRIDGEPORT

The characters arrive in Bridgeport as the annual spring festival is in full swing. It takes place each year in Freyrmond (March). The Festival of Blooms celebrates the equinox (Imbolg) and the sowing of new crops so vital to the area.

THE FESTIVAL OF BLOOMS

When you are ready to start this encounter, please read or paraphrase the following to the players:

You find yourselves in the bustling seaport of Bridgeport on a warm and sunny early spring day, Freyrmond 20th, 3517 I.R. It is midafternoon, and the crisp smell of sea air combined with the aromas from a variety of outdoor food vendors make a heady mix as you move toward the busiest part of town — the Trademoot. This small coastal city is astir with excitement because Bridgeport's annual spring festival, the Festival of Blooms, is underway.

The local citizenry seems to be wearing their best and brightest, if a bit rustic, attire, and most buildings are festooned with streamers of bright paper and chains of radiant and fragrant floral blossoms.

As you approach the Trademoot, the town's central open-air market, the sense of excitement only increases.

You hear many different minstrels vying for attention in the din among a cacophony of celebratory sounds and voices. However, as you take all of this in, one clear and penetrating voice rises above the tumult:

"Step forward my lords and ladies! Come forward and compete in contests of strength, grace, and wit to determine who will be this year's Master of the Blooms! Don't be shy! Any and all are welcome to give it a go! Step up and try to cover yourself in endless glory!"

As you move forward to take a closer look, the crowd parts to reveal an open space where a series of contests have been set up. The barker whose voice you so clearly heard is owned by a middle-aged man bearing an outlandish top hat and a bright blue sash over his dark topcoat. Seeming to catch your eye, he waves you forward to take part in the contests.

The purpose of these contests (beyond determining the winner of the title of Master of the Blooms!) is to allow the characters to show what they can do as well as to see what their soon-to-be party members are capable of.

At this point, explain the nature of each contest and then run each of them. The participant with the most contest wins is the overall winner.

One of the enduring traditions of the Festival of Blooms is a series of friendly contests that are scored to determine a winner who is then crowned the "Master of the Blooms." Contests include mock fighting (strength), lifting (constitution), juggling (dexterity), archery (dexterity), oration (charisma), and history (intelligence).

RULES

Each contest is resolved by d20 rolls. Each participant adds at least their base ability bonus to the called for skill roll. Further, allow characters to use a relevant proficiency bonus whenever possible. In addition, you might want to give the players advantage when their characters have a background that ties into the contest. The characters should shine in these contests among normal citizens, so allow any reasonable bonuses to apply. There can be two or more winners of any contest.

Other townspeople (half the total number of characters) should participate in the contest along with the characters. Use a standard +2 modifier to all the NPC contestants' rolls. The contests that call for judging are decided by a variety of local potentates, including guild leaders and well-to-do farmers.

To track the outcome of each contest, award 5 points to the participant who gets first place, 3 points for second, and 1 point for third. Then simply total each participants' points; the contestant with the most overall points wins and is crowned, "Master of Blooms."

Mock Fighting (Strength): The mock fighting contests involve squaring off with a padded baton against a single opponent in a 10-foot-diameter circle. After the "go" signal, the first participant knocked out of the circle loses. It is a double elimination tournament. This means each participant is not out of the tournament until they have been bested two times. The initial winner takes on all comers until they either beat everyone or are themselves beaten. That initial winner can try again, as can each participant who has been bested once. Each participant in this contest gets one try to knock off the winner of the previous match and then defend the circle. The winner is the contestant that remains with only one or zero losses in the circle. Second place is awarded to whoever had the second most wins before suffering their second loss, and so on.

Lifting Contest (Constitution): The lifting contest involves lifting a series of heavy casks off the ground and stacking them onto a sturdy platform while being timed by a one-minute glass. All entrants participate at once. The participant who stacks the most casks (the die roll number plus constitution bonus) on the platform in one minute wins.

Juggling Contest (Dexterity): The juggling contest requires all entrants to participate at once. Each entrant starts with one papaya and starts tossing it up and down. Each contestant must succeed on a DC 13 Dexterity check to keep from dropping the fruit. Each participant is then thrown another papaya that the participant must catch and incorporate into the juggling attempt. The same DC check needs to be made to keep from dropping a papaya, with the check being repeated each time a new piece of fruit is added. A participant who drops a piece of fruit is out. When only one entrant remains, he or she is the winner. The top three places are determined by how many total papayas the contestants were able to juggle.

Archery Contest (Dexterity): The archery contest involves each participant shooting arrows from a pedestrian shortbow at a horsehair target 25 yards away. Each entrant gets 5 arrows. The participant with the most bullseyes wins. The bullseye is effectively AC 17. As with the other contests, the top three score points.

Oration Contest (Charisma): The oration contest is a judged event where each participant recites a poem, story, joke, limerick, or just about anything else. The entrants whose oration is judged to be the best wins. For this contest, the contestant with the highest check result wins. Performance, persuasion, or even intimidation might be used effectively.

History Contest (Intelligence): The history contest is another judged event. Each entrant recites what they believe to be the most meaningful historical fact. The participant whose historical recitation is judged to be the best wins. This contest works exactly like the oration contest above. This is a good contest to allow some flexibility with proficiency use. Arcana, Medicine, or even Animal Handling could

all allow somebody to know a meaningful bit of history. A Charisma (Deception) check might be in order for a character that wants to bluff.

IMPORTANT: For the history portion of the contest, one of the participants, a retired sailor named Joshua Cree (**commoner**), steps forward and states, "I was a sailor on the research vessel *Discovery* out of Brookmere. Among the marvels we experienced, our captain and ships' officers met with emissaries from the sea elf kingdom of Azurelume." What, if anything, the characters do with this information remains to be seen.

This exposition by Joshua Cree is an important story hook. Should the characters talk to Cree following the contest, he reveals that he became violently ill while serving as a deckhand on the *Discovery* and that while healing from the ship's cleric made him feel temporarily better, it did not last.

So as a mutual decision between the *Discovery's* captain, Zeb Quindal, and himself, he was put on another passing ship, the *Spirit* out of Tindledusk, and returned to port. If pressed on the nature of his illness, he somewhat embarrassedly admits that he was likely suffering from some sort of stress-induced illness ("I was feeling all nervy!") while serving on the ship and that once ashore, he has felt much better. He is now retired from sailing for good as a result.

Finally, Joshua Cree relates that after reaching the port city of Tindledusk, he made his way overland back home to Bridgeport and has taken on work as a farmhand on a pineapple plantation owned by Orth Grisk. The farm is located a bit south and east of Bridgeport. He is in town just for the afternoon to take part in the contest and is then returning to the plantation. He has nothing further of interest to tell the party at this point.

Once the contests are over and a winner is determined, please read or paraphrase the following to the party:

As soon as the last contest concludes, the same ostentatious gentleman who started the event moves over to confer with the judges. After a few moments of huddled consultation, he breaks from this group and shouts:

"Ladies and gentlemen. I am very pleased to announce that the winner of this year's Master of the Blooms contest is ..."

With that, he strides over to the winner and places a laurel crown of beautiful flowers on the winner's head and then continues, "Please join me in congratulating our most worthwhile champion."

After the applause subsides, the same gentleman says, "Now that we have a Master of the Blooms, it is my honor to order, as baron of Bridgeport, that a keg of chilled Bridgeport Reserve be brought forward so that all of our esteemed participants may slake their thirst following their arduous labors!"

And just like that, two porters rush forward bearing a keg and place it on the same stage that was used for one of the strength contests. They work quickly with a mallet and spigot to tap the keg. As soon as the golden liquid contained therein begins to pour, they start filling up wooden tankards to pass out to all the contest participants.

After being handed a tankard and taking a sip, you find the cold beverage to be some sort of citrus ale that is aromatic, strong, and wonderfully refreshing.

The characters can then talk amongst themselves, regaling each other in explanations of near contest defeats and retelling their own contest victories, or do anything else that they want to do at the festival.

As the characters mill around after the contest, Baron Goron Ulien (**noble** with AC 11), the emcee of the contest, approaches the party and says, "You lot look like you can handle yourselves better than most. If you are looking for work, Jaxon Brand, a merchant captain here in town, is putting together an expedition. If this sort of thing is of interest to you, head out to the Brand Estate, which is just out of town to the east. Feel free to use my name and tell them that I sent you."

As the afternoon wears to evening, the characters should resolve what to do next, which could include finding lodging or trying to find work. However, in the very likely event that one of the characters is crowned Master of Blooms, it is expected that this individual mingles at the festival and takes part in further celebrations throughout the evening in Bridgeport's various inns and taverns.

Meeting Jaxon Brand

As the characters explore town, they find Bridgeport to be a prosperous and friendly city, especially with the current festival as its backdrop. Inquiries made anywhere about work yields the universal answers that that the Galley's Hands guild is always looking for strong rowers and that field hand help in many of the surrounding farms is always in short supply. However, with a successful DC 10 Charisma (Persuasion) check, any inquiry about work beyond simple menial labor — after a thoughtful moment of reflection on the part of the NPC — results in a statement to the effect of "I heard that Jaxon Brand is putting some sort of expedition together, and he is paying top coin to those who sign on."

Any Bridgeporter who is asked volunteers that Jaxon Brand is head of the Brand family, which owns Zephyr Assimilated, the largest mercantile shipping company in Bridgeport. Further, a character who asks where to find Jaxon Brand is directed to the Brand estate that is located directly east just out of town, and told to look for the large white manse with the Zephyr Assimilated sign (a stylized sloop riding a gust of wind) at the beginning of the approach to the manse.

The characters can easily find their way to Jaxon Brand's estate, which is just a few minutes' walk outside of Bridgeport proper. If this visit happens during the day, they find a large ornate archway that features open iron gates (closed after dark) that lead up to a magnolia tree-lined path of pea gravel wide enough for two carriages or carts to pass. On the very top of the arch is a large sign bearing the Zephyr Assimilated logo. Beneath the sign in raised letters painted with gold are the words "Estate Brand."

The characters see the manse before them as they walk up the approach. The mansion is a sprawling affair, two stories tall, with a broad, open-air veranda on the front. As the party approaches the front steps, a smiling liveried servant moves to greet them. This servant (a middle-aged man with a pale complexion) cheerfully and simply asks, "Good day. What brings you to the Brand Estate?" Any answer relating to the expedition that Jaxon Brand is assembling combined with a successful DC 13 Charisma (Persuasion) check (made with advantage if Baron Ulien's name is used) results in the following response: "Please come with me then. I will take you to Mr. Brand forthwith."

Failed checks or inquiries made of other subjects result in a courteous, "Please wait here," followed by a 15-minute wait while that servant goes off to find Martin Brand (**noble**), Jaxon's younger son, who handles many of the day-to-day affairs of the estate. When Martin arrives (a young man; short, dark hair; wearing a creased and well-worn vest that looks like it was slept in), he is mildly annoyed and put out by the interruption. A DC 15 Charisma (Persuasion) check improves his mood and makes him more tractable with respect to getting questions answered and finding out about the expedition. He leads those asking about the expedition to his father. In this case, modify the following text to

apply to Martin rather than the servant leading the party to meet with Jaxon Brand.

If the characters are escorted to meet Jaxon Brand, please read or paraphrase the following:

The liveried servant you are following takes you into and through the house, passing a variety of well-appointed rooms. The tour takes you seemingly all the way to the back of the house and into an open-air study that faces an elaborate and well-sculpted walking garden full of brightly blooming shrubs, flowers, and trees. The back wall of the room that faces the gardens is comprised of hinged panel doors that can apparently be closed in inclement weather.

The room itself contains an imposing desk made of some sort of lacquered dark wood, walls covered with charts and maps of many places that you do not immediately recognize, a large table covered with yet more maps and papers, and a set of more casual furniture made of wicker that is arrayed to face the gardens. One of those wicker chairs is filled with a middle-aged man with dark hair now peppered with streaks of gray wearing a loose-fitting white shirt. He is sipping some steaming beverage as you enter.

After you file in, he turns to face you all. With a smile he says, "Welcome friends. What can I help you with today?" As you take a better look at this fellow, you see that despite the smile, his face bears the signs of obvious strain and his eyes look tired.

Zephyr Assimilated

The Brand family owns Zephyr Assimilated. Jaxon Brand, the current head of the family, has done an amazing job of expanding the business over the past 20 years. He has improved and added to the fleet, adding a number of carvels and cogs, while enlarging the number of overall routes. Regular expeditions now include routes to Bret Harth, Martyn's Next, the city of Reme, and even to the distant ports of Quy Tai, Turkad, and San Caseo City. All of this is common knowledge among the residents of Bridgeport.

Jaxon patiently listens to whatever the characters have to say. If the characters are too coy and are not straightforward with their desire for employment, Jaxon quickly dismisses them and directs them to his second, Martin Brand (his second son), who offers the party only menial work around the estate and on the docks.

However, if the party asks about adventuring work, the expedition Jaxon is rumored to be starting, or any sort of straightforward inquiry about employment, Jaxon states:

"I have a problem. The flagship of my fleet, the *Z.A. Zephyr*, is captained by my eldest, Elisa. I fear that something has befallen her and the *Zephyr*.

"She left Bridgeport four months ago on an expedition taking the *Zephyr* south and east first to Warsley and then across the Sinnar to San Caseo City. Well, I know that she arrived at Warsley as expected, about three months ago, and offloaded her cargo as planned. She then reloaded the hold with goods from Warsley to transport and sell at San Caseo. She used a mage of our acquaintance in Warsley to cast *sending* to contact me, so I know these things and that she left Warsley in good order on Yule (December) 11 or so.

"The journey to San Caseo from Warsley should take about a month. But as far as I can tell, she and the *Zephyr* have not arrived. The seas are fickle, so being a bit late is never anything an experienced sailor can get too excited about, but there's been no sending from San Caseo. When the days dragged on without hearing from Elisa or getting any word about the arrival of the *Zephyr* to San Caseo, I became increasingly concerned. She is now over two months late in getting to San Caseo. Elisa is my most competent and efficient captain. However, it is as if Elisa and the *Zephyr* have vanished. I've been seeking the services of a spellcaster powerful enough to cast *scrying* but have so far been unsuccessful.

"Something has happened, I just know it! I cannot tell you how frustrating it is to sit here day after day with no news. So, I have decided to do something about it. I am putting together an expedition captained by my eldest son, Timothy, who will search for the *Zephyr* on the fastest ship of our fleet, the *Z.A. Bounty*, a two-masted schooner. Having no idea what happened to the *Zephyr* or Elisa, I want to be prepared for anything. Therefore, I am looking for capable and brave adventurers to accompany the mission."

A Note on Scrying

A 5th-level spell is well beyond the capabilities of the party at this point and a 9th- or higher-level wizard is not common. Even if the party tracked down a mage of enough power to cast this powerful *divination* spell, please see the **General Notes on Crocodile Island** sidebar and note the magic field that surrounds Crocodile Island that effectively blocks *divination* magic.

Through further question-and-answer roleplaying, the party can learn any of the following:
- Elisa is 28 years old and a veteran of many voyages.
- Elisa is slender and stands about 5 feet 6 inches tall. She has long dark hair.
- Her first command was at age 22, and she has proven to be one of the finest captains in the entire region.
- Timothy is Jaxon's second child and is 25 years old. He has proven to be an average captain, sometimes not using the best of judgment. But Jaxon has great hopes for him nonetheless.
- Jaxon's other children are Martin (23), and his youngest, Tina (19).
- The *Zephyr* is a three-masted clipper built for speed and cargo capacity.
- The *Zephyr's* mission was a lengthy loop beginning by heading to Warsley with a hold full of durable local Bridgeport agricultural products such as cotton and preserved fruits and vegetables. After arriving at Warsley, Captain Brand was to sell the Bridgeport goods to acquire as much grain and copper ore as she could buy; she would then sail across the Sinnar to San Caseo City to sell the grain and ore, both of which are much sought after in San Caseo. Finally, Elisa

Roleplaying Jaxon Brand

Jaxon Brand is a forthright and no-nonsense sort of person. He is a ruthless but fair negotiator. He takes the long view on negotiations, recognizing that getting the best deal now might not be the best path to a lasting and mutually profitable relationship. He values family, community, and order. He is good-natured while being naturally reserved.

Common Sayings

- "I like this idea. Maybe we can work something out to our mutual benefit."
- "We have no place for that sort of behavior in this company — only the best from us and for our partners."

was to negotiate and buy whatever local products from San Caseo City she thought would sell well in this region before returning.
- The whole mission was to take no more than four months.
- Being a merchant captain involves a lot more than being a good sailor. You must know how to negotiate and have an eye for a good deal.
- The one other ship that Jaxon knows about that could have been in the same approximate part of the Sinnar Ocean as the *Zephyr* is a research mission out of Brookmere called the *Discovery*. Jaxon has checked and learned that the *Discovery* is still at sea and is not expected to return to Bridgeport for several more months.
- He knows that the research cog was funded by Bram Zander out of Brookmere and that the ship is captained by Zeb Quindal, who is well known to Jaxon Brand as he has worked for Zephyr Assimilated in the past. Jaxon further knows that Bram Zander owns the merchant company Judicious Passage. They have a small office in Bridgeport down by the docks.
- Jaxon knows that the *Zephyr* made it to Warsley, offloaded all of its cargo, and took on a hold full of grain and copper ore. The *Zephyr* then departed, heading southeast.
- That departure was more than three months ago in mid Yule (December).
- The *Zephyr* should have reached San Caseo City two months ago.
- Jaxon has received no *sending* from Elisa and has not received any sort of information of any sort concerning her whereabouts or those of the *Zephyr*.
- Jaxon will pay 500 gp for any reliable information about the *Zephyr* or his daughter. And, he offers 2,000 gp each to the party members to undertake this mission: 1,000 gp each now and 1,000 gp upon their successful return with Elisa in hand or with definitive information regarding her ultimate fate.
- Finally, if the characterss agree, Jaxon informs them that the *Bounty* is set to depart in two days, the close of the Festival of Blooms. They are to report to the ZA pier and board the *Bounty*.

Should the characters reveal that they met a sailor from the *Discovery* named Joshua Cree, Jaxon is astounded. He says things such as "What?! This is amazing! This Cree fellow may have information regarding my Elisa and the *Zephyr*! Do you know where he is? You have already proven your worth! Well done!" and so on. If the characters accept the mission and do not indicate that their priority is to track down and interrogate Cree, Jaxon Brand strongly urges them to do so.

If the characters fail to connect the sailor from the contest to the current situation, call for a DC 12 Intelligence check. A successful check reminds them that they heard a sailor named Joshua Cree talk about serving on a ship called the *Discovery* at the festival. Inquiries after Joshua Cree in town (accompanied by a successful DC 15 Charisma [Persuasion] check) result in the characters being directed to the Grisk pineapple plantation, about a two hour walk east of town.

Joshua Cree

Finding Joshua Cree is easy enough. The land immediately around Bridgeport is almost completely cultivated. Asking anyone for directions gets the players to the Grisk pineapple plantation. It is about a two-hour walk from the Brand estate. The plantation is fairly typical in that it has a main house owned and occupied by Mr. Grisk and his family, a series of smaller residences for the farmhands and whatever other servants Grisk employs, as well as outbuildings used for a variety of agricultural purposes.

The plantation itself features large flat fields filled with pineapple plants in various stages of maturity. When looked at from afar, the fields look as if they are filled with mounds of green blades stuck up in the air in an endless array of angles.

Anyone who asks after Cree is are pointed to the far end of the plantation where Cree and a few others have been sent to work on clearing more arable space from the nearby forest.

If the characters follow the instructions they were given, they cross nearly a half-dozen pineapple fields before they see the approach of the wood's edge and hear the unmistakable sound of axes striking wood. If the characters make no effort to hide their approach, the four field hands (treat as **commoners**; substitute wood-splitting axes for clubs) are quite surprised to see them; it is not often that an armed party visits the fields. If the party calls out and asks for Cree, one of the men somewhat nervously steps forward. If the characters interacted with Joshua Cree at the festival, he smiles in greeting as he recognizes them.

However, before any sort of colloquy can take place, please read or paraphrase the following to the party:

> One of the men you recognize as the sailor you spoke with at the festival somewhat nervously steps forward. You hear the unmistakable sounds of cracking and crunching branches emanating from the nearby woods, indicating that something large is heading this way. As everyone shifts nervously toward the source of the cracking sounds, the air is suddenly pierced by a terrifying screech. A huge creature that looks like some kind of massive bear crossed with an owl breaks from the edge of the forest and rushes directly toward you and the field hands. This beast seems quite upset!

The field hands apparently got a bit too close to an **owlbear** nest, which causes the beast to attack. As this owlbear is defending its nest, she fights to the death. The owlbear attacks the field hands and characters indiscriminately. Should the party survive the attack and search for where the owlbear came from, a successful DC 12 Wisdom (Survival) check discovers tracks to the nest about 50 yards into the forest from where the field hands were working. Nothing of value is in the nest except the two owl bear eggs that are each worth 250 gp in town. Whether Mr. Grisk lays claim to those eggs since they were on his property is, of course, up to you and likely depends on how the characters handle the situation.

Once the owlbear threat is handled, the party is free to question Joshua Cree. He knows everything stated in the **What Joshua Cree Knows** sidebar. He freely shares what he knows as he has no reason at all to keep any of it a secret. Finally, if necessary, a successful DC 13 Wisdom (Insight) check reveals that Cree is being honest and forthright.

The Discovery

Should the characters decide to follow up on the additional information about the *Discovery* provided by Jaxon Brand, they easily find a small storefront in the docks ward that bears a sign that reads "Judicious Passage." If the party visits during normal business hours, they find the shop manned by a half-elf named Shaleen Brindlewood (**commoner**).

There is not much to this shop. It is 15 feet wide and 20 feet deep. Empty benches sit to the left and right as the characters enter the

What Joshua Cree Knows

Joshua Cree was a deckhand on the *Discovery* when they encountered the *Zephyr* on the Sinnar. When each boat recognized the other's colors, they pulled up broadside, which is quite normal, in order to exchange information and to see if the other needed anything. An away boat carrying the officers from the *Zephyr* made the short trip to the *Discovery*. Cree witnessed this meeting, and it was obvious to him that the captain of the *Zephyr*, a dark-haired woman, and his captain, Zeb Quindal, knew each other and were friends. In fact, the captain of the *Zephyr* dined with Captain Quindal that evening on the *Discovery*.

This afforded the chance for Joshua Cree to gossip with some of the crew from the *Zephyr*. Cree learned that the *Zephyr* was heading for some island far to the south before turning north and east for San Caseo City, the *Zephyr's* scheduled destination. The *Zephyr* crewmembers that Cree talked with boasted that they were going to find "great riches" on this small uncharted island. They further bragged that precious gems were lying around the place just waiting to be picked up.

This encounter happened about a month ago.

As stated in more detail above in **The Festival of Blooms** section, Joshua Cree had been suffering from bouts of violent illness while serving on the *Discovery*. Shortly after witnessing the meeting between Captain Brand and Captain Quindal, Cree was put on another passing ship, the *Spirit* out of Tindledusk, and returned to port. After reaching the port city of Tindledusk, he then made his way overland back home to Bridgeport. He arrived only about a week or so ago and has since taken on work as a farmhand.

store. A counter spans the back of the store from left to right. Shaleen stands behind the counter. She greets any visitor warmly, "Welcome to Judicious Passage. How may we be of service?"

If the party asks about the missing research vessel, Shaleen gives a mildly surprised and puzzled response to the inquiry. A successful DC 12 Charisma (Persuasion) check convinces Shaleen to reveal what she knows:

- Judicious Passage is primarily a passenger transport company but does some shipping as well.
- They specialize in custom destination travel options.
- Bram Zander, the owner of Judicious Passage, commissioned the cog *Discovery* to do just that: Explore the southern section of the Sinnar Ocean to chart it and discover new routes.
- The *Discovery* left Bridgeport in Daan (June) approximately nine months ago.
- The *Discovery* is a big boat, a cog, with three masts and a crew of nearly 50.
- It is big enough to survive just about any ocean storm, and the crew was well enough armed to repel just about any conceivable threat.
- Three sages had been hired to do the charting and record all the ship's findings.
- The *Discovery* was not on a strict schedule due to the nature of its work. It was expected that the entire expedition would take approximately one year.
- Despite the *Discovery* still being out to sea on its mission, one sailor on board named Joshua Cree returned early due to an illness. He returned to Bridgeport only about a week ago and now works on a pineapple plantation owned by Orth Grisk. Shaleen can provide directions to this farm should the characters ask.
- Shaleen knows nothing about the fate of the *Zephyr*.

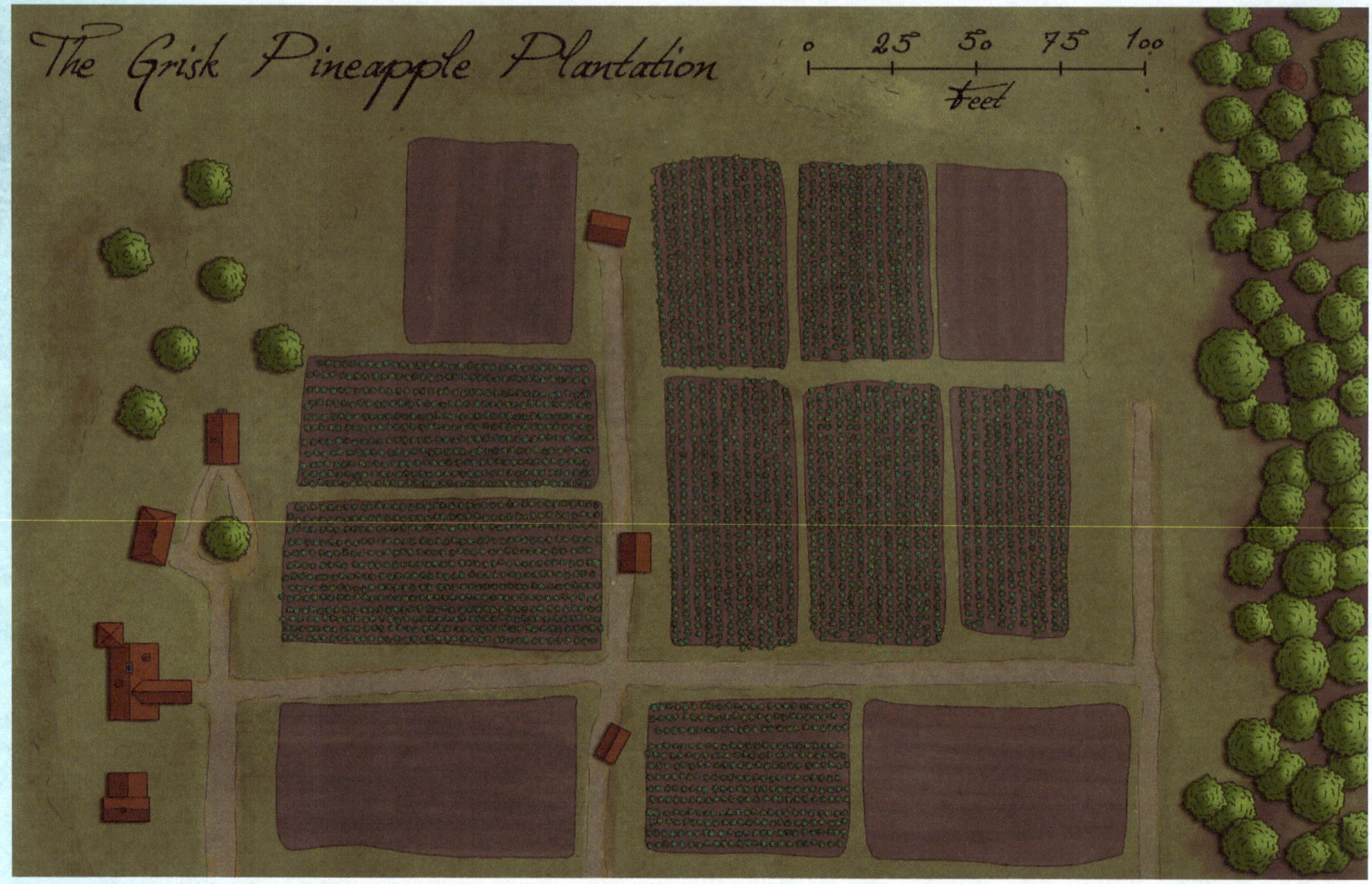

The Grisk Pineapple Plantation
0   25   50   75   100
Feet

1 Square - 5 Feet

Chapter Two: Departure

After a raucous close to the Festival of Blooms the night before (featuring a parade followed by a big outdoor party in the Trademoot), the next day dawns clear and bright with a light easterly wind. The Zephyr Assimilated pier is easy to find based on its sheer size and its signage.

But before arriving at the Zephyr Assimilated pier, the characters cannot help but notice copies of a broadsheet posted at various places throughout Bridgeport as they make their way through town. This broadsheet was published by Timothy Brand, the captain of the *Bounty* whom the party will meet shorty. (Give the players **Handout 1: Timothy Brand's Broadsheet** to set the stage for their meeting with the one and only Captain Timothy).

At the end of the pier, the party notices a series of large rowboats that are in various stages of being loaded and rowed out to a ship at anchor a few hundred yards out into the bay. As the characters move forward on the pier, please read or paraphrase the following:

The day has opened bright and clear, but the same cannot be said of many of the sailors and dockworkers around you who all look as if they enjoyed the close of the Festival of Blooms last night immensely. Ahead of you, three bench-seat rowboats are being loaded and rowed to a boat at anchor out in the bay about 200 yards from the end of the pier. As Jaxon Brand described, it is a two-masted schooner. From here, you can see that it is certainly a handsome ship, sleek and complete with a masthead carved like a muscular godlike man at full draw with a longbow.

As you get closer to the activity at the end of the dock, it seems that you were expected. A man with short, sand-colored hair and bearing a clipboard greets you. "Good day masters. Right this way please." He gestures to an open rowboat. After clambering aboard, a sleeveless man already sitting in the rower position silently nods to you all as he grabs the oars and starts rowing you out into the bay. In short order, his sure and practiced strokes take you to a rope accommodation ladder hung over the side of the schooner. After a somewhat awkward climb up the rope ladder, you find yourself on the aft deck of the boat.

The ship is a hive of activity with sailors rushing hither and yon. About 15 feet in front of you, striking a somewhat staged and outlandish pose, is a young man in bright silks complete with a feathered cap and a soft leather booted foot up on an overturned barrel. As he sees you, as if on cue, he finishes a flourish with an incredibly ornate cutlass, neatly and crisply sheathing it with a practiced and pompous air. As the last of you boards the ship, he shouts a greeting: "Welcome to my ship, the *Bounty*! I am Captain Timothy Brand. You may call me "captain" or "sir" or "my lord." I hear you are brave adventurers hired to assist in our rescue mission of my wayward sister. I warned my father that this day would come. But anyway, I am in command here. You will find me a stalwart, brave, and true leader."

Without pause, he gestures to a woman behind him. She wears a black vest over a white shirt; she looks as if she wants to be anywhere but here at the moment. Timothy continues, "This is Jace, my first mate. She will see to all your needs and will show you to your staterooms, for I am far too busy to be bothered with such trifles. It is a great day for sailing! The winds favor us. Greetings and welcome aboard!" With that, Captain Timothy strides away shouting unnecessary and random orders, all of which seem to be completely ignored.

As the captain strides off, Jace stands there shaking her head in apparent embarrassment. Jace then says, "Right this way, masters. Let me show you to your rooms." Jace then starts walking toward the bow of the ship, expecting you to follow.

After crossing the aft deck and taking the stairs down to the main deck, the characters cross the main deck where the hatch doors remain open as supplies continue to be loaded onto the ship. Jace then leads the party, should they continue to follow, to a covered set of staterooms in the bow of the ship. A total of four staterooms easily accommodate two characters per room.

The characters are free to ask Jace any questions they want and to interact with any of the rest of the crew. Otherwise, Jace unceremoniously gestures to the staterooms and begs off as she is needed in order to see that the ship is adequately and properly loaded for departure.

A full stat block for the *Bounty* can be found in **Appendix E**.

The loading of the ship finishes around noon and without further ceremony, anchor is weighed. The *Bounty* starts across the bay heading west and then south toward the Strait of Praeis.

Should the party seek to talk to Captain Timothy, he tells them he is busy getting the mission underway and does not have time now. He tells them that they will be paid the honor of being invited to dinner in his cabin this evening.

If any of the characters ask about the *Bounty's* destination, First Mate Jace replies somewhat uncertainly, "South then east toward Warsley."

Should the party seek to talk to any of the crew or officers, they find everyone busy at a variety of tasks. The sailors politely answer the characters' questions, but clearly want to get back to their work.

Roleplaying Captain Timothy Brand

Timothy Brand feels he has always been in the shadow of his older sister Elisa, and for good reason. While Elisa has excelled at virtually every task and challenge, Timothy has struggled. And as is the wont of siblings in such a situation, he resents his big sister. This has made the young man quite insecure, forcing him to constantly attempt to compensate. In turn, he has become impulsive, vain, and a poor leader. He is not a bad or evil person, just one who endlessly compensates for shortcomings that he most of all perceives. His moods wax and wane. Because of this, he can be emotionally inappropriate and says things for no apparent reason. He is the kind of leader who freezes at the worst time and is not one to make good decisions even under the most favorable of circumstances.

Timothy is not comfortable with the characters being on board. This is because they work directly for Jaxon Brand, his father, and as such, enjoy a special status. He is bossy and petulant to the party as a result.

Common Sayings

- "An extra jot of rum for all the crew!" (With no apparent reason for this)
- "Will this cursed voyage never end!" (Despite fair weather)

If asked about where they are going, no one really knows exactly and simply answers "South, as far as I know." If asked how they feel about Captain Timothy, they answer that he is fine and is their captain. But their answers lack enthusiasm and suggest to the characters that the crew has their doubts about the captain. That said, none express those doubts out loud at this point.

Stowaway

A few hours after departure and once the *Bounty* leaves the safety of Bridgeport and the bay, the party hears shouting from the main deck. If they investigate, they find many of the crew gathered there along with the captain. One of the crew has what looks like a young boy by the collar of his shirt and is thrusting him in the direction of the captain: "It seems we have a stowaway, Captain. What should we do with him?" After a long and somewhat awkward pause while he struggles to find something to say, Captain Timothy finally responds, "Well, he seems like a fine lad. I admire his spirit! Put him to work so that he may earn his keep." And with that, the captain turns on his heel and strides back toward his stateroom.

The rest of the crew then slowly starts to disperse, some of them muttering to themselves about "bad luck" and "ill omens." Shortly, no one is left except a puzzled-looking crewman holding the boy. A quick glance at the boy reveals a kid about 12 years old wearing a slightly smug expression without any outward signs of fear.

The characters may approach and interrogate the boy if they like.

The stowaway says his name is Gar Turnbull and that he ran away from home because he did not want to grow up to be a farmhand like his father.

None of this is true except his first name. Gar is really a **doppelganger** who is simply joyriding and seeking to wreak some

Getting Seasick

After an hour or so on the water, consider having the characters attempt DC 12 constitution saving throws to keep from becoming seasick from the rolling motion of the ship. Any character with a sailor background automatically makes the save. Further, consider giving advantage to those characters who have some sailing experience. Just because a given character is amphibious as a racial feature does not make them immune to seasickness, which is caused by the motion of the boat, not by the water itself. Characters who fail rush to the gunwale and enjoy their breakfast for a second time. The affected characters quickly acclimate thereafter.

havoc for the fun of it. His plan is to cause as much chaos as he can, maybe by starting a fire. When the jig is up, he transforms into a sahuagin, jumps overboard, and swims away to new adventures elsewhere. A successful DC 13 Wisdom (Insight) check reveals that Gar is not telling the truth and that he is up to something. Such is the indifference of the doppelganger that he takes very little care to hide his intentions.

What happens from here is of course up to the players and you. If the characters take their concerns to the captain, he shrugs them off and mocks the characters for being afraid of a little boy. If the party attacks the doppelganger, he fights back viciously and quickly reveals his true shape.

If the characters do nothing, it is up to you to decide when and in what form Gar's hijinks take shape. Gar may cut a mainstay and send some of the crew in the riggings flying. He may try to light a fire somewhere on the boat. Gar may also get caught trying to poison the food or water supply. It doesn't take long for something to happen as Gar is unwilling to play the role of cabin boy. If he is asked to work, he sulkily refuses.

Whenever and however the confrontation happens, Gar fights until he is reduced to less than one-third of his hit points. He then attempts to flee as outlined above.

All this, of course, scores no points in the captain's favor with the crew. This is just another example of his poor leadership, and the mutterings among the crew to this effect only increase.

Dinner with the Captain

Captain Timothy has the characters to dinner on the evening of their first night at sea. His purpose is to learn about the characters and to see if any of them are a threat to his command.

While Captain Timothy's cabin is certainly fine, it is ill suited for an event such as this as it is simply too small. He has ordered two sea tables to be set up and set with fine china and glassware such as one would find at a high society dinner party. Glassware and china tip and slide with the motion of the boat, frequently spilling onto the white — and once clean — tablecloth. The odd and cramped setting is completed by an embarrassed looking First Mate Jace who was ordered to don an ill-fitting black coat and to serve as the butler for the evening's meal. Captain Timothy either pointedly ignores or simply does not appreciate the incongruity of the scene.

He is high-handed and insulting. However, the characters cannot do much about it given their position on the ship and the fact that Captain Timothy is in charge. If any of the party responds with anything that the captain would deem as "insolence!" he states that the next such incident will find that character in the brig. And the captain is more than petty enough to follow through with that threat.

If asked about the broadsheet essay that the characters found in town, Timothy proudly states that it was of his authorship and that these essays are his way of doing his part to better Bridgeport. He un-ironically relates that he selflessly shares these thoughts and wisdoms in order to improve the lives of his fellow citizens.

Some examples of what the captain might say to the party are as follows:

- "Oh, I thought you were far more experienced adventurers than that. Hell, my greenest crewmember has wetted his blade more than you!"
- "You all are as green as grass!"
- "Well, if a fight ever breaks out, young ones, stay close to me. You will be safe, and you may even learn something."
- "You can do magic? Can you fly? Can you hurl fire great distances? Can you transport yourself across great distances? Well, what good are you? Any huckster at the carnival can do more magic than you!"
- "Have you ever been to The Green Realm? No? Well, I have."
- "I have a girlfriend from Qui Tai." (If asked what her name is, he embarrassingly and obviously makes up a name on the spot.)
- "I cannot wait to see the look on my sister's face when I rescue her from whatever mess she has gotten herself into!"
- "Oh, my sister! She is such a simpleton! She is really not good at much. It is amazing that father put her in charge of anything, let alone our flagship. It must have been out of pity for her."

Some good roleplaying along the lines of "Why are you being such a jerk?" while reminding the captain that the characters work for Jaxon Brand and not him (accompanied by a successful DC 14 Charisma [Persuasion] check) earns a halfhearted apology from Timothy. He then ceases the verbal abuse.

Castaways

At some point as the ship passes near the island of Greenreach as it heads south toward the Strait of Praeis, the barrelman calls out: "Ahoy! Looks to be a small craft or raft port (left) side ahead about two cables (240 fathoms)!"

Should the party move to the foredeck and look for themselves, they see a raft, about 20 feet by 20 feet with about 6–8 smallish robed figures trying to hail the ship. They are waving their hands and jumping up and down. A successful DC 15 Wisdom (Perception) check reveals that the figures are all wearing hoods covering their heads; a check of DC 20 or higher reveals a clawed reptilian foot peeking out from underneath one of the robed figures.

As the *Bounty* moves within 15 fathoms (30 yards), the party is able to see that the seven robed figures are each around four feet tall.

The robed figures are **kobolds** who have grandiose plans of seizing a ship. Normally, kobolds would be way too craven to attempt such piracy, but they are emboldened by the presence of 6 **lacedons**[D] clinging to the bottom of the raft. This pack of kobolds has formed a symbiotic relationship with these terrible creatures in that they provide the lacedons fresh meat while the kobolds gleefully pick their victims' bodies clean of any treasure.

When the raft gets within a few fathoms of the ship, the lacedons let go of the raft, swim under the ship, and seek to scale the far side of the ship while the attention remains on the raft. Meanwhile, the kobolds call out in Common for help, wail about being shipwrecked, and generally stall for time. As soon as the lacedons attack, the kobolds leap to the attack as well, attempting to climb up the side of the ship. The lacedons fight to the death. But if the tide of the battle turns against the kobolds, they try to make it back to their raft and flee.

The captain is noticeably absent during this entire encounter.

CHAPTER THREE: THE OPEN SEA

Once through the Strait of Praeis, the *Bounty* turns southeast toward open ocean. The Sinnar spreads out in its vast blue glory before the Bridgeport vessel. Good weather and fair winds still accompany the mission, and but for the high-handed presence of Captain Timothy, everyone should be settling into the rhythm of sea life. After a week on board, the characters have met and interacted with most of the officers and crew. Bonds or grudges form as you orchestrate.

What follows are a series of encounters that take place on the open sea. It is important to have the storm encounter occur before the *Bounty* encounters the *Discovery*. Encountering the wreckage of the *Discovery* must be the last in the series, and it takes place approximately two months after the *Bounty* leaves Bridgeport.

DRAGON TURTLE

Please read or paraphrase the following:

After a couple of weeks on the *Bounty*, you have settled into the rhythm of life at sea. Despite the questionable leadership of Captain Timothy, the *Bounty's* crew dispatches their daily duties with a practiced efficiency. The weather has been fair and the winds favorable. Land has been out of sight now for a couple of days. Other than the occasional pod of dolphins that has accompanied the *Bounty* for short stretches, the voyage thus far has been almost boring.

That is, until the normal creak of riggings and usual banter among the crew is broken by a sharp cry from the barrelman, "Ahoy! Starboard!" As all eyes swing in that direction, you see quite the sight. Scores of large fish, maybe a school of tuna, break the surface of the water porpoising at high speed. Suddenly, a pointed maw attached to a reptilian head the size of a carriage breaks the surface of the sea and engulfs maybe a dozen of the big silver fish in one swallow. As this monstrosity continues to breach, the ship lists suddenly to port under your feet due to the water displaced by this massive creature.

After regaining your balance, your eyes swing back to the source of the disturbance: a huge turtle-like creature with a long tail and neck with large, taloned flippers. This massive creature is easily as large, if not larger, than your ship in length and width. As water continues to stream off the crenulations of its shell, its huge head swings in your direction. With baleful eyes fixed on the *Bounty*, it surprisingly speaks in Common; its powerful voice sounds like a combination of hissing and a beast clearing its throat: "Well, what do we have here? It has been many moons since I have tasted landbound flesh. Maybe you have something delicious for me?"

Just as the characters are taking in the **dragon turtle** and trying to get their bearings, a high and panicked voice shrieks out, "What is that thing?! Kill it! Destroy it!" The voice belongs to the obviously

A TRIP TO WARSLEY?

The characters may decide that a good place to stop and seek information concerning Elisa Brand and her ship is the port city of Warsley. Captain Brand had gotten word to her father that she had arrived, offloaded her cargo, refilled her hold, and departed from Warsley all in good order approximately three months ago.

If the characters suggest this course to Captain Timothy, he brushes it off as "foolishness" and "a wild goose chase." However, should they convince him with a successful DC 17 Charisma (Persuasion) or (Intimidation) check, Warsley is roughly a one-week journey east from the Strait of Praeis. Warsley is a city of 3,500 inhabitants with primary industries of agriculture, mining, and shipping trade.

Sailors frequent a small temple to Quell located near the docks. The head cleric is named Jesmond Mald (use **priest** stats). A successful DC 14 Charisma (Persuasion) check (advantage if accompanied by an offering) gets Mald to volunteer that he is familiar with Zephyr Assimilated, Captain Elisa Brand, and the *Zephyr*. He can confirm that the *Zephyr* was in port approximately three months ago and that there were no incidents or troubles, at least as far as he was aware of. He further directs the characters to a ramshackle dockside tavern called The Tangled Rigging in order to search out a sailor named Jasper Cronks. Mald believes Cronks used to sail for Zephyr Assimilated before he was terminated for his endless and excessive drinking.

Alternately, asking around the docks after Captain Elisa Brand, the *Zephyr*, or Zephyr Assimilated accompanied by a successful DC 15 Charisma (Persuasion) check directs the characters to The Tangled Rigging where they learn the same information as above. Warsley's Harbormaster is Gand Adams.

The Tangled Rigging was in fact the place where Elisa Brand encountered Cronks months before. It was at this meeting where Cronks filled her head with tales of a small island filled with easy riches. He convinced her that the island really exists. Captain Brand then decided to take Cronks with her to help find the island. Captain Elisa Brand, Cronks, and the *Zephyr* are long gone by the time the party arrives at Warsley.

Minna Buckley (**commoner**), the proprietress of The Rigging, readily relates that Cronks was filled with absurd and wild tales of "vast riches" on a small tropical island he called "Crocodile Island." She further informs the party that Cronks used to go on and on about the active volcanoes on the island. Finally, she tells the character that she, along with the rest of her bar patrons, laughed these stories off as being the typical ravings of a hopelessly drunken and delusional sailor. Minna also relates that Captain Brand visited The Rigging three months or so ago and had a lengthy meeting with "the filthy drunk" Cronks. Finally, Minna Buckley tells the party that when Captain Brand shipped out, she took Cronks with her.

That is the extent of useful information the characters can obtain in Warsley.

A list of the names of some of the sailors on board the *Zephyr*:

Farren Uberto, bosun
Benton Snowdon, bull ensign
Shelley Stonebridge, helmsman
Joss Raven, carpenter
Wystan Shell, conning officer
Albertina Netle, ensign
Claribel Merton, ensign
Idell Notleigh, purser
Gene "Brown Tooth" Dewl, pilot
Ludie Sharman, sailor
Winona "No Cash" Smit, sailor
Faith Shirley, sailor
Quince Taylor, sailor
Elwell Stevens, sailor
Halsey Claridge, sailor
Gilmer Trollope, sailor
Tarleton "Whale" Whulsup, sailor
Burgess Salvodore, sailor
Edbert "Squealer" Zeph, sailor
Rawlins "Three-Teeth" Fawcett, sailor

panicked Captain Timothy who is heading toward the characters from his quarters.

This outburst draws nervous and dark looks from the crew as they stare in shock at Captain Timothy's outburst.

The dragon turtle, having just eaten, patiently awaits a response from the *Bounty*. Fortunately, First Mate Jace has not lost her nerve and steps forward and yells in response, "O Great One! What could we have that would please you? We are nothing more than a mere sailing vessel."

The dragon turtle then responds, "Certainly you must have an extra crewman or two for me to snack on?" A croaking noise that is the creature's laugh follows this question.

At this point, Captain Timothy completely loses control. In a fit of swearing, he orders the crew to attack and destroy the beast. The now-unhinged Captain Timothy shouts things like, "Give it nothing!" and, "Destroy the beast!"

The dragon turtle is more than a match for the *Bounty* and the characters at this point. All of the crew, excepting Captain Timothy, knows this. Random crewmembers hiss statements like "Shut him up!" at the characters.

A successful DC 13 Intelligence (Nature) check makes it quite clear that the dragon turtle is not amused by the ongoing antics of Captain Timothy. It starts to turn from a relaxed broadside position to one facing the Zephyr in a posture ready to attack.

Quick intervention by the characters at this point can save the day. They can either calm Captain Timothy down — requiring a DC 15 Charisma (Persuasion or Intimidation) check — or bodily restrain (grapple) him — a Strength (Athletics) check contested by Captain Timothy's Athletics (+4) check. If Captain Timothy is successfully grappled, he is so embarrassed that he does not attempt to break free.

Meanwhile, First Mate Jace works on a solution. She knows that dragon turtles, like their airborne relatives, love flattery and meat. As the characters are dealing with Captain Timothy, she orders a cask of preserved pork back thrown overboard for the monster while she delivers the following flattery, "O Magnificent One! Please accept this trifle as a thank you for gracing us with your noble presence!"

If the characters keep Captain Timothy under control while First Mate Jace treats with the dragon turtle, the dragon turtle scoops up the offering and, without a backward glance, disappears into the briny deep from which it came.

If the dragon turtle makes an attack on the ship, and the ship survives, there will likely be considerable damage. If the characters opt to help look for damage, allow them to make a DC 14 Wisdom (Perception) check to find the damaged sheet that might otherwise play a pivotal role in the upcoming storm encounter.

Because the dragon turtle has a full belly, it is not spoiling for a fight. However, if attacked, it attacks the ship for two rounds and then swims off, bored by the whole thing.

The crew notes a successful intervention with the dragon turtle, which results in many nods and smiles of appreciation and even a few "Huzzahs!"

DOLDRUMS

After several weeks at sea and with the *Bounty* heading ever southward, the ship encounters a stretch of calm that challenges the nerve of the crew and sees even more erratic behavior on the part of Captain Timothy.

Please read or paraphrase the following to the party:

While the characters can do nothing about the weather (presumably), they can try to improve the morale of the crew. If the above was not clear enough, a successful DC 10 Wisdom (Insight) check informs the party that the morale of the crew is becoming dangerously low.

The characters can do several things to try to improve the situation. Through effective roleplaying and successful DC 12 Charisma (Persuasion) checks, the characters can improve the mood of individual crewmembers by doing things such as sharing kind words, asking after families back home, or even leading the crew in song.

A successful DC 12 Intelligence check gives the characters the idea that opening up a cask of rum and throwing an impromptu party might be just the thing to turn the mood of the crew around. If suggested to anyone but Captain Timothy, the characters' suggestion is received with gusto. Again, that goes for everyone except Captain Timothy. The captain does not protest too stridently, however, as he knows that

he is on tenuous footing with the characters due to their being hired directly by his father and, as a result, not under his command.

Should the characters go ahead with this plan, a cask gets opened and the crew cheerfully partakes, even offering up some "huzzahs!" for the party. However, after a few minutes of merriment, Captain Timothy storms out of his stateroom, his face reddened with rage and flecked with spittle, and demands, "Who ordered that spirits be opened?! This is a mutiny!"

The mood darkens quickly, with many crewmembers reaching for their weapons and shifting their bodies around in anticipation of violence.

Any party member may diffuse the situation by answering the captain and giving reasonable explanations such as "Because we thought it was the right thing to do" along with a successful DC 13 Charisma (Persuasion or Intimidation) check. If successful, Captain Timothy stomps off after delivering an awkward, "Well all right then. Carry on."

If unsuccessful, First Mate Westhoff forcibly intervenes by bodily dragging Captain Timothy back to the captain's quarters. No one sees anything of Captain Timothy for the rest of the day. Fortunately, the next day dawns bright and clear and brings with it a return of the favorable winds. The *Bounty* once again is able to resume its course. The morale of the crew, still improved from the party the day before, is buoyed and the crisis is past.

Oddly, when Captain Timothy emerges the next day, he acts as if nothing untoward happened the day before and actually acts with a sort of manic and over-the-top cheerfulness that only results in puzzled looks from the crew.

STORM

Many weeks into the voyage and with memories of land recalled like wistful dreams, a violent storm strikes the *Bounty*. The storm builds quickly, starting with increasing winds that change direction by the minute, followed by dark and ominous clouds that appear to stack densely over the ship. When the storm strikes, it is with tremendous violence and requires courageous and composed actions by the crew and the characters to survive it.

When you are ready to run this encounter, please read or paraphrase the following to the party:

Swift action by the characters can save poor Quince, but doing so will not be easy. First, any party member seeking to get to the rope on which Quince clings must make a DC 14 Dexterity (Acrobatics) check to keep from losing balance in the lashing wind and rain, and to keep from being swept overboard (see **giant sharks** below). If aided by a fellow party member, that check is made with advantage.

Assuming that step one is successful, the character must make a DC 13 Strength (Athletics) check in order to grab the rope on which Quince clutches and haul him back aboard. Again, creative solutions should be rewarded with checks made with advantage. However, if the dragon turtle attacked and damaged the rigging previously, and the damage was not found and repaired, this Strength check is made with disadvantage.

As bad as the storm is, this is not the end of the party's peril. Using the storm as cover, a band of **merrow** are in the process of climbing the side of the ship seeking some easy prey. They correctly assume that the ship's crew are unprepared for such a raid because of the storm.

Anyone outside of the staterooms on any of the decks sees the merrow creeping over the gunwale of the ship with a successful DC 15 (Wisdom) Perception check. Any party members in their staterooms spot the invading merrow with a successful DC 22 (Wisdom) Perception check out of one of their porthole windows.

If the merrow are not seen by the party, the characters hear a scream and upon investigating, they see a merrow plunging over the side of the ship with a helpless crewmember in its clutches. At this point, they cannot miss the rest of the raiders.

Ten merrow are taking part in the raid. They are roughly equidistant from each other on the main deck as they climb the side of the ship. Each merrow tries to escape if it can subdue and abduct a crewmember, or the remaining merrow flee if half of their number are slain.

Due to the terrible conditions, any character attempting to move anywhere on the deck must make a DC 14 Dexterity (Acrobatics) check to keep from losing balance and falling in the lashing wind, rain, and the huge waves crashing onto and over the ship. A character who falls must succeed on a second DC 14 Dexterity (Acrobatics) or Strength (Athletics) check to keep from being swept over the railing and into the water below.

Because of the heaving and pitching deck, the huge waves crashing over the ship, and the heavy wind and rain, the upper decks are considered difficult terrain. For the same reasons, all ranged attacks are made at disadvantage and every character attempting to cast a spell must first succeed on a concentration check, a DC 10 Constitution saving throw. Failure means that the spell is interrupted by the extremely difficult conditions and is lost. This concentration check does not apply to cantrips. However, if the cantrip involves a ranged spell attack, that attack, like all other ranged attacks, is made with disadvantage.

In an effort to keep this combat manageable, consider rolling $1d4 - 2$ (minimum 0) each round and having the result be the number of crew members incapacitated and snatched by the merrow. Use that same number to reflect the number of merrow that perish that round as well.

The party should face their own group of merrow. The characters are likely 4th level at this point. For four characters at that level, two merrow is a medium encounter, three merrow is a hard encounter, and four is a potential deadly encounter.

When facing off against characters, the merrow attempt to strike them with their harpoons and, if successful, leverage them via strength contests overboard and into the shark-filled waters below.

In addition to the merrow, 3 **giant sharks** patrol the waters around the *Bounty* hoping that the merrow's efforts result in an easy meal for them.

The officers and crew join the party in battling the merrow. Captain Timothy is noticeably absent from this fight. If confronted about this later, he claims that he was unaware of the attack because of the din from the storm, a claim everyone finds hard to credit.

Adrift Research Ship: The Discovery

The *Discovery* is a three-masted cog. A full stat block for it can be found in **Appendix E** against the unlikely event that the shipped is towed into a harbor and repaired.

Several uneventful days after surviving the terrible storm and the merrow attack, the *Bounty* encounters a drifting ship listing badly to port with two of its three masts destroyed. Once approached and boarded, the characters find that this ship is the *Discovery* out of Bridgeport. Unfortunately, they find the crew all slain, but find some important clues that help them on their quest to find Elisa Brand and the *Zephyr*.

When ready to start this encounter, please read or paraphrase the following:

The crew of the *Bounty* is quick to point out (and are clearly chagrined at their captain's inability to tell) that this adrift vessel cannot be the *Zephyr* based on the ship's shape and size alone. The *Zephyr* was a clipper; the boat before them is a cog, a much wider and slower ship.

Crewmembers speculate that the storm must have hulled the boat to cause it to be in this sorry state. Any character making a successful DC 16 Wisdom (Perception) check catches signs of damage beyond what the recent, terrible storm could have caused. Those who are successful spot gashes and gouges likely caused by edged weapons. Further, any character that makes a successful DC 16 Intelligence (Arcana) check notices a broad swath of charred railing on the drifting ship that was almost certainly caused by magical fire. (The pattern of scorch marks squares with the sequelae of a *burning hands* spell.)

This ship is in fact the *Discovery* commissioned from Brookmere. A successful DC 13 Intelligence check (with advantage if the character is a native of Bridgeport) allows any character to recognize that the tattered colors indicate that Bridgeport was the ship's port of origin. If the party fails to realize the identity of the boat, several sailors shout this information out loud.

As thick as Captain Timothy is, he is quickly forced to accept that the unmoored and severely damaged ship before them is clearly not the *Zephyr*. Obviously disappointed and with visible effort, Captain

Timothy restrains himself and says, "Well, we may as well approach and see who we are dealing with."

He then shouts orders to the helm to turn starboard on an intercept course. At this point, please read or paraphrase the following to the characters:

While Captain Tim is not well liked, his suggestion seems to make sense with the rest of the crew. Everyone turns expectantly toward the characters. Assuming the party assents, a dinghy (or two) is lowered and two crewmembers are assigned to row the party over to the drifting boat.

The characters are quickly and efficiently rowed over to the apparently deserted boat. The rowers maneuver the dinghy up to the port side of the ship. The gunwale of the canted ship is only 10 feet or so above the heads of the seated party. Any effort to throw a rope over the side of the ship is successful. It is then a short and easy climb to board this drifting ship. As the characters approach the damaged ship, they cannot help but see the damage to the ship's rudder and the large hole on the ship's port side.

The deck of the ship is tipped at an angle, but not so severely so that walking is impossible. However, the tilted deck does constitute difficult terrain. Once on board, the party sees that no one is on any of the decks. They also see the "stumps" of the forward two masts. It is clear that they were torn off with a great deal of force. They further notice obvious signs of combat: congealed blood, scorch marks, and scattered rents and cuts made by edged weapons on the railings and surfaces of the ship. All of this confirms the characters' initial observations. Finally, at the aft end of the main deck, they find the tattered remnants of the ship's colors.

As the party begins moving around on the deck of the *Discovery*, a DC 13 Wisdom (Perception) check reveals the sounds of bumping and scraping from belowdecks, as if heavy objects are being moved around in the hold. See **Area 8** below for more information on this.

When the characters deal with the trouble belowdecks (see **Area 7**), they can explore the rest of the ship at their leisure. Specific locations of the *Discovery* are as follows:

Area 1: Main Deck

Beyond the broken mast, four hatches to access the hold below, steps up to the aft deck, steps up to the forecastle, and the detritus and wreckage from the storm, nothing of interest is here. With respect to the access points to the hold below, all four hatches are on this deck. The two fore hatches are open, and the two aft ones are closed. Each hatch is supplied with a set of stairs down.

What Happened to the Discovery?

The *Discovery* in fact encountered the *Zephyr* and Elisa Brand many weeks before, leagues to the south and east of the party's current location. The *Discovery*, captained by Zeb Quindal, was engaged in its charting mission when the *Zephyr* was sighted. When the *Zephyr* was approached and hailed, Elisa Brand came aboard and had dinner with Captain Quindal. That evening over dinner, she excitedly described a large island far to the south located out in the middle of the Sinnar Ocean called "Crocodile Island." She was very excited about the prospects of exploring the island. She learned of the island from Jasper Cronks (see Elisa Brand's journal excerpts found on the *Zephyr* in **Chapter 4** for more information regarding Cronks), who spoke of a bounty of peridot and onyx on the small island. She and the *Zephyr* had left Warsley and were headed to this previously unknown island when they encountered the *Discovery*.

Elisa confided all this to Captain Quindal, including map coordinates to "Crocodile Island," because she and the captain were already familiar with each other, as Captain Quindal had occasionally worked for her father. Knowing and trusting Captain Quindal as she did, Elisa was excited to share this information with her friend and colleague. See **Player Handout 2: Captain Zeb Quindal's Journal (Excerpt)** and the ship's manifest below.

Unfortunately, a safe return to Bridgeport was not in the cards for either Captain Quindal or the *Discovery*. While riding out the same terrible storm that the *Bounty* survived just days before, the *Discovery* was beset by one of the most fearsome and legendary sea creatures in existence: a kraken.

Such was the ferocity of the storm that it roused the kraken from its fathomless rift in the depths of the Sinnar. This beast had not seen the surface in years and when it felt the savagery of the storm, it came as if summoned to celebrate its destructive power.

The kraken severely damaged the *Discovery* quite by accident. When it broke the surface in a flurry of tentacles and ferocity in joyous homage to the raging storm, the *Discovery* just happened to be close by. The sheer force of the cresting kraken ripped off two of the *Discovery's* masts and damaged the third, severely damaged its rudder, and holed the ship just above the waterline on the port side. The *Discovery* then took on a good deal of water that caused it to list, which is the state in which the party finds it. The kraken moved on, not even noticing the *Discovery* in its passing.

Unfortunately, this was not the end of the *Discovery's* woes. The storm eventually stilled, but it left the ship seriously and obviously disabled. Then, just the day before the characters and the *Bounty* discover it, a force of sahuagin raiders from the distant sahuagin realm of King Bachzarisaa attacked the *Discovery*. The severely damaged *Discovery* was easy pickings for the merciless sahuagin. When the characters board the *Discovery*, most of the raiders had previously departed, leaving only a handful of sea devils lingering belowdecks to torture the few remaining survivors.

AREA 2: FORECASTLE

This is the crew's quarters. Dozens of individual berths have been thoroughly tossed. Clothing and mesh hammocks are scattered and torn up. A successful DC 12 Wisdom (Perception) check reveals the presence of many bloodstains but no bodies. A check of DC 18 or more divulges signs of bodies being dragged out of this part of the ship toward the main deck. Finally, a successful DC 16 Intelligence (Investigation) check locates some scattered valuables amounting to 8 gp, 35 sp, and a small leather bag of 6 garnets valued at 20 gp each.

AREA 3: HELM (AFT DECK)

This is where the wheel and binnacle are located. The wheel is bent and bears marks from something blunt repeatedly striking it. The compass mounted on the binnacle has been smashed. Nothing else of interest is in this area.

AREA 4: PILOT'S QUARTERS (AFT STATEROOMS)

This stateroom is in a sorry state. The raiding sahuagin thoroughly looted it. Clothing and mundane personal items are scattered about. A successful DC 14 Intelligence (Investigation) check (with advantage if a character has the sailor background) reveals two nautical navigation tools. One is a brass sextant, bent and unusable. The other is an azimuth compass set in a small wooden box made of some dark wood that has mother of pearl inlay that was apparently missed by the sahuagin (value 65 gp). Beyond that, the room contains a myriad of torn and damaged charts, the creation of which was the *Discovery's* mission in the first place.

Area 5: Officers' Quarters (Aft Staterooms)

This stateroom contained three individual berths. The former occupants are now deceased because of either the storm and kraken or the sahuagin raiders. Personal effects are scattered everywhere. What little furniture there was is smashed. Nothing of value is here.

Area 6: Officers' Quarters (Aft Staterooms)

Same as **Area 5** above except that a successful DC 13 Intelligence (Investigation) check finds a spellbook that belonged to one of the wizards hired to help with the charting and protecting the ship. The spellbook contains the following wizard spells: 1st level—*burning hands*, *color spray*, *feather fall*, *grease*; 2nd level—*arcane lock*, *darkness*, *misty step*; 3rd level—*blink*, *haste*, *water breathing*.

Area 7: Captain's Quarters (Aft Staterooms)

When the characters enter this area, please read or paraphrase the following:

> This formerly elegant stateroom has seen better days. The few pieces of furniture have been smashed into kindling. Feathers are everywhere, the scattered remains of the bedding that once adorned the hinged sea bed that was mounted on the wall. Unlike the rest of the staterooms on the ship, this one has more woodwork and other small refined touches. You surmise that this must have been the captain's quarters. As you stand in this room trying to puzzle out what the layout was before being ransacked, you see the remnants of a small writing desk in the corner, a bed on the other side of the room, and a small wardrobe.

Several things of interest are in the captain's stateroom that the party can find. They are as follows with the attendant Intelligence (Investigation) DC numbers:

DC 10 — Captain Zeb Quindal's Journal: This leather-bound journal (**Player Handout 2: Captain Zeb Quindal's Journal [Excerpt]**) is on the floor and is mostly obscured by some torn cloth that may have once been a shirt. This journal provides the characters with some important information about the possible location of Elisa Brand, including a hand-drawn portolan chart showing the location of Crocodile Island (**Player Handout 3: Crocodile Island**). The chart is tucked in at the location of a specific journal entry, Foeros 16th. This entry is from a couple of weeks ago and discusses encountering the *Zephyr* and Captain Brand. This same entry specifically mentions that Captain Brand is headed to a previously unchartered island called "Crocodile Island" and that she wishes for Captain Quindal to inform her father of this detour when the *Discovery* returns to Bridgeport. Finally, the entry states that Elisa was pursuing tales of "vast riches" on this island. The rest of the journal contains mundane details of the voyage and is of no interest to the party.

Specifically, with regard to the map, a successful DC 13 Intelligence check informs that the location marked on the hand-drawn map is in a previously uncharted section of the Sinnar Ocean, thousands of leagues away from any known civilized habitation. Consulting with

the helmsman, pilot, or first mate of the *Bounty* reveals the same.

DC 12 — Ship's Manifest: This large folio is under the detritus that was formerly the desk. It contains a list of all the officers and crew onboard; all the supplies taken on when they departed from Bridgeport months ago, Daan (June) 10th; and of most interest to the party, it notes the date the *Discovery* encountered the *Zephyr*, Freyrmond (March) 16th.

DC 15 — Captain Quindal's Saber: Unfortunately, the sahuagin raiders caught Captain Quindal without his family heirloom, his saber. It is a *+1 saber* (use longsword stats) and bears a large ornate "Q" on the butt end of the pommel. It is deeply buried under what is left of his bed and bedding. The sahuagin must have missed it as they tore apart the ship.

DC 19 — Captain Quindal's Treasure Cache: If the characters carefully examine the floorboards, they find one that is loose. Once found, it is then a simple matter to pry it up to reveal a coffer containing the following: 75 pp, 2 diamonds worth 500 gp each, a *potion of superior healing*, two *potions of water breathing*, and a *necklace of adaptation*.

Area 8: Hold

Most of the sahuagin left, but a small group remains torturing two remaining *Discovery* crewmembers as more winnow and destroy the contents in the hold. There are 8 sahuagin in the hold. A **sahuagin priestess**[D] and 2 **Sinnar sahuagin**[D] are busily and lustily torturing the two remaining crewmen: Halen Drand (use **bandit** stats), a rank-and-file crewmember, and Sylros Clearsky (use **bandit captain** stats), a half-elf ensign. The remaining 5 **Sinnar sahuagin**[D] are rifling through the stores in the hold.

As stated in **Area 1**, 4 access points to the hold are on the main deck. The two fore hatches are open, and the two aft ones are closed. Each hatch is supplied with its own set of stairs down.

The sahuagin below are quite preoccupied with their current endeavors and are convinced that they are alone on the ship. So any attempt at stealth by the characters is made with advantage against the sahuagins' perception.

When the party is ready to descend into the hold, please read or paraphrase the following to the characters:

> As you descend into the darkness of the hold, you hear sloshing water, the sound of crates and casks being moved around with considerable violence, and the sound of an odd slurry-sounding language being spoken by several individuals. Underneath all of this, you hear the faint sounds of someone whimpering in pain.
>
> As your eyes adjust to the dim, you see many dark green, toothy, and clearly marine humanoids of some sort busily tearing apart the hold while three of them loom over two severely injured looking humans. Water is everywhere, deeper on the port side of the hold matching the overall cant of the ship.

The lighting conditions are dim light, and the entire hold is considered difficult terrain because of the water and scattered cargo.

The sahuagin savagely attack as soon as they become aware of the characters' presence. They fight until either half of their number are slain or the sahuagin priestess is killed. At either of these two points, the survivors attempt to flee through the hull breach located in the aft portion of the port-side hold.

If the characters subdue and question one of the sahuagin, please refer to the **Why Take Live Prisoners?** sidebar below. This is an opportunity for the characters to learn just how terrible the sahuagin are.

Halen (human) and Sylros (half-elf), the two surviving crewmembers, are both alive but badly injured. They are extremely grateful for the rescue and happily join the crew of the *Bounty*. Either of them can relate as much of the material as you wish from the **What Happened to the *Discovery*?** section above, importantly including the *Discovery's* rendezvous with the *Zephyr* and Captain Elisa Brand's supping with Captain Quindal.

In addition, these rescued sailors describe a bizarre and macabre scene they witnessed just hours before. It involved the sahuagin surfacing with what appeared to be a partially inflated jellyfish, loading a couple of alive but unconscious captives into the creature, including Captain Quindal, and then submerging. They have no further information to share about this strange event. For more information, see the **Why Take Live Prisoners?** sidebar as well as The Meat Locker (**Area K-2b** in **Chapter Five**).

Nothing else is of immediate use to the party. When the party returns to the *Bounty* and reports what they found, Captain Timothy orders the *Bounty* tied up to the *Discovery* for salvage efforts. After tying up, the rest of the day is spent with the crew scavenging everything useful from the *Discovery*. There is no further sign of the sahuagin.

MUTINY ON THE BOUNTY

With map coordinates in hand, the *Bounty* now heads toward the mysterious and previously unknown "Crocodile Island" with the hope of finding Elisa Brand and the *Zephyr*.

However, weeks of service on the *Bounty* under Captain Timothy have worn on the crew, officers included. One night, the characters hear a polite knock on their stateroom door to find First Mate Jace Westhoff standing there. After asking to come in and after the party acquiesces, please read or paraphrase the following to the characters:

Before you stands the first mate, hat literally in hand, looking a bit embarrassed and nervous at the same time. After a few uncomfortable seconds of silence, the first mate speaks, "Good evening, masters. I come to you with a matter most grave and urgent. As you certainly know, Captain Timothy is not well liked by the crew. However, that happens on long voyages. Such is the sailor's life. What is happening on the *Bounty* is something else, something more dangerous. The captain's reckless decisions, his obvious lack of courage, and his constant highhanded and insulting ways have worn dangerously thin on the crew. They are on the brink of rebellion, a mutiny. And, after discussing this with my fellow officers, I cannot disagree as much as it shames me to admit. The crew is openly calling for a change in leadership. The crew want me to take command.

"As reluctant as I am to take command under these circumstances, I worry that if I decline, the crew will choose someone else who does not have my, well, restrained temperament. What I am saying is that if I took command, I assure you that no harm would come to Timothy Brand. He would not be turned out of his quarters or imprisoned. He would simply become a passenger with no duties on the ship.

"What say you?"

The characters have a decision to make. First Mate Jace has proven her worth many times over on this voyage and certainly would be a much better sea captain than Timothy Brand. However, Timothy is the son of the characters' employer. Because Jaxon Brand hired the party, they enjoy a special status on the *Bounty*. If they decide to back the crew's wishes and agree to allow Jace to replace Captain Timothy, then she likely asks the characters to provide some support for her decision to remove Timothy Brand as captain to Jaxon Brand when, and if, they return to Bridgeport.

On the other hand, the party can counsel caution and restraint. With a successful DC 15 Charisma (Diplomacy) check, the characters convince Jace and the crew to grudgingly allow Captain Timothy to retain command and for them to go back to their duties.

Should the characters confront Captain Timothy, he is indignant and outraged: "How dare you insult your betters in such a base manner?!" "You sirrahs, are no gentlemen!" "My father will be outraged at this slight!"

But when facing the reality of unanimous opposition and rightly fearing for his own safety, he sullenly relents.

In any event, whatever the party decides to do with Captain Timothy, this leadership crisis breaks him. Going forward, he is extremely deferential to the characters and sullenly, but silently, accepts his fate, whatever it may be. Fortunately, whether the characters decide to back the crew led coup to install Jace as the new captain or if they urge restraint in support of Captain Timothy, the rest of the journey to Crocodile Island is uneventful.

Chapter Four: Crocodile Island

The *Bounty* has an uneventful 10 days or so of travel as the crew follows the chart found on the *Discovery* in search of the mysterious Crocodile Island. The characters should be at least 5th level to have a reasonable chance of surviving this next section of the adventure.

As the *Bounty* comes within view of Crocodile Island for the first time, please read or paraphrase the following to the party:

> After spending nearly a month on the open sea in pursuit of what at times has felt like a fool's errand, the ship's pilot informs you that you could sight Crocodile Island at literally any moment. With viral speed, this welcome news quickly spreads through the crew. Because of this hopeful development, members of the crew now scan the surrounding water in all directions with the hope of catching a glimpse of the fanciful and mysterious island that is the object of your expedition. After an entire morning is spent in suspenseful expectancy, a sudden cry comes from the nest on the main mast, "Land ho! Starboard! 35 degrees!"
>
> Everyone not engaged in some vital operation on the ship rushes to the starboard rail, straining to see the object of the hue and cry. And sure enough, as the *Bounty* crests each wave, you see a dot on the horizon that must be the enigmatic island. The helmsman shouts order for a change in direction. A fair wind assists as the ship begins its turn to starboard, now heading directly toward the distant and secretive island.
>
> After this exciting turn of events, the next hour spent cleaving through the waves toward the island seems interminable. Finally, you hear the helmsman shout orders for the *Bounty* to be brought about to starboard. As the ship settles in broadside facing the island, you can finally take in the full panorama of the land mass. You immediately see that the island is aptly named. At about a quarter-mile distant, the island indeed looks like a massive crocodile patiently floating in brooding menace. You estimate that it must be at least fifty miles long from tail to snout. From your current vantage, you see that a small set of hills rises in the location of the crocodile's "head" following a dip down to the neck. Then, just like the profile of a real crocodile, the land rises again in a ridge of low-lying mountains to a high point in the middle of the beast's back, followed again by a gradual descent to a low point at the far end of the island, the tip of the crocodile's tail. The head of the island is facing north.
>
> Finally, you see that the island is surrounded by intermittent sandy beaches interspersed with a rocky shoreline. The entirety of the landmass is blanketed by dense tropical forest and at the spot where the crest of the creature's back would be, at least a couple of peaks produce some sort of white smoke. This smoke partially obscures the top ridgeline of the island and explains the slightly acrid and sulfuric smell that you cannot help but notice. You immediately suspect some sort of volcanic activity.

It is assumed that the *Bounty* approaches Crocodile Island from the west or northwest. From this vantage, the characters will not see the *Zephyr* as it is at anchor on the far side of the island (the east side). The *Bounty* can anchor virtually anywhere around the island. Due to rising shallows, the ship runs aground if it gets closer than 200 feet to the island. This fact is immediately apparent to any of the ship's sailors.

General Notes on Crocodile Island

Crocodile Island is a volcanic island that has been active for thousands of years. As a result, areas of the island contain concentrations of caustic sulfur dioxide gas that belch forth from volcanic vents. These areas of higher gas concentration are indicated on the map of the island. In those areas, air-breathing creatures who are not immune to poison damage or the poisoned condition and who remain in the gaseous area for one hour must succeed on a DC 14 Constitution saving throw or sustain 3 levels of exhaustion. A character who continues to remain in the area must make another saving throw or suffer an additional 3 levels of exhaustion. If they have not been cured of at least one level of exhaustion in the meantime, this means death. After leaving the gaseous area, those affected by the gas can reattempt the save once per hour while outside of the gaseous area. A successful save outside of a gaseous area resolves all exhaustion. If the repeated save attempts all fail, the exhaustion resolves on its own after 8 hours of being outside the affected area. Suffering from 3 levels of exhaustion means disadvantage on ability checks, attack rolls, and saving throws, as well as having speed halved.

Further, like a beacon, centuries ago the volcanic activity of this remote island caught the attention of the grand duke of the City of Brass. This efreet often visited the molten depths of the island to relish the extreme heat of the volcano — a heat level that is unusual on the Prime Material Plane. Because of his repeated and extensive cavorting in the volcanic depths of the island, a bridge to the Elemental Plane of Fire formed, which in turn created an extraplanar field that surrounds the island. It is not visible, and the characters will not feel it in any tangible way. If *detect magic* or another similar spell is cast, the entire area radiates faint *conjuration* magic. The only practical effect of the field is that it interferes with certain types of magic, specifically Divination spells.

Any Divination spells cast within the region or aimed at the region have a 50% chance of failure. If the spell fails, it just does not work, and nothing happens. Some exemplar spells are *comprehend languages*, *detect evil and good*, *detect magic*, *find traps*, and *identify*. Finally, some Divination spells just don't work under any circumstances. These are spells that involve communication or remote sensory inputs that are foiled by the extraplanar field. Examples of Divination spells that never work on or near Crocodile Island are *arcane eye*, *clairvoyance*, *commune*, *locate creature*, *locate object*, and *scrying*. All other magic operates normally. In addition, Divination spells cast by the long-term residents of the island (namely the craniform) are not affected by this field.

ENTERING THE WRONG SIDE OF THE ISLAND?

The adventure contemplates the characters' arriving on the western side of Crocodile Island on board the *Bounty*. Seeing nothing of note on that side of the island, most parties will want to circle the small island before deciding on a course of action. And, in the process of doing so, they find the *Zephyr*, at anchor, on the east side of the island. After picking up the trail of the object of their quest, Elisa Brand, the characters follow her trail inland going from east to west.

The critical encounter on the island lies at the very center of the island as part of the Hidden Valley section below. So, if a group of characters lands on the west side of the island and then goes inland, it is a simple matter to run all of the encounters as written east-to-west instead of west-to-east. Characters still arrive at the same crucial location: the salt water lagoon detailed in the Hidden Valley section.

If the *Bounty* circumnavigates the island, they do not see any sort of structures or other signs of an intelligent or structured society. However, the anchored *Zephyr* is easily spotted. The direction of approach is irrelevant, but as the *Bounty* rounds the island and approaches the east side of the island, please read or paraphrase the following:

Now that the *Bounty* is closer to the island as it circles the landmass, you more clearly see the island's rugged geography and that its heights are obscured with some clinging fog or mist that is slightly yellow in color. You also cannot help but notice the sour and acrid smell of sulfur that seems to suffuse the entire area. The odor is caustic enough to cause your eyes to water and your nostrils to sting. Despite this seemingly tainted air, the island is far from lifeless. You hear the hoots and calls of innumerable birds and other animals and easily spot the bright plumage of a great variety of tropical looking birds as they swoop and caper among the tall, dense, and lush trees.

As you stare transfixed at the verdant island, your reverie is interrupted by a sharp call from the watch, "Ship, ho! Straight ahead! Four cables!" In response, you and most of the crew rush forward to the bow rail. As you find a position among the press of bodies to see what lies ahead, you spot a three-masted clipper that matches the description of the *Zephyr*, but do not see any signs of movement on the ship or any colors flying.

WHY TAKE LIVE PRISONERS?

The sahuagin are famous for their cruelty and brutality. In fact, one of their most notorious hallmarks is not leaving behind survivors of any attack. So why did they take Captain Brand and at least one of her officers and undertake the effort to deliver them alive to King Bachzarisaa? The reason is the influence of King Bachzarisaa's wife, Enzu, a high priestess of Dajobas, the Shark God. Devotees of Dajobas, who is also known as the Devourer, believe that eating the fresh blood and flesh of the powerful increases the strength of the consumer. As a result, King Bachzarisaa believes that eating recently slain "important" air-breathing humanoids further bolsters his power and venerates Dajobas. In an effort to curry favor with their barbarous king, sahuagin raiders scour the area seas for likely targets, especially sea captains, to eventually grace King Bachzarisaa's dinner table.

This is in fact the *Zephyr*. However, all the crew were either slain or captured by sahuagin, so it is deserted. Likely, the characters want to investigate the ship. As with the exploration of the *Discovery*, longboats are lowered and the short distance between the two ships is quickly covered. The ship is eerily silent as the characters approach, with the only sound being the rhythmic lapping of waves against the *Zephyr's* hull.

No convenience ladder or lines hang over the ship's side to assist with boarding. So, boarding the ship requires a successful DC 14 Strength (Athletics) check to climb up the side of the *Zephyr*. Once accomplished, it is a simple matter to drop a line to assist those who follow. With a rope in place, the climb check is made with advantage.

Once above decks, the signs of combat are obvious. Rents and nicks are on nearly every surface, obviously caused by edged weapons, and copious bloodstains are everywhere. A successful DC 15 Wisdom (Nature) check reveals the presence of claw marks on the decking comparable to what the party found on the *Discovery*.

Further, a successful DC 13 Wisdom (Perception) or Intelligence (Investigation) check finds the remnants of the *Zephyr's* colors, a corner of which peek out from underneath a pile of damaged rigging and sail.

Finally, any characters that look to shore from the decks of the *Zephyr* cannot help but notice the smashed remnants of two longboats on the beach.

The *Zephyr's* sails are damaged but reparable. By using the extra yard stored on the *Bounty*, the *Zephyr* could be made seaworthy with 24 hours of concerted effort. A stat block for the *Zephyr* can be found in **Appendix E**.

Overall, the characters find a ship that was thoroughly tossed. The hold has been ransacked and is now full of smashed crates and jumbled cargo. Grain and copper ore are scattered everywhere. The grain is ruined, but the copper ore is salvageable. However, all the tuns that held the ore are smashed. The sahuagin had no use for either grain or copper ore, so they did their best to destroy it all.

Characters looking to shore from the either of the two boats see the destroyed remnants of two away boats about 20 feet up on the beach away from the water's edge. At this point, they also notice the flotsam of various crate remnants and barrel staves washed ashore as a result of the sahuagin rampage through the *Zephyr's* cargo.

The officer's quarters are on the aft deck. Four separate staterooms are on this deck. A search of them reveals heavily damaged furniture and personal effects. In the first three, nothing of value or particular interest remains.

However, the captain's quarters are easy to find based on their size and quality (despite the damage) of the accommodations. As the characters enter this stateroom with its obviously broken lock, please read or paraphrase the following:

> This once-handsome stateroom has certainly seen better days. Despite the riot of smashed furniture, rent fabric, and scattered papers, it remains obvious that this is the nicest room on the ship. Some scratches and dents aside, the woodwork remains mostly intact and the two porthole casings are of obvious high quality. A cursory search reveals scattered personal items: an ivory hairbrush; a pair of hair sticks that seem to be made of ebony; many pieces of well-made clothing, now torn and rent, fitting someone slight and of short stature; a drawer that formerly resided in a writing desk containing a small coffer that appears to have been forced open and is now empty; and many damaged books covering an array of subjects from history to nautical charting.

Among the smashed sea bed, splintered wardrobe, and damaged writing desk, a successful DC 13 Wisdom (Perception) or Intelligence (Investigation) check finds an intact leather-bound journal that bears the Brand crest embossed on its cover. This is Elisa Brand's journal and provides the characters with some useful information and answers. It contains notes from years of sailing, the vast majority of which are

FLORA AND FAUNA OF CROCODILE ISLAND

Because of the ancient and active volcanoes that created this island, there are some unusual genetic variations and adaptations based on the unique environmental conditions on the island. Generations of flora and fauna on Crocodile Island have been exposed to the caustic gases from the incessant volcanic activity, and now, all plants, animals, and creatures are immune to the toxic volcanic gases on and around the island. Further, all such lifeforms are immune to poison damage and the poisoned condition.

of no help or interest to the characters. The excerpts from her journal (contained in **Player Handout 4: Elisa Brand's Journal**), however, should prove most illuminating to the party.

As is common, while the ship's purser oversees all financial matters relevant to the ship, the ship's captain maintains actual physical possession of the ship's coffer. The coffer was in Elisa's now destroyed desk. The sahuagin raiders found the strongbox and looted it, but they missed something. The drawer containing the coffer has a false bottom. A successful DC 15 Intelligence (Investigation) check discovers the false bottom. This check is made with advantage if the drawer is picked up off the floor and examined.

Once discovered, the false bottom contains a gold Zephyr Assimilated signet ring (value 200 gp, but worth three times that to the Brand family) and a leather purse with 100 pp and 6 garnets worth 300 gp each.

At this point, the characters will most likely want to go ashore to determine the final fate of Elisa Brand. The information provided in her journal excerpts should make that plan of action the most reasonable.

The characters may be tempted to mount a huge expedition by largely emptying the ship and moving onto the island with a large force of sailors. Any such suggestion is met with strong disapproval by any and all of the *Bounty's* officers and sailors at large.

The deserted and recently attacked *Zephyr* has everyone spooked, and the officers argue that they need every able-bodied sailor to defend the *Bounty* and recover the *Zephyr* as well. However, a successful DC 16 Charisma (Persuasion) check results in the unenthusiastic agreement to send an equal number of sailors (use **bandit** stats) as there are characters. These unfortunate and sulking "volunteers" are selected by drawing lots. It should be very clear to the characters that these men and women do not want to accompany them onto the island, but that they will grudgingly follow the orders they were given.

TO SHORE

One or two away rowboats are sufficient to bring the party to the island's sandy shore. Once disembarked from the boats and on the beach itself, please read or paraphrase the following:

> The short but tense ride from the *Bounty* to shore is now behind you. You now find yourselves standing on the sandy beach of Crocodile Island. After so many weeks at sea, it feels disorienting to be standing on solid ground again. As you look around, you see that your compatriots are experiencing the same as they seem to weave slightly in place as they struggle to get their bearings.
>
> The raucous hoots and calls from the jungle ahead of you are even louder now that you are on shore. The dense canopy, starting approximately 30 feet from shore, looks like a solid

CROCODILE ISLAND
Path of Elisa Brand
N
W
E
S
0 2 4 6 8 10
MILES
Caustic Gas Zone
Brand/Sahuagin Attack
Craniform Colony
Pass
High Moor
Zephyr
Uder
Blackbeard's Cave
Bounty
Caustic Gas Zone
HIDDEN VALLEY
1 Square - 5 Feet
Marshland
Path up to Pass
To Ocean (Underground)
Underground Entrance to Craniform Colony
BLACKBEARD'S CAVE
1 Square - 5 Feet
Sail Cloth
Sleeping Mat
Up

wall of vegetation. And the stinging and burning sulfur smell that you could not help noticing from the deck of your ship is that much stronger now that you are actually on the island. Your eyes sting and your nostrils burn as you take in the scene around you.

After reconciling your senses to being on solid ground as opposed to a pitching deck, and after observing the lush, verdant jungle ahead of you, you sight the remnants of two thoroughly smashed away boats about 20 feet inland from shore. The entire area you stand in seems churned by different footprints. Many of the prints were obviously made by booted individuals, likely members of the *Zephyr's* crew, but others are strangely shaped.

As the characters have already encountered sahuagin, a successful DC 10 Wisdom (Survival) or Intelligence (Nature) check confirms that sahuagin made these other tracks.

As noted above, the characters see obvious tracks leading from this place directly inland into the canopy. A successful DC 15 Wisdom (Survival) check informs them that approximately 15 humanoids left the beach and headed inland, but that there appear to be sahuagin tracks in the sand as well. If the check succeeds by 5 or more, the party learns that the sahuagin prints overlay the humanoid prints, suggesting that the sahuagin arrived at this spot after the humanoids and then followed them inland.

Interestingly, a check made at 20 or higher also reveals that sahuagin prints go both inland and back toward the water. As the sahuagin must be periodically submerged in water, they followed Brand and the *Zephyr* crew trail inland for about an hour before giving up and turning around to head back to the soothing waters of the Sinnar.

If the characters take the time to search the beach in this area for any of the gems referenced in Elisa Brand's journal, a successful DC 16 Intelligence (Investigation) check discovers a handful of small peridot and onyx stones after approximately 30 minutes of careful searching. These small stones seem to have been mixed into the sand as a result of all the recent foot traffic. The party can find 10 stones total, with an average value of 25 gp each.

Should the party decide to broaden their gem search either up or down the beach away from their landfall spot, call for a Perception check after every 15 minutes of searching in either direction. With each successful DC 16 Wisdom (Perception) check, the characters find a mixture of 5 peridot and onyx stones with an average of value of 50 gp each. After moving away and searching for more than an hour in either direction from their original landing spot, the party notices that

Getting Lost in the Jungle

The trail left by Elisa Brand and company and, for a short while, the pursuing sahuagin is easy to follow and leads directly to a small break in the jungle heading directly inland. However, once off the beach and attempting to follow Elisa Brand's trail farther inland, at least one of the characters must succeed on a DC 15 Wisdom (Survival) check every hour of travel in order to keep heading in the right direction. If two such checks are failed in succession, the party wanders into a concentration of caustic volcanic gas and has to make a DC 14 Constitution saving throw consistent with the information contained in the **General Notes on Crocodile Island** sidebar. After those saves are attempted, the characters experience a **saber-toothed jaguar**[D] attack. See the **Spending the Night** sidebar below for tactics and further information.

Volcanic Gases and the Characters' Route

The caustic gases that belch forth from several active volcanos on the island generally suffuse the entire island, depending on the winds. However, in times when the winds are down, the gases pool around the cones of the volcanos themselves. That is the case when the characters arrive at Crocodile Island. Presently, the north and south ends of the island each contain heavy concentrations of sulfur dioxide (as indicated on the map of the island). Fortunately for the party, and due to the laxity of the winds, the middle band of the island is free of these heavy gas concentrations. This area is still saturated with the terrible smell and irritants that plague the characters, but they are not subject to the more serious effects of the sulfur dioxide gas. That is, unless the characters stray far from the path either to the north or to the south, consistent with the effects stated in the **General Notes on Crocodile Island** sidebar.

At the point where the party enters the jungle, the island is a bit less than 20 miles across as a parrot flies. It is a very rough and winding trail that requires an ascent replete with many switchbacks before encountering a pass between the volcanic peaks followed by a descent to a valley in the approximate center of the island. Should the characters follow Elisa Brand's tracks to their conclusion, it requires three days of travel up and over the volcanic range and then down to the valley containing the saltwater lagoon, to the location where the sahuagin overpowered and captured Elisa and company.

the sulfur smell intensifies and goes from annoying to being caustic. At this point, they are close to entering the marked areas on the map containing denser concentrations of sulfur dioxide. See the **General Notes on Crocodile Island** sidebar for the effects of prolonged exposure to the island's caustic volcanic gases.

The trail that leads inland starts out sandy, but quickly turns to soft and loamy soil interspersed with large patches of rough volcanic rock. The characters notice two things immediately after leaving the beach and walking underneath the canopy: 1) the ground begins to rise as they head inland; and 2) the temperature and humidity increase dramatically. After a few minutes of following Elisa and company's apparent tracks inland, please read or paraphrase the following:

With just a few steps into the jungle, the beach behind you and the glimmering Sinnar Ocean are quickly swallowed by the heavy emerald-green canopy. You still catch occasional glimpses of the sky through small fissures in the dense and enveloping foliage above. The briny, crisp air behind you is now replaced with stagnant, humid, and burning ventilation seemingly caused by the heavy jungle and the volcanic activity of this island.

As you proceed inland, you feel the ground beneath your feet gradually incline as you wind around massive tree trunks and outcroppings of volcanic rock. Your clothing and armor stick to you unpleasantly, and the hum of biting insects accompany each of your steps. You feel like you are being engulfed by the cacophony of jungle sounds, including the warbles and calls of countless colorful birds and the hoots

After 100 feet or so in, the trail that the characters follow narrows, allowing only single-file travel. Should the party spend time to search for precious stones, they find them using the same check DC and frequency as noted above for similar exploration efforts as on the beach. The difference is that the stones will not be in loose sand but are encased in the ubiquitous and sharp formations of igneous rock. Any such stones found are easily pried out of the enfolding rock. Finally, if the characters decide to do an extended gem hunt, use the same limits and toxic gas effects as stated above in the beach exploration section.

As mentioned above, if any of the characters are making regular Wisdom (Survival) checks to stay on the trail and follow the tracks of Elisa Brand and company, they notice that the trailing sahuagin prints stop after about an hour's travel in from the beach. A successful DC 17 check indicates that the sahuagin doubled back at this point. A successful DC 15 Intelligence (Nature) check informs the characters that sahuagin, based on their amphibious nature, cannot stay out of the water for more than a few hours.

Unwitting Allies

Unfortunately for the party, after Elisa Brand and her away team passed this way, a **deathwatch beetle**[D] settled in near the trail hoping to catch an easy meal. The beetle is carefully camouflaged; thus, it takes a successful DC 20 Wisdom (Perception) check to notice that the vegetation-covered mound along the righthand side of the trail is something more than it appears. If not noticed, it attacks the lead character with surprise.

Complicating things is the presence of 4 **spell parrots**[D] in the trees above. The characters should not take any notice of them since they look exactly like normal parrots. The jungle is full of a vast array of brightly plumed birds including many parrots and macaws, so encountering them here should not be of any moment to the party.

If the party attacks the beetle with any arcane spells, there is a chance that each of the parrots may mimic the spell and affect a target at random, including the characters and the beetle. As these are very rare creatures, only a successful DC 18 Intelligence (Arcana) check reveals that these spell effects are coming from the parrots above.

The mindless predator attacks the party until it is killed. The beetle does not have anything of value. If attacked, the parrots fly away.

Dangerous Flora

At any point that makes sense (but while still ascending), the characters encounter an aggressive plant-like creature. Among the many colorful blooms of the jungle, a **blood orchid**[D] sits near the trail looking for some easy prey.

Because of its large size and bright red hue, only a DC 12 Wisdom (Perception) check is required to notice it provided that the characters are within 50 feet of the plant. However, if noticed, it merely looks like a big flower with three downward-curving petals of flesh with dark, pebbly outer hides and pallid whitish undersides. A DC 20 Wisdom (Nature) check is necessary to recognize that it is dangerous. If any of the characters come within 30 feet of the plant, it flies and attacks. Should the party steer around the blood orchid and stay at least 30 feet away from it in doing so, it remains quiescent.

If attacked by multiple adversaries and reduced by more than half its hit points, the blood orchid attempts to flee.

Spending the Night

Crocodile Island is a verdant and dangerous place. For each eight hours spent camping or resting in one place, there is a 50% chance of an encounter. If an encounter happens, either choose one of the following that suits the situation or determine one with a 1d6 roll:

1d6	Encounter
1	Saber-toothed jaguar
2	Giant sloth
3	Mobat
4	Prehistoric honey badger
5	Giant fly
6	Allosaurus

Saber-toothed jaguar[D] **attack.** This nocturnal hunter smells the party's camp and approaches. The large cat circles the camp looking for a good place to attack, seeking to surprise its prey and drag off a delicious character. If reduced to less than 50% of its hit points, it flees to seek easier prey.

Giant sloth[D] **at graze.** At some point while camping, anyone serving watch duty hears the unmistakable sound of something large moving through the jungle near them. It is a giant sloth foraging. The massive herbivore ignores the characters if unmolested, and the creature moves on after a few minutes, barely taking notice of the party. However, if it is attacked, it fights back to the best of its ability.

Mobat[D] **attack.** As the party rests, the characters are attacked by an equal number of mobats. They press the attack until half of their number are killed.

Prehistoric honey badger[D] **encounter.** While this campsite may have seemed like a safe and reasonable location, the party did not realize that they were setting up camp close to an underground honey badger lair. At some point, the five-foot-long, aggressive, weasel-like creature investigates who has come for a visit. It is very interested in the characters' food supplies and rends and tears backpacks to pieces to get what it wants. If reduced to less than 50% of its hit points, it retreats to its hidden lair.

Giant fly[D] **visit.** Just like real-life flies, this encounter is not dangerous, just annoying. As the characters rest, six giant flies descend on the camp to investigate the delicious smells they detected. They hover and fly around for several minutes looking for food. They buzz off if one of their number is killed or leave on their own after 10 minutes of thoroughly annoying the party.

Allosaurus[D] **attack.** No uncharted, tropical, and volcanic island would be complete without a dinosaur or two. As the party camps, they are set upon by a vicious allosaurus. The mindless predator attacks until it is slain.

The High Moor

Depending on their rate of travel, but likely early in Day 2 of following Elisa Brand's trail, the party notices that the ground here surprisingly flattens. They further notice that the already damp air becomes even more humid and that the ever-present stinging insects become even more numerous. Over the millennia, a small fen developed here in this slight depression on the slope of the volcanoes. The roughly circular moor is about 100 yards in diameter.

The trail skirts the swamp to the south. Depending on how the party proceeds, they may be able to pass this locale without event. However, if they fail to make attempts to be quiet and careful in their passage (requiring a group DC 14 Dexterity [Stealth] check), they attract the attention of a mated pair of **bog beasts**^D that call this small marsh home.

The creatures are quite territorial and resent any intrusions. As a result, they viciously attack until one of their number is slain and the other is reduced by 75% or more of its hit points.

Should the party strike out across the fen instead of around it, they are attacked by 4 **swarms of poisonous frogs**^D in succession.

Nothing of value is in this moor.

Pass

Based on speed of travel, the party should reach the pass between two adjacent calderas sometime in the middle of Day 2. At this spot above the tree line of the jungle, the characters are afforded a spectacular view of the island and the surrounding sea. They can look behind them and see the two ships at anchor on the east side of the island. After moving 50 feet or so along the length of the rocky pass, they can see down into a valley featuring a small sparkling lake surrounded by sandy beach. Beyond the valley with the small lake at the bottom, the characters see the volcanic hills rise to form the far side of the valley.

From this spot, it looks as if it would take a few hours to reach the floor of the valley ahead of them. This is the approximate center of the island with respect to east and west. A successful DC 16 Intelligence check confirms this for the characters.

As to the pass itself, a successful DC 12 Wisdom (Survival or Perception) check reveals a smaller trail leading away to the right (north) and winding farther up the side of that volcanic peak. The main trail bears the unmistakable signs of recent passage continuing west. However, this small side trail shows no such recent traffic. A DC 14 Wisdom (Survival) check indicates that this newly discovered side trail bears signs of aged tracks heading north and up toward the eastern face of the peak. A barefoot human appears to have made these sparse tracks. There is no way to accurately date these tracks beyond recognizing that they are longstanding. This trail leads to Captain Garth Blackbeard's hideout.

Captain Garth Blackbeard's Cavern Complex

The steep and winding trail leads to the hidden cave where Captain Garth Blackbeard made the best life he could for himself while marooned on this island many years ago. The single-track winds for about 300 yards, making for a total ascent from the pass of approximately 50 feet. The mouth of the cave is not visible from anywhere on the pass. Once the party rounds a final bend in the trail, they see the cave mouth, facing east, a mere 20 feet away from them. There are no signs of movement in the cave mouth nor any sounds emanating from within.

As the party approaches Captain Blackbeard's cave, please read or paraphrase the following:

If the party searches for tracks, they find none on this windswept mesa. The cave opening is approximately six feet tall and eight feet wide. It is made of the same igneous rock that dominates the entire island. Sunlight entering the cave entrance illuminates the cave with dim light. The cave widens after the opening to approximately a 12-foot-wide-by-15-foot-deep chamber. The ceiling remains the same six feet or so as the cave aperture.

The floor is littered with fish bones, cracked shells, and the desiccated husks of some sort of large seed or fruit. Nothing else of interest immediately presents itself.

The Sad Tale of Captain Garth Blackbeard

A score of years ago, Captain Blackbeard was leading a trade expedition across the Sinnar Ocean out of the port city of Freegate aboard his ship, the *Dauntless*. Beset by a terrible storm, his ship was torn asunder, resulting in a complete loss of almost all hands onboard. Captain Blackbeard survived by clutching a large piece of floating spar and also due to his wonderous magical ring, a *ring of water breathing*^B. He floated for countless days until the currents deposited him on the shores of Crocodile Island. Exhausted and severely dehydrated, Captain Blackbeard made his way into the jungle where he fortunately found some sweet water in the form of a small stream. After reviving a bit, he made his way inland to try to figure out where he was. Wandering the same trail that Elisa Brand would take many years later, he discovered a small cavern complex high up on the slopes of one of the volcanic peaks. He had no supplies other than the clothes he wore, the few weapons he bore when the storm stuck, and the spar and piece of sail, left on the beach, that kept him afloat all those days on the open water.

Captain Blackbeard spent many years exploring the island while carefully surviving the dangers of the jungle. He observed the craniform colony from a distance but never made contact with them out of fear. Other than taking the steps necessary to keep himself alive, he spent his days sitting in front of his cave keeping a vigil for any ship that might pass near the island. After many such years spent on his aerie, hoping in vain for a glimpse of any vessel and more than just a little insane at this point, he finally died in his sleep one night while secure in his cavernous home.

However, after entering the cave, a successful DC 20 Wisdom (Perception) check alerts characters to a slight draft coming from deeper within the cave. A successful DC 16 Intelligence (Investigation) check reveals a narrow fissure in the very back of the cave covered with a cleverly fit piece of heavy canvas. Any careful examination of the canvas leads the characters to recognize it as a piece of sail.

The fissure is not perfectly oriented straight up and down but rather is diagonal going from left to right and from floor to ceiling. The fissure is approximately three feet deep before a larger space opens beyond it. It is completely dark beyond the fissure.

While a tight fit, a medium creature can squeeze through this opening. If anyone examines the crevice itself, they see that the leading edges and inner faces of it seem worn smooth. This was due, of course, to the repeated passage of Captain Blackbeard. A DC 15 Intelligence (Nature) check informs the characters that the wear is from some repeated passage by some unknown creature pushing through the crevice.

Beyond the fissure was Captain Blackbeard's residence until he died of natural causes, greatly accelerated by malnutrition and poor mental health.

Not comfortable relying on his camouflaged door alone, Captain Blackbeard rigged a trap on the far side of the crevice as a further line of protection. Two inches or so above the floor on the far end of the crevice, Captain Blackbeard rigged a trip "wire" (thinly woven vine strands) that triggered a spring type scythe trap.

SIMPLE SCYTHE SPRING TRAP

Trigger. Any jostling or "tripping" of the tripwire pulls the restraining peg free and allows the spring-loaded wooden arm to violently snap toward the opening of the fissure.

HANDAXE OF LIGHTNING

Handaxe, very rare (requires attunement)

You gain a +2 bonus to attack and damage rolls made with this weapon. When you hit with an attack with this weapon, the target takes an additional 1d6 lightning damage. Further, the weapon bears the additional minor property:

Aqueous: While you are attuned to this item, you attack underwater without the normal underwater melee penalty and you have advantage on Strength (Athletics) checks to swim.

RING OF WATER BREATHING

Ring, uncommon (requires attunement)

While wearing this ring you can breathe normally underwater.

Effect. Captain Blackbeard built this trap out of a bamboo-like wood. He then mounted a long, dagger-shaped piece of volcanic rock on the end that was designed to impale any would-be invader. Fortunately, the years have dried the spring-loaded wooden arm and made it less effective than it was when the trap was first set. **To hit:** +10; **Hit:** (3) 1d6 slashing damage.

Countermeasures. A successful DC 18 Wisdom (Perception) or Intelligence (Investigation) check reveals the tripwire. If recognized, it is a simple matter to step over the wire. Once on the other side and in the far chamber, any reasonable attempt succeeds at disarming the trap. However, a character trying to disarm it while in the fissure itself must succeed on a DC 16 Dexterity check while using thieves' tools or a DC 16 Dexterity (Sleight of Hand) check. Failure triggers the trap.

Beyond the crevice is Captain Garth Blackbeard's former quarters and his final resting place. This lentiform natural cavern is quite narrow but quickly widens to a space of nearly eight feet across before tapering to a point in the far end of the cavern, roughly 10 feet away from the fissure.

Beyond the trap on the eastern end of this small and vaguely turnip-shaped room, there is a sleeping mat that contains the remains of Captain Blackbeard and a small set of crude wooden shelves adjacent to the mat before the room tapers to the west. After the characters enter this room and clear the trap, please read or paraphrase the following:

After clearing the crude but dangerous trap at the far end of the fissure, you find yourself in a cramped cavern that widens as you move away from the fissure to a width of nearly eight feet. At the midpoint of the room, it begins to taper down again until the chamber terminates in a punctiform fashion roughly ten feet away from you to the west.

Beyond the vaguely turnip shape of the room, you immediately notice two features: one appears to be a sleeping pallet or mat made of desiccated fronds and leaves, on top of which lies a supine skeletal body clad in tattered bits of clothing; next to and a bit behind the pallet and body stands a small crude shelf, about three feet tall with two shelves. The shelves appear to be heaped with all kinds of shells and rocks.

The body is that of Captain Garth Blackbeard. The poor and tormented captain died in his sleep. Besides the tattered remains of his clothing, his body bears his magic ring: a *ring of water breathing*[B]. It is on the corpse's second finger on its left hand. Lying next to the body's right hand is a handaxe that glimmers faintly if any light source is brought into the room. If examined, it shows no signs of rust or wear. It is a *handaxe of lightning*. It was Captain Garth's prized possession, and its magic played a big role in helping him survive on this island for as long as he did.

On the small shelving unit that Captain Blackbeard fashioned sits his collection of odds and ends that he gathered on the island over his years of being marooned here. Among the interesting shells and the pretty but worthless rocks are the following gemstones: 5 peridots worth 100 gp each, 3 peridots worth 200 gp each, 6 onyx gems worth 50 gp each, and 2 fire agates worth 500 gp each.

THE SULKING GIANT

Whether or not the party investigates Captain Blackbeard's hideout, they likely continue to follow the trail of Elisa Brand as it continues west. The trail now descends back into the dense jungle toward the valley below after leaving the pass behind. As they reach the end of the pass and before they start down the other side of this mountain, please read or paraphrase the following:

> As you reach the end of this high pass, you realize that the island is not composed of volcanic peaks all arrayed in a perfect line. Your eyes are immediately drawn to a small sparkling blue lake far below you. It seems that a valley is hidden among the peaks in the center of this island. The lake or lagoon is outlined by a beach that surrounds it and stands between the water's edge and the encroaching dense jungle. The trail you follow heads down and toward this distant valley.

However, before getting back into the jungle proper and only a few hundred yards down from the pass the characters just navigated, they see a strange sight: a brooding **volcano giant**[D] lost in thought, staring out over the valley below. As the party approaches, please read or paraphrase the following:

> As you make your way down the rocky trail still heading west on the trail of Elisa Brand, you come upon a most strange and startling sight. About 25 yards farther downslope and still above the jungle sits a very large humanoid of some sort. It seems to be staring down at the valley below. You can see its broad back as it sits on a boulder; the boulder itself is at least six feet tall. You see that its skin is a leathery dark brown and that it wears only a wrap by way of clothing around its waist. The creature must be 18 feet tall or so. Propped up next to the rock is a massive spear that looks to be at least 12 feet in length. As you stand there taking in this amazing creature, its head turns toward you, clearly seeing you all. Its heavyset features take you in evenly and dispassionately. If anything, the large humanoid bears a slightly mournful expression.

This is Uder Conbar, a volcano giant brought to this remote island to serve at the pleasure of the grand duke of the City of Brass. The efreet visits the island frequently and sought a servant suited to the intense temperatures and conditions of a series of active volcanos. Uder was taken from the rest of his tribe who reside under the Hellsgate Peaks mountains. He now serves at the grand duke's pleasure here on this remote island far away from his family and friends. This all makes for a sad giant.

Uder is not looking for a fight but certainly battles with gusto if given an excuse. At CR 13, he would likely be more than a match for the party, so caution should be the order of the moment. Please note

HELPING UDER

If the characters are willing to help Uder and say anything to that effect to him, he mentions that the grand duke brought him here through a planar portal. This portal is in the depths of the volcano and Uder has not seen the grand duke use it since. Uder can lead the party there, and after a one-hour winding descent through hot, stale, and acrid (sulfur) air-filled tunnels, the group arrives at a landing 400 feet above a large lake of molten lava. The heat here is nearly unbearable.

In the middle of this landing is a 10-foot-diameter circle of inscribed arcane runes on the ground. A successful DC 18 Intelligence (Arcana) check is necessary to activate the portal. If successful, the earth shakes as the portal blazes with magical energy. A hazy image of a view from the Hellsgate Peaks mountains appears within the circle's bounds. Uder immediately recognizes what he is seeing and without a backward glance, strides into the circle and immediately disappears. The circle then stills, and the runes go dark.

that volcano giants feel that their shadows are actually their souls and will not suffer any creature who dares trod upon it.

If the characters are cautious and not overtly hostile, Uder can actually be a good source of information for them. Any sort of approach made with non-threatening gestures and words accompanying a successful DC 13 Charisma (Persuasion) check makes Uder well-disposed to the characters. As he is exceptionally bored, he is happy to speak with them.

Finally, if any of the characters get near Uder, they will feel powerful heat radiating off the giant. This heat is not dangerous as long as the characters do not get too close.

In the course of conversation, the party can learn the following from Uder:

• Uder Conbar hails from the Hellsgate Peaks mountains.
• He was convinced to come here and serve the grand duke of the City of Brass, an efreet who was not entirely honest with him about the terms of his servitude.
• He was under the impression that he could return to his home whenever he wished, but he came to learn that this is not the case.
• Uder longs to return to his home, his tribe, and his family.
• The grand duke is not present currently.
• The grand duke comes and goes without warning.
• Uder comes to this spot occasionally to watch the valley below and to pass the time.
• There is a surface vent a few hundred yards to the north of where he currently sits that he uses to access the surface.
• He did not see a party of humans pass this way but did note some sort

ROLEPLAYING UDER CONBAR

Uder Conbar is a mature male volcano giant. He is reasonably good-natured, but his forced servitude has made him resentful and melancholy. Overall, he is largely indifferent to the affairs of humans and their related "little people" races. He misses his tribe and his homeland. Had he not been taken, he likely would have a wife by now. He longs to return home and responds very positively to any suggestion of help in accomplishing that goal (see the **Helping Uder** sidebar). While not overtly aggressive, he is quick to anger and responds to anything that he takes as an insult with violence.

COMMON SAYINGS

• "Easy for you to say. Once you are done here, you have the means to return to your homes and to your people."
• "Tribe and honor are everything."
• "The twisting caverns of this island are beautiful, but I miss my home."

of disturbance or fight between humans and some sort of aquatic-looking creatures many days ago.

• He was able to watch it unfold from this very spot.
• The fight took place in the valley below, near the beach at the edge of the tree line on the shore of the lagoon below.
• He could not tell who prevailed.
• He does not care who prevailed.
• He thinks the disturbance took place 14 days ago but is not exactly sure about that.
• He did notice some of the craniform observing the conflict.
• A colony of humanoid craniform live in a series of underwater caverns somewhere underneath the lagoon.
• He does not know anything more about the craniform, the humans, or the aquatic creatures.

Uder is willing to talk with the characters for as long as they like, for as long as they are respectful, because he really has nothing better to do. If asked, he respectfully declines an invitation to join the party as his duties to the grand duke continue.

Should the characters survive their interaction with Uder, the trail beckons leading down the mountain and into the valley below. Likely, the party wants to head to the location that Uder indicated, or if they did not talk to Uder, the path they follow takes them eventually to that spot anyway.

Dangerous Pet

Not all of the grand duke's minions are as welcoming and amiable as Uder. Knowing that his pet would enjoy the unique mineral composition of the volcanic island, the grand duke brought his **red bulette**[D] to Crocodile Island years ago. It usually spends its time in the depths of the island as it eagerly consumes the rare minerals embedded in the volcanic rock. But unfortunately for the party, it is grazing on mineral clusters just 20 feet below the surface and about 50 yards downslope from the spot where the characters met Uder.

As the character pass overhead, it is attracted by the unusual metals they carry and bursts up in the middle of the party to randomly attack a character. To keep from being surprised takes a successful DC 20 Wisdom (Perception) check to detect the slight rumbling beneath their feet while quickly putting together that something is approaching the party at speed from underground.

Because it is not carnivorous and is interested in the party only because of the refined metals they carry, the bulette dives back into the metamorphic rock of the island and flees if it is reduced to fewer than half of its hit points.

In the event that Uder remains where the party met him, he watches the attack with amusement. He does not intervene unless it looks as if the party is in serious trouble. In that event, Uder heaves his massive spear through the air to strike the bulette broadside. This blow drives off the bulette. If asked, Uder states that he "never liked the dirty beast anyway."

It takes half a day to get down from the pass and down to the floor of the valley if the characters are traveling on foot. The hot, humid, and pungent-smelling jungle remains their constant companion.

Mud Slide

As the party continues to plow through the oppressive and damp jungle while continuing to stay on the trail of Elisa Brand, the characters have to endure one more hazard before reaching the valley floor and the small lake at its center.

The steep grade of the descent into the valley, the shallow topsoil, and the heavy humidity have made for perfect mudslide conditions. About an hour after fighting off the bulette, the soft ground suddenly shifts under the characters' feet. With astonishing speed, a huge swath of jungle ferociously tumbles down the side of the mountain and sweeps up everything in its path, including the characters.

Everyone must succeed on a DC 15 Dexterity (Acrobatics) check

or take 35 (8d6) bludgeoning damage and be buried alive and begin to suffocate. Those who succeed take 10 (3d6) bludgeoning damage and are able to avoid being buried. For those buried, see the rules for suffocating (a creature can hold its breath for a number of minutes equal to 1 + its Constitution modifier for a minimum of 30 seconds). A character can dig itself or another character out with two successful DC 15 Strength (Athletics) checks. Finding a buried creature requires a successful DC 14 Wisdom (Perception) check.

Assuming the characters extricate themselves from this muddy morass, the rest of their journey to the valley floor is uneventful.

The Hidden Valley

The characters should be at least 7th level at this point of the adventure.

After several days of hot and harrowing travel through the tangle of the island, the characters arrive at the spot where Elisa Brand's away team was assailed by the sahuagin. The exact spot of the confrontation is a small, sandy clearing at the edge of the jungle where it meets the beach of the lagoon. As the party arrives, please read or paraphrase the following:

> At this point, you are thoroughly tired of this godforsaken island with its stinging insects, dangerous plants, and poisoned air. Your eyes burn, and your nose is raw from wiping. At least you have descended from the heights to this scenic valley while following the trail of the elusive Elisa Brand and her away team.
>
> While the tracks you have followed these few days have remained consistent, you have yet to sight any of the *Zephyr's* crew. However, immediately before you lies a small, sandy clearing that sits on the edge of the jungle where the jungle meets the narrow beach surrounding the small lake you spotted from the pass above. You notice that the sand looks heavily churned, and you see what appear to be the remains of a few broken weapons. It is then that you notice a foul odor separate from the sulfur smells of the island. You cannot deny the stench of animal decomposition. Finally, you note a few oddly-shaped lumps at the edge of the clearing and just under the surrounding verge. As your eyes focus, you recognize that what you are seeing are the shapes of several bodies tangled together and lying at impossible angles.

If the characters investigate, a successful DC 13 Wisdom (Survival) check reveals that a melee fight involving at least 10 combatants occurred in this clearing and spilled over onto the

A Saltwater Lake in the Middle of the Island?

The saltwater lagoon in the middle of the island is fed by underground water-filled passages that extend out to the surrounding ocean. However, without knowing this geography, an inland saltwater lake with sandy beaches might strike the characters as odd. As the characters approach the lake, a successful DC 13 Wisdom (Perception) check reveals the brine smell of salt water over the pervasive smell of sulfur. If the check succeeds by 3 or more, those successful further notice the telltale signs of a gentle tide affecting this lake. They are able to pick out the striated layers of sand deposited by the tide on the beach surrounding the lagoon.

HIDDEN VALLEY CRANIFORM

The craniform are an intelligent race of humanoids that inhabit the still and temperate waters of this saltwater lagoon. Their colony is located in a series of submerged caverns on the eastern side of the lagoon, a bit south of where the characters first encounter them. The waters of the brine lagoon are fed by passages that lead to the greater sea around the island. While these tunnels are vital to the survival of the craniform colony and allow them to access the sea in order to hunt and forage for food, they are also the means by which they were first visited by the marauding sahuagin.

Since this first raid decades ago, this intelligent and peaceful race has been preyed upon for generations by the predatory sahuagin whose city, Tzar'Grandula, is not far to the south and west in the depths of the Sinnar Ocean. In order to keep from being completely wiped out by the marauding sahuagin, the craniform pay tribute to the sahuagin by offering some of their young craniform to be taken back to the King Bachzarisaa's submerged city to serve as slaves and, ultimately, as food for the terrible sahuagin. These steps have helped preserve this peaceful race. The craniform speak Aquan and Craniform.

---

beach. Because this fight took place nearly two weeks ago, some of the signs are harder to pick up than others. A successful DC 15 Wisdom (Survival) check picks up traces of sahuagin prints moving both away from the water's edge and into the clearing as well as toward the lagoon. A check of DC 18 or more reveals faint traces of blood mixed into the sand in the clearing that have mostly faded away. Finally, a check of DC 20 or more seems to indicate that several booted figures walked toward the lagoon amid many sahuagin prints heading in the same direction. These prints halt at the edge of the water.

If the characters investigate, they find the remains of four mangled humanoid bodies that are the source of the powerful rotting stench that suffuses the entire area. There are two females (both human) and two males (one human and one elf), and all appear to have been sailors. While the characters do not recognize any of the decedents, they do recognize the general garb and kit the bodies bear, all of which identifies them as sailors. These unfortunate sailors were part of Elisa Brand's away team who were caught and beset by the sahuagin. These four were killed in the recent attack. The marauding sahuagin stripped the sailors of anything of value, including their weapons.

Importantly, none of the bodies matches the description of Elisa Brand.

If the characters try to discern how exactly these people were killed, a successful DC 12 Wisdom (Medicine) check reveals that these poor souls bear wounds inflicted by sahuagin claws, teeth, and spears.

Unfortunately for the party, the scent of the ripening bodies has caught the attention of a pair of **trolls** that call this part of the island home. The trolls arrive shortly after the characters start examining the bodies. The badly decomposed bodies smell delicious to the trolls and they will not be driven off this find — along with the fresh meat that the party represents. They fight to the death to defend their planned meal.

THE CRANIFORM

Unbeknownst to the characters, a contingent of **craniform**[D] have been watching them from just under the surface of the water close to shore. Shortly after the fight with the terrible trolls, please read or paraphrase the following:

Just when you thought things could not get any stranger on this bizarre and pungent island in the middle of nowhere, 15 or so impossibly strange crab-like humanoids break the surface of the water and walk up the beach toward you. They each bear an obsidian-tipped spear. They stop at least 25 feet away from you and one, the leader of the group, steps forward and lays its spear on the ground. It then extends its lower set of arms toward you, pincers pointed upward in a sign of non-aggression. The trailing creatures then each sink to their knees and bow forward, cancriform heads almost touching the sand, in clear genuflection toward you. As they kneel, each places their spear flat on the sand.

The creatures themselves appear to be some sort of cancriform humanoid. Each of them bears a carapace of chitinous composition, eyestalks that fixate on your group, antennae, and a pair of mandibles set to either side of a complementary set of horizontally-aligned maxillae that constitute the creatures' mouths. Extending outward from the neck of each crab creature is a set of short but large chitinous arms, each of which terminates in a seemingly oversized claw. Below these larger claws is another set of arms. These extend from either side of the upper torso, not unlike how arms extend from shoulders in more familiar humanoids. This second set of smaller chitinous arms each ends with a smaller pincer. The creatures' torsos and legs are covered by the same chitinous exoskeleton that extends to cover their clawed feet.

As you try to make sense of what you see before you, the leading crab creature takes a step forward and slightly bows its head toward you and speaks. Well, at least you think it is speaking. After a moment, you realize that it is speaking to you in Common, of sorts. As you listen, you sort out what it is saying. Its odd voice is a collection of rasping sounds and clicks. You are able to make out: "You are most welcome breathers of air. Long have the folk awaited your coming. Please. Only your friendship do we want. Welcome to the embrace of the Sea Mother."

And with that, the crab creature looks at you, awaiting your response.

The characters are faced by Jyrcyx, a **craniform priestess**[D] and spiritual leader, and 14 **craniform**[D]. They hope and sincerely believe that the characters are their promised saviors. Jyrcyx speaks a stilted form of Common after engaging her *tongues* spell and speaks for the craniform. Should the characters attack or make any overt hostile gestures, the craniform flee back to the lagoon and return to the safety of their underwater caverns in order to consider their existential crisis brought on by the party's hostilities toward them. However, should the party take a "see what happens next" approach or even move toward the craniform without obvious aggression, Jyrcyx is more than happy to speak with them.

This encounter is likely unnerving to the characters. The craniform will not move until the party does something. The priestess that addressed them is ready and eager to speak further with the characters. She answers any questions the characters pose to the best of her ability. Even though strange and foreign looking, a successful DC 12 Wisdom (Insight) roll inform the characters that Jyrcyx is being truthful and honest.

Unfortunately for Elisa Brand and her sailors, her arrival at this fascinating and hidden saltwater lagoon coincided with a visit by the

CRANIFORM COLONY
1 Square – 5 Feet
6
4
5
3
2
1
N
E
S
W

ROLEPLAYING JYRCYX

While able to speak Common, Jyrcyx and all craniform are quite foreign to land dwellers. They have a fundamentally different understanding of the world around them than that of the characters. For the craniform, the sea is everything. The characters' world is of course much broader. The characters should find Jyrcyx's communication stilted and odd. Her sentences are short, and it is often hard to figure out exactly what she means. Jyrcyx — as well as any other craniform trying to communicate with the characters — are prone to unneeded corrections and repetitions. Because the craniform are so foreign, they are almost impossible to offend. Many basic terms that normal humanoids use are completely foreign and unknown to the craniform. Finally, Jyrcyx and all the craniform are peaceful and nonaggressive people.

COMMON SAYINGS

• "Everything is Sea Mother and Sea Mother is everything."
• "Without the sea, there is nothing."
• "The tides provide."
• "The craniform are the true vision of the Sea Mother."

dreadful sahuagin there to pick up their doomed craniform tribute. The sahuagin knew that there were air-breathers on the island as they had attacked the *Zephyr*. They then tracked the team inland a bit before returning to the safety of the water. The sahuagin were delighted to see Elisa Brand and company appear on the shore of the lagoon so close to the home of their servitor craniform.

As evidenced by the remains in the clearing, the crew of the *Zephyr* did not go quietly. They battled the sahuagin until they were overwhelmed by the superior numbers of the aquatic predators.

Elisa Brand and three of her fellow crewmembers were taken alive. Two more slain crewmembers were also taken to serve as immediate food for the sahuagin.

The craniform observed the fight between the sahuagin and Elisa Brand's party as well as the characters' clash with the trolls. The bravery and fierceness exhibited by both groups merely confirms what the craniform believe, that the characters represent salvation and their deliverance from the depredations of the sahuagin (see **The Prophecy** sidebar below).

Speaking with Jyrcyx can be frustrating, but she is eager to communicate with the characters. This of course is a very fluid encounter. The characters can speak to her at length here on this strand. Should a lengthy colloquy take place here or not, Jyrcyx invites the party to join her and the rest of her clan in their colony, about 100 feet to the south. Jyrcyx reassures the characters that the journey underwater is short ("Just a few grasses down," see the **Craniform Units of Measurement** sidebar), and that some of their subterranean caves are not water-filled but are filled with air and are dry.

What follows summarizes what the characters can learn from Jyrcyx. There is a lot here, and it could very well come out in a series

The Prophecy

Generations of craniform have suffered at the clawed hands of the sahuagin. Over the ages, every attempt to fight back was met by a brutal repression. The craniform survived through the years only by appeasing the voracious appetites of the sahuagin by sacrificing a percentage of each generation of craniform young. For an intelligent species, this makes for a terrible existence.

While the concept of pulling up stakes and moving is inconceivable to the craniform, they are not completely unaware of the greater outside world. The craniforms' oral traditions tell of past terrestrial visitors to the island and tales of a savior group of air-breathers who will free the craniform from the subjugation at the hands of the vicious sahuagin. The central tenet of this belief is that the craniform must be true in their faith and believe in this salvation, and only then will the promised succor be delivered to free them from this terrible reality. This one hope has afforded the craniform the will to persevere in the face of the relentless depredations by the sahuagin.

of conversations. It can be delivered either in summary fashion or roleplayed out in all of its oddness. What Jyrcyx knows:
- We have lived in the shoals and shallows in this sanctuary (the saltwater lagoon) for many birthings (generations).
- We have no memory of living anywhere else.
- Sea Mother (the sea itself and their deity — distinct concepts) provides all.
- We reach the embrace of the Sea Mother (the greater sea) by ways (submerged tunnels under the island).
- The vile (sahuagin) used to regularly raid our colony.
- They attacked us until we were nearly sand (dead or gone).
- Before we returned to the sand, we had to make a shift (deal or exchange).
- Once every third moon (month), we must deliver five of our young to the vile.
- Choice is made by driftless selection (drawing lots).
- They use them as servants and food.
- This sacrifice is terrible, but it must be.
- It is the deepest sadness of the folk.
- Buoyancy (hope or faith) keeps us swimming.
- Because of an oracle (vision or prophecy) many birthings ago by a great Gifted (priestess), we have kept buoyancy.
- The oracle tells of a group of air-breathers that will free us from the vile.
- Fifteen sunsets ago the vile came for their price (tribute of young slaves).
- At the same time, a different group of air-breathers arrived at our shores.
- They were attacked by a large school of vile.
- They tried to help us and save our cherished (young craniform).
- The air-breathers fought fiercely despite having a much smaller school.
- Several air-breathers died.
- Four were taken alive by the vile into the waves.
- Four air-breathers walked into the waves, and two were dragged.
- The four walking air-breathers were different sizes.
- Two others not alive were dragged into the waves.
- Whether they live or die, only Sea Mother knows.
- The vile forced the air-breathers to take air bladders that the vile use to swim air-breathers down to their reef.
- What is hair? (If asked about identifying characteristics such as hair or hair color.)
- The king of the vile is called Bachzarisaa.
- His city is many kelps from here.

- The city is called Tzar'Grandula, which means "City of Feasts."
- It is in the deep and warm blue water. (Points to the south.)
- Your fierceness is effervescent.
- You must be the air-breathers that were oracled!
- You will destroy King Bachzarisaa and free us from the viles!
- This tide has been awaited for many birthings!
- We can help you!
- We can help you survive the waves!
- The folk have a ritual that will deliver the Blessing of the Sea Mother!
- You can be like the folk then, breathe both above and below the waves.
- Will you take the ritual and free us from the vile?!

The Craniform Colony

One hundred feet down the beach to the south, Jyrcyx indicates that the craniforms' home is down underwater and then back and up underneath the beach to the east. As the characters inspect the beach, they notice that the beach itself slopes appreciably down to the surface of the lake. The pitch is such that a successful DC 12 Intelligence check reveals that the drop from the clearing where the characters fought the trolls to the surface of the water is currently approximately 10 feet.

Craniform Colony General Conditions

All areas in the craniform cavern complex are completely dark. The volcanic rock walls are slick. Specific areas in the colony are underwater during high tide. The Sea Mother's Shrine (**Area 6**) is always dry. It is the high point in the cavern complex. Unless otherwise stated, the approximate ceiling height in each cave is 10 feet.

At any given time, at least 100 craniform, including young, are present in the colony. Sixty or so of these are fully grown and capable of defending the colony. Another 25 craniform are out foraging and hunting in the sea to help meet the colony's food needs.

The craniform are curious but respectful of the characters. The principle of the saviors is commonly known and understood in this community. However, only Jyrcyx and her two disciples have the *tongues* ability, so unless the characters undertake special communication efforts such as casting *comprehend languages* (for one-way communication) or *tongues* (both Divination spells, and consequently 50% ikely to fail), or if any of the characters speak Aquan, the party will not be able to speak with any of the other craniform colony members.

If the characters search the caverns, they find loose and uncut volcanic gems collected in various places. In fact, they are so common that craniform young play with them. Unless the party tries to completely "clear out" the craniform of their gems, they do not object to the characters taking any since gems like these are just that common on the island. The scattered gems are peridot and onyx stones. Their values range between 25 gp, 50 gp, and 100 gp each. There are literally dozens of each type of precious stone present. If the characters spend the time necessary to do so, they find 30 of each type of stone of the various values indicated above.

In any event, Jyrcyx suggests that it is easiest for air-breathers to approach the craniforms' colony during low tide. Despite being a saltwater lake in the middle of the island, due to the tunnels connecting the lake to the greater sea, the water level of the lagoon is affected by the tides. It is assumed that the characters follow this suggestion. If not, many of the areas described below are filled with water.

She further relates that waiting for the water lever to lower will make the approach much easier for air-breathers. If the characters wait two hours, the water level drops nearly five feet, at which time Jyrcyx indicates that now is a good time to make the short swim down.

Assuming the characters explore during low tide where Jyrcyx indicates, after wading out from the sandy beach they discover that the floor of the lagoon suddenly drops to surprising depths. They further find that a sheer volcanic rock headwall extends about five feet down until there is a broad opening that allows a swimmer to head east toward the side of the island where the *Zephyr* and *Bounty* are moored.

By this point, the party should have at least one magic device or potion that allows them to explore underwater without concern for drowning. In the unlikely event that they are not so equipped, it is a swim of less than one minute.

Jyrcyx and her people guide and even help characters who cannot swim well.

After getting under the imposing headwall and a swim of less than 20 feet back to the east (underneath the island), the party ascends to the surface of the water and find themselves treading water in an underground and circular subterranean pool roughly 30 feet or so in diameter. The rest of the walls surrounding the pool are sheer rock that terminate in a low ceiling just five feet above the water's surface. Finally, they see a rocky ledge on the far eastern side of the pool that slopes down and into the water.

The rock shield that slopes into the subterranean pool is slick but should pose no challenge to the characters. A short climb up brings them to the entrance to craniforms' home and their network of caverns under the island.

Area 1: Entrance Chamber

This area is submerged at high tide. As the characters enter this area, please read or paraphrase the following:

Denizens of the craniform colony gather to stare at the air-breathers, but they do not crowd or impede the progress of the party in any way. Unless the characters have other ideas, Jyrcyx leads them to the Sea Mother's Shrine (**Area 6**). As they proceed, the characters are able to look into the side chambers as Jyrcyx leads them steadily east. They also notice that the floor rises steadily the deeper they go into the cavern complex.

Area 2: Craniform Nursery

This area is submerged at high tide. This cavern is full of shallow pools, even at low tide, which makes it suitable for the care of craniform young. After hatching and for the first 8–12 months of their lives, craniform cannot breathe air and require constant submersion. This chamber is guarded at all times by at least 6 armed **craniform**[D]. However, the characters are not stopped if they wish to enter.

Area 3: Craniform Egg Pools

This area is submerged at high tide. The female craniform lay their eggs here. A series of shallow pools are in this chamber, even at low tide. As with **Area 2**, this part of the colony is similarly supervised. While they may enter this area, the characters are not allowed to touch or interfere in any way with the laid eggs resting in the pools.

Area 4: Craniform General Living Cavern

This western/lower portion of this cavern is submerged at high tide. The bulk of the craniform colony resides here. At any given time, food preparation, spear fashioning, resting, playing, and any other possible activity can take place. The characters can enter this chamber at any time.

Area 5: Craniform General Living Cavern

This western/lower portion of the cavern is submerged at high tide. Other than the dimensions, it is exactly the same as **Area 4**.

Area 6: Shrine to the Sea Mother

This area is never submerged, even during high tide. As the characters enter this area, please read or paraphrase the following:

As you approach what seems to be the very end of the warren, a final cavern mouth stands open directly ahead of you. Jyrcyx slows her pace, and you slow yours to match. While still moving forward, she bows her head slightly as she enters this unknown cave.

Entering, you are greeted by an even stranger sight. This roughly oval cavern is approximately 40 feet long and 20 feet deep and is a place of great significance to the craniform. The far wall is covered with a series of paintings or murals. Looking closer reveals that these images are a series of depictions of the subjugation and enslavement the craniform have suffered at the hands of the sahuagin. The panels show sahuagin slaughtering craniform, with craniform of all sizes being led off in bondage. They show images of apparent sadness with the craniform with their heads bowed standing around bodies of presumably dead craniform. However, the final panel shows something completely different. It appears to be an image of a ship, and on that ship are sailors hewing and hacking sahuagin apart with swords and axes.

Looking then to the left of this last mural, and at the highest point in the room, there lies a three-stepped dais topped with a statue or carving of some sort hewn out of dark black stone. Kneeling at either side of the statue are two craniform, their heads bowed in apparent reverence. As your group fully enters the cavern, both kneeling craniform take notice of you. No other craniform are in the room.

The two craniform flanking the statue are Zogren and Tati, two fellow **craniform priestesses**[D]. Along with Jyrcyx, they are the only craniform who can speak with the characters. In addition to the above from Jyrcyx, the party can learn any of the following from any of the three:

- Only female craniform can become priestesses.
- A priestess is a favored of the Sea Mother.
- They are referred to as "Gifted" among the folk.
- The first awareness of this favor comes in the form of a vision from the Sea Mother.
- This vision reveals the Sea Mother's true form: a massive sea turtle.
- The statue is a likeness of the Sea Mother (a sea turtle roughly carved out of obsidian).
- This chamber is a holy and important place for the craniform.
- Everything from education of the young to fertility ceremonies takes place here.
- The sahuagin have plagued the craniform for many birthings (generations).
- These three priestesses and the whole colony believe that the characters are their prophesized saviors.
- The priestesses are ready to perform the ritual — the Sea Mother's Blessing — whenever the characters are.
- The vile worship a terrible god called Dajobas the Devourer.
- The vile yearn for the release of the terrible Dajobas and believe that sacrificing to Dajobas by feasting on weaker species hastens the terrible god's return.

The characters are free to go anywhere in the craniform caverns that they wish and can leave entirely should they so desire. Jyrcyx, Zogren,

and Tati are willing to answer any questions the characters may have to the best of their ability. They are also prepared and ready to perform the ritual to give the characters the ability to pursue the sahuagin under the waves and to the sahuagin city whenever the characters wish. After all, the craniform have been waiting a long time for this day and are eager to be free of the sahuagin yoke.

THE RITUAL

The ritual itself is straightforward. The three craniform priestesses have a mildly caustic concoction that renders the imbiber temporarily unconscious and triggers a dream-like state that allows that subject to experience a connection with the Sea Mother herself.

The actual mechanics of the ritual require the priestesses to serve each participating person a shell filled with some thick and inky black liquid. The mixture is made up of sea anemone poison, octopus ink, lionfish blood, and gelatinous jellyfish tissue.

The ritual can accommodate as many of the characters as are willing to go through it at once. The priestesses simply produce as many shellfulls of the pungent brew as necessary. The party may elect to designate one of their number to go through it alone first as a sort of trial balloon for the rest of the group.

Regardless of the number of participants, when ready, the ritual begins with a craniform kneeling before each supplicant with head bowed while holding forth a shell of the liquid described above. They then encourage each petitioner to drink deeply of the "bounty of the sea."

As each character drinks, the priestesses collectively chant in their stilted and odd Common:

To those not participating in the ritual, they see each imbiber who drinks any amount of the liquid slump immediately to the ground unconscious. They see that each comatose character seems to be breathing, but if checked, they do not detect any sign of a heartbeat. This unconscious state lasts for approximately five minutes and the blacked-out character(s) cannot be revived by any means.

For those who participate in the ritual, they experience a powerfully transitive and psychedelic episode. This hallucinatory journey culminates in the characters having a brief encounter with the Sea Mother herself and confers upon them the abilities they need to confront the sahuagin in their own element.

For characters who do participate in the ritual, please read or paraphrase the following:

With an immense amount of trepidation, you follow the craniforms' guidance and sit on the stone floor in this hallowed chamber. The cave drawings seem to sit in mute judgment of you as you wonder what is going to happen next. After sitting, one craniform kneels before you, bows its head, and with extended arms, thrusts a shell filled with some sort of thick, oily, and inky black liquid toward you. Their direction and meaning are clear: You are to drink this stuff.

As you raise the shell to your lips, you catch the heavy fish smell of the chunky concoction, and as you taste it, you notice its sharp brine taste.

Your starting to drink must have been a signal to the craniform, because the three priestesses start to chant in their weird voices:

"You must die before you live, drink deeply and drown in what is she, swim larvae swim, to the Sea Mother you must

join, hatch reborn and perfect."

After your first swallow, you gag as your stomach roils in response to the noxious beverage. Then you feel a moment of panic as you realize that you cannot breathe. As hard as you try to pull air into your lungs, all that you get in return is the sensation of feeling faint. That is the last thing you remember as darkness washes over you.

As you come to, you immediately realize that you are not you. You are now something tiny and insignificant. This out-of-body experience has brought you somewhere deep underwater. You are swimming, sort of. It is more of a wiggle. Somehow your wiggling motion propels you forward. You realize that you are not alone. All around you are thousands more that look exactly like you — some sort of underwater larvae all struggling toward the same goal. You are struck by how exposed and vulnerable you are in this vast and deep place.

With a lurch, your existence suddenly shifts. You are still swimming, but now it feels more purposeful and controlled. While still small, you realize that you are some sort of shrimp-like creature that uses a miniature version of a lobster tail to propel itself forward. As before, you are not alone. You are surrounded by other prawn-shaped creatures all struggling toward the same unknown goal.

With another lurch, your experience shifts again. You quickly appreciate that you are no longer swimming. You are now on the floor of a massive and deep sea, walking up a sandy rise on spindly and armored legs. You then realize that you are taking in your surroundings through a pair of eyestalks that not only see your two large and chitinous claws that seem to lead the way before you, but also that you again are not alone. Other hard-shelled crabs scramble and struggle along with you to climb this sandy slope toward an unknown goal.

After an interminable battle against the loose sand, you finally attain the summit of this sandy rise. Before you is a truly awe-inspiring sight: Resting in a valley of inestimable size is a massive sea turtle that looks as big as the sea itself. This massive creature seems to be holding court as thousands of other sea creatures, from the smallest plankton to colossal squid, surround her on all sides in apparent homage. As you try to make sense of what you see before you, the titanic creature turns its head in your direction. Its amber-colored eyes seem to be the size of moons. As you lock your gaze with this creature, you again feel a shift. But this time it is different. With a rush you feel that your spirit is flung far and wide through the vast sea. During this bizarre and dizzying journey, you witness innumerable forms of sea life and seascapes.

Finally, with a spinning lurch, you come to, back in your own body, coughing violently, on your back but completely dry. You are back in the holy cavern of the craniform, the place where you started your most strange hallucinatory odyssey. Above you stand the same craniform that gave you the caustic liquid to drink. As you reacquaint yourself with your body and your surroundings, you cannot help but realize one thing: You now feel a deep affinity for the sea and are quite convinced that you would feel quite comfortable submerged in its depths.

The Sea Mother's Blessing

Successfully completing the Sea Mother's Blessing ritual confers the following abilities on the characters:

Amphibious. The characters can breathe air and water.

Depth resistance. Characters are immune to the effects of water pressure and cold water at any depth.

Slime skin. The affected character's skin becomes translucent and slimy, and the creature can't regain hit points unless submerged in saltwater (even by magical means). When the creature is outside a body of saltwater for more than three hours, it takes 6 (1d12) acid damage every hour unless saltwater is applied to the skin.

Sunlight sensitivity. While in sunlight, characters gain disadvantage on attack rolls and on Wisdom (Perception) checks that rely on sight.

Swim. Characters gain a swim speed of 40 ft.

Understand Aquan. Characters gain the ability to understand but not speak Aquan.

Underwater Attack. Characters may make melee attacks underwater without the normal underwater melee penalty (disadvantage).

All armor, weapons, and possessions borne by the character are transformed in that they do not affect the characters' swim speed or ability to move and act underwater. Finally, a *remove curse* spell ends the blessing and removes all effects.

The Sea Mother's Blessing Effects

In addition to the effects above, roll or have each character who undergoes the ritual of the craniform roll 1d12 for one additional effect each. If two different characters end up getting the same effect, considering having one of those characters re-roll to ensure variety in the party:

1d12	Effect*
1	The character's teeth fall out and, in their place, they grow tiny tentacles. The character gains the ability to speak Aquan.
2	The character's eyes grow disproportionately large, solid black, and glassy. The character gains darkvision 60 feet. If the character already possesses darkvision, the range increases by 60 feet.
3	The character grows a stalk from his or her forehead with a two-inch-diameter phosphorescent ball on the end. The character gains the ability to cast *light* at will through the phosphorescent ball.
4	The character's fingers grow webbing between them and the character gains +10 ft. to swim speed.
5	The character's teeth grow and distort in such a way as to allow that character to unhinge their jaw for a bite attack. The teeth are natural weapons. The character is proficient with the natural weapon and uses their Strength modifier to hit. If the character hits with them, they deal slashing damage equal to 1d4 + their Strength modifier.
6	The character becomes translucent while completely submerged in saltwater. While submerged, the character is invisible per the spell *invisibility* except that only the character's body becomes invisible—equipment, clothing, etc. remains visible.
7	The character gains the capacity to ingest a large amount of saltwater and then forcefully eject it in any direction. Thus, while submerged in saltwater, the character can use the dash action as a bonus action.
8	The character gains an affinity for electric eels. As a bonus action while completely submerged in saltwater, at will, the character may emanate a field of electrical energy that causes all creatures within five feet to make a Dexterity saving throw, taking 2d6 lightning damage on a failure or half as much on a success. The character also gains resistance to lightning damage.
9	The character's body becomes covered in tightknit and iridescent green fish scales gaining a natural armor class of 16. A dexterity bonus does stack with this effect, but the protections of other armor do not.
10	The character's skin becomes dusky and mottled in appearance while underwater, resulting in a form of underwater camouflage. The character has advantage on Dexterity (Stealth) checks made while underwater.
11	The character sprouts tiny anemone tentacles on its face and, like an anemone, is immune to poison.
12	A large claw replaces one of the character's hands. For to-hit purposes, the strength of the claw is 15 (+2, plus proficiency bonus) and the reach is 5 ft. A successful hit does 6 (1d8 + 2) bludgeoning damage, and the target (if size medium or smaller) is grappled (escape DC 12). Actions that require two hands, e.g. wielding a two-handed weapon, are no longer possible.

*Please note that should any character wild shape or transform into any other sort of creature through whatever means, these above effects do not alter the assumed shape that character takes. These effects only manifest when characters are in their native forms.

TIP

The ritual — which involves the characters drinking some unknown substance that does who knows what to them — should be a moment of great tension. If some portion of the party less than the whole group undertakes the ritual at once, those who participate in the ritual should have the below read or paraphrased to them outside of the presence of those who do not. Each character should experience this moment of uncertainty and unease before hearing what others of their party have gone through.

Thus, the characters have completed the ritual and received the Sea Mother's Blessing. The characters quickly come to understand the benefits and drawbacks associated with their new state. They also quickly appreciate that their appearances have changed. A successful DC 14 Wisdom (Medicine or Insight) check informs the specific character of all the details in **The Sea Mother's Blessing** sidebar.

This is obviously not an insignificant experience for the characters. They have been fundamentally altered in obvious ways. In the event the characters are upset with the craniform, other than being confused by the characters' reaction to these gifts, the craniform can do nothing to reverse the effects of the ritual.

Kzanto's Story

The characters likely want to spend some time experimenting with their new abilities. Other than being able to communicate that they can now "breathe as we," Jyrcyx, Zogren, and Tati cannot give the characters any further specifics.

However, Jyrcyx, Zogren, and Tati can offer the characters some direction from here. If the party does not think to ask, any one of the craniform priestesses approaches the party at some point after the ritual to tell them some specifics concerning the location of the sahuagin stronghold where they believe Captain Brand and company were taken.

The priestess explains that the sahuagin inhabit a city called Tzar'Grandula many kelps (about 3 miles) to the south and west. The city sits in a deep basin. From the sea floor in that basin springs a series of low rising spires that compromise the largest structures of the city. The largest of these spires and the grounds around it in the very center of Tzar'Grandula is the seat of King Bachzarisaa, his court, and his guards. It is called "the Tooth." From this spire, King Bachzarisaa rules Tzar'Grandula. She explains that it lies "75–80 kelps away, as the fish swims." Additionally, she explains that the entire region is teeming with patrolling sahuagin and their dangerous allies, including several species of sharks.

The priestesses do offer at least a partial solution to this problem and that is in the form of Kzanto, a half-grown **craniform**[D] male (not that the characters can readily tell male from female) who had been sacrificed as a slave to the vile many moons (16 months or so) ago. He quite unexpectedly returned to the craniform colony one moon ago. He brought with him tales of the ineffable cruelty of his sahuagin captors — stories of torture and blood sport — as well as of how he made his escape. While characters who accepted the Sea Mother's Blessing can understand Aquan, the priestesses eagerly act as translators should the characters want to converse with Kzanto.

If they are interested, Kzanto relates the following:

One moon ago or so, Kzanto was discharging his daily cleaning duties in and around the Tooth. More specifically, he was cleaning the king's coral gardens that surround the base of the Tooth. King Bachzarisaa is obsessed with his coral gardens and will not suffer the merest imperfection in them. One of King Bachzarisaa's favorite pets, a massive shark called "the beast," lives in the coral gardens to ensure that no undesirables intrude anywhere near the grounds surrounding the Tooth.

That day, Kzanto was disposing of some waste in a downward flowing vent located in the gardens used solely for waste discharge. So sickened and saddened by his terrible existence was he that Kzanto conceived on the spot to "throw himself away." He then climbed into this waste vent full of detritus from the gardens and the inedible parts of the beast's victims and swam and crawled his way down into and through the filth. To his surprise, the volcanically created vent flattened out after a few grasses. He then followed this passage for what he describes as feeling like "many tides" but readily admits that he does not know how long in either time or distance his journey really was, other than that it was "many kelps."

He finally located an exit to this tunnel-like vent and after cautiously peering out, he realized that he could not see any of the sahuagin city, any of the sahuagin spires, or any of their patrols. After emerging from this hidden vent entrance, he was then able to swim safely back to his colony. In summary, Kzanto can tell the characters that:

- The tallest and most central spire in Tzar'Grandula, called "the Tooth," is where King Bachzarisaa lives and rules.
- This spire is surrounded by a series of elaborate coral reef gardens which in turn are patrolled and guarded by a massive shark called "the beast."
- Kzanto escaped via a vent used for waste disposal. The vent surfaces in the middle of the coral gardens, about 10 grasses (60 feet) away from the base of the tooth.
- Kzanto knows of only one entrance into the tooth and that is through the top of the caldera.

The Effects of the Depths

Characters who do not partake of the blessing because they have a magic item or ability that allows them to breath underwater are in for an unfortunate surprise. Swimming through deep water is much like traveling at high altitudes because of the water's pressure and cold temperature. For a creature without a swimming speed, each hour spent swimming at a depth greater than 100 feet counts as 2 hours for the purpose of determining exhaustion. Swimming for an hour at a depth greater than 200 feet counts as 4 hours. As a result, those who did not accept the blessing or who don't have a swimming speed from another source must succeed on a DC 16 Constitution saving throw after swimming for more than two hours or sustain one level of exhaustion per hour of additional swimming.

Where from Here?

At this point, the characters should be in the approximate middle of Crocodile Island among the craniform. The *Bounty* and *Zephyr* are at anchor on the eastern side of the island. Now that the characters are such adept swimmers, it would be a simple matter to swim back east through the submerged tunnels in order to rejoin the two ships. However, the appearances and physical natures of the characters have been dramatically changed. How will the crew react? The question of what to do with the two ships and how exactly the party goes about involving these ships is, of course, completely up to them. Tzar'Grandula is to the south and west of Crocodile Island.

- The very top of the Tooth is an arena in which King Bachzarisaa entertains by putting on a number of blood sports.
- This area is not heavily patrolled because no creature would be able to make its way through the city to the Tooth unchallenged.
- He and his fellow slaves, prisoners, and future arena combatants were housed in the level underneath the arena.
- The level underneath this slaves' level is where King Bachzarisaa's guard is garrisoned.
- He believes that the temple to the sahuagin god is somewhere underneath that.
- He also believes that King Bachzarisaa's court and residence is somewhere underneath that, but his duties never took him to either the temple or the King's court.
- Many dozens of sahuagin and other creatures are in the Tooth at any one time.
- Kzanto can guide the characters back to the mouth of this vent from which he made his escape.
- If asked, he can also draw a crude map of the king's spire.
- Finally, he did not see the humans that the characters describe, but he does know of at least one location where captives are held and can indicate that on the map (**Level 3: The Prison**).

Provide the characters with **Player Handout 5: Kzanto's Map**.

What he will not do under any circumstances is venture back through the waste vent or go anywhere near the sahuagin city. He would rather die than return.

Chapter Five: Into the Depths

The characters should be 8th level at the start of this part of the adventure.

Tzar'Grandula sits at the bottom of a deep basin three or so miles southwest of Crocodile Island. The main structures of the city are a series of volcanic spires or stalagmites of sorts that lie along the same fault line that created Crocodile Island and its currently active volcanos. The central spire from which King Bachzarisaa rules is called "the Tooth." It is immediately surrounded by a series of coral gardens. Radiating outward, a visitor would find smaller spires inhabited by sahuagin princes and barons, hundreds of common residences, mussel beds, more coral reefs, and finally a series of guard structures at the perimeter of the city.

The journey to that part of the Sinnar Ocean where Tzar'Grandula lies from Crocodile Island is a short one. The characters likely either swim there led by Kzanto or might take the two ships to the spot, again with the aid of Kzanto. That short journey can be as eventful as you like.

Potential Aquatic Encounters

1d4	Result
1	As the characters swim along, a massive shadow moves over them. A successful DC 15 Wisdom (Nature) check reveals that the huge shape was a passing whale.
2	The party encounters a random hunting party of 10 **merrow**. They believe the odd-looking swimmers to be easy prey. They press the attack until half of their number are slain.
3	The characters are spotted by a pair of **killer whales** that think they look delicious. When one is slain, the other thinks better of its menu choice and flees.
4	Shark attack! It seems that everything in the depths is hungry and that the characters look like easy kills. A **giant shark** attempts to take the characters by surprise and make one of them a meal. It does not flee unless it has a chance to do so after being severely wounded.

Light and Sound Underwater

Despite the depth, 500 feet is still within the sunlight zone. So during the daytime, Tzar'Grandula is suffused with bright light.

As to sound, under normal circumstances, vocalization — the use of air pressure to cause vocal cords to vibrate resulting in sound — is vastly diminished underwater. Fortunately, the Sea Mother's Blessing conferred upon the characters affords them the ability to speak and be heard underwater. Any character with the amphibious racial feature or who can breathe underwater for any other reason can speak normally underwater as well.

Tzar'Grandula
200 Feet
8 Squares
The Tooth
Tunnel
Section Through

In any event, the party reaches the obscured vent access point from which Kzanto made his escape some weeks before. It is roughly 500 feet under the surface of the ocean. The entrance is obscured by a stand of some sort of long brown fronds that root on the ocean floor in front of the entrance. Kzanto quickly parts the thick stalks and moves confidently into the grove.

The entrance lies at the far side of this 20-foot-deep or so stand of long, broad-leafed tangle. It is roughly circular in shape, and the edges of the portal are very smooth. The entrance sits about five feet off the floor of the sea on the vertical surface of a large ridge of rocky hills that runs approximately east and west. A successful DC 14 Intelligence (Nature) check informs characters that this tunnel was likely created by volcanic activity, but that this vent was created long ago.

Kzanto knows that this ridge forms the edge of the undersea basin wherein Tzar'Grandula sits and shares this fact with the party. Unless the characters contrived a way to speak to Kzanto (e.g. a *tongues* spell), he becomes agitated if any of the characters indicate that they want to swim up and over the ridge to take a look. Kzanto knows that there is a chance of being spotted by the sahuagin perimeter if they were to carelessly swim up and over this ridge. He strenuously urges caution if any of the party members declare their intention to go take a look at the city. The profile of this ridge varies, but it averages 50 feet or so in height.

Should the characters look over the ridge, they see the city of Tzar'Grandula spread out before them. It is quite a vista. It is assumed that the characters attempt this during the day. If it is at night, please adjust the following text as necessary. As the characters look at the city, please read or paraphrase the following:

Arrayed before you on the far side of this low range of rocky hills is quite the sight. The sahuagin city of Tzar'Grandula sits brooding before you. Such is its breadth that you are pretty certain that you cannot see the far side of the city. You first recognize what must be watchtowers arrayed along the outer edge of the city. The closest one to you is less than 200 feet away. It is approximately 40 feet tall and has a domed gallery on top. Towers are located at regular intervals, around 500 feet apart, along the entire perimeter of the city.

From your vantage you also notice numerous depressions in the seafloor, some covered in nets, a much larger depression that seems to be an underwater amphitheater, hundreds of low domed structures that you assume to be residences, and kelp and coral gardens everywhere. All that aside, the most prominent feature that you cannot help but notice is the series of spires that thrust upward from the seafloor. They form a line that runs right through the middle of the city. The spires vary in size, with the shortest being near the outer limit of the city. You would guess that these smaller towers are roughly 50 to 60 feet tall. They increase in height as they approach the center of the city. The tallest one, shaped like a massive, roughhewn villiform tooth, lies in the very center of the city, and that spire appears to be more than 150 feet tall. This must be the spire of which your escaped craniform spoke.

Amid these physical structures, the sahuagin city is astir with activity. You see what likely amount to hundreds of sahuagin engaging in a variety of activities along with dozens of sharks and other creatures that you are too far away to recognize.

One thing is abundantly clear and that is that Tzar'Grandula is a busy and dangerous place.

Just as Kzanto warned, there are patrols. Unless those characters who climbed up to take a look succeeded on a group DC 17 Dexterity (Stealth) check (everyone in the group makes the ability check; if at least half the group succeeds, the whole group succeeds), they catch the attention of a sahuagin patrol. The patrol is composed of 5 **Sinnar sahuagin**[D] and 2 **hunter sharks**. The characters notice the patrol as well and see them coming, which allows them to drop back down behind the ridge. The zealous patrol follows and fights to the death.

The passage itself is completely dark and has a diameter of approximately four feet, which is more than large enough to accommodate any medium-sized swimming creature. After entering, the vent runs roughly south toward the heart of the sahuagin city. The characters have to swim in single file if they elect to follow Kzanto's escape route. It is completely dark.

The meandering tunnel descends slightly over 1,500 yards. The characters encounter many brightly hued fish, many forms of coral growth, waving stalks from countless plants, and dozens of different crab species while traversing the passage. Fortunately, all of them are harmless.

The same cannot be said though of the end of the passage where it turns and ascends. From this "elbow" in the tunnel, it is only 20 feet or so to the surface of the seafloor and to the access point Kzanto described as King Bachzarisaa's coral gardens. At this elbow of the passageway, a **giant anemone**[D] has taken up residence. Because of the refuse regularly deposited by King Bachzarisaa's slaves, this creature is provided with a steady and regular food source.

Kzanto failed to mention this creature because he would have hardly noticed it during his passage. The combination of their exoskeleton and the poison immunity conferred by Crocodile Island results in craniform all but ignoring these sorts of creatures. The characters will not be so lucky.

The anemone blends in extremely well with the other growths in the passage. The characters need to succeed on a Wisdom (Perception) check opposed by the anemone's Dexterity (Stealth) check (made with advantage) to recognize the mass of brightly colored and waving tendrils to be anything other than standard sea flora. If they recognize it, they realize that it is quite large and that it effectively blankets this entire section of passage. The tunnel is too narrow to allow anyone to go past the creature without coming close enough for the creature to strike with its tendrils. Consider allowing creative solutions for bypassing this

Spellcasting Underwater

Under normal circumstances, an air-breather would have a very hard time casting a spell with a verbal component underwater. However, those characters who underwent the Sea Mother's Blessing will not have to deal with that hurdle. As a result, because of the benefits of the blessing, spells are cast as normal. However, that does not mean their effect is normal or unchanged. Take fire-based spells for example: Keep in mind that creatures fully immersed in water have resistance to fire damage.

Shark Wild Shape and Sahuagin Shark Telepathy

Every sahuagin has the ability to command any shark within 120 feet of them. If a character in shark form approaches a sahuagin, that sahuagin may attempt to command that character. In that event, the character in shark form must succeed on a DC 15 Wisdom saving throw or must obey the command given to them. At the end of each of its turns, an affected character can make a Wisdom saving throw. If it succeeds, this effect ends for that character and the character is immune to commands from that sahuagin for 24 hours.

creature without killing it such as forcibly moving it up and out of the way or temporarily covering it with a blanket or bed roll.

After getting past the anemone, it is a simple matter to ascend the 20 feet or so past and through the accumulated refuse from the gardens and emerge on the seafloor in the middle of King Bachzarisaa's coral gardens. When they emerge, please read or paraphrase the following:

As you peer out of the waste vent and take in your surroundings, you immediately recognize that you are in a spectacular coral garden. If not for the tense circumstances, the amazing array of colors, shapes, and life around you would be breathtaking. The reefs vary in height with a range of five to fifteen feet.

You see that the topographically complex coral reefs are laid out to form a sort of a maze that circles the entire base of the massive spire before you. Throughways dissecting the reefs radiate in every direction through the gardens.

The base of the huge spire is no more than 60 feet away from you. Its diameter here at the seafloor must be a couple of hundred feet at least. It towers to a height of well over 100 feet above you where it terminates in a broad, flat top. You know from Kzanto's description that the top is open and forms the entrance to the spire.

Other than the dizzying array of brightly colored fish and the unbelievable variety of small invertebrates that teem among the corals, there is no sign of movement anywhere near the spire.

No sahuagin sentries are anywhere in immediate view as the characters emerge from the waste disposal vent. They are free to explore the coral gardens immediately adjacent to the vent access point without risk of being seen by anyone. However, once they venture either up toward the top of the spire to enter it, or if they swim to the other side of the spire, they encounter the Beast.

Run of the Beast

The reason there are no sentries immediately around the Tooth is because this area is regularly patrolled by a **wereshark**[D] who is a favorite of King Bachzarisaa. No one, sahuagin or otherwise, approaches the spire without good reason because of the presence of this creature. The wereshark, a sahuagin named Trantiztua, almost always stays in giant shark form and is in that form when the characters encounter him. He is always accompanied by his 2 pet **hunter sharks**.

Trantiztua is the king's champion, and he immediately and viciously attacks anyone or anything that looks as if it does not belong.

Trantiztua formerly was a successful member of the King's Guard. This means that he was among the most capable and terrifying of all of the sahuagin warriors. How he contracted lycanthropy is unknown. However, it immediately put him in a precarious position with his people.

The sahuagin loath any sort of deformity or deviation from the physical norm. Hatchlings that display just about any unusual characteristics (other than the mutation that results in a second set of arms) are quickly put to death.

However, lycanthropes enjoy an odd position in sahuagin society. While definitely pariahs, they do enjoy a status of sorts in that the sahuagin believe that lycanthropes have been shown the direct favor of their shark god and view the lycanthropy as more of a gift than as a curse.

From the coral gardens looking up, a successful DC 13 Wisdom (Perception) check reveals the shapes of several sharks performing lazy circles around the circumference of the Tooth about 60 feet up from the sea floor. Unless the characters conceive of a way to get past Trantiztua without the creature noticing them, the wereshark attacks and fights to the death. The rest of the residents of Tzar'Grandula give the Tooth a wide berth because of Trantiztua. Because of this fact, no alarm is raised if open combat results.

Either bypassing or slaying Trantiztua allows the characters access to the top of the Tooth, the only way to enter the central spire.

THE TOOTH

LEVEL 4: ARENA

The Tooth functions as the seat of Tzar'Grandula's government in addition to being the residence of King Bachzarisaa. Every important administrative and religious function is performed in this long-quiescent volcanic spire.

The top of the caldera is open to the surrounding water. Its rim towers over the rest of the city. After dealing with Trantiztua, the characters may ascend the exterior of the spire without event. Once they reach the top and look down into the top of the spire, please read or paraphrase the following:

After ascending the exterior of the old volcano that makes up the tallest spire in the very middle of this underwater city, you recognize that the top of the spire is open to the surrounding water. The rim or opening on the top is probably 75 to 100 feet in diameter.

Looking down over the rim and into the spire, you see that it forms a natural bowl. Your eyes are immediately drawn to what appear to be two sahuagin combatants close to the bottom of the bowl. They appear to be battling just above two pieces of opposing grating that are partially open at the very bottom of the bowl, 40 feet below you. You readily understand that this opening would allow access to the deeper sections of the spire. They each wield some sort of long spear.

While keeping an eye on the sahuagin combatants who do not seem to see you yet, you also surmise that this caldera has been turned into an arena or amphitheater of sorts. Not far down from your current position is a rectangular-shaped platform that is skirted with low walls and contains a handful of carved stone chairs or maybe even thrones. Opposite this platform on the other side of the arena you notice a stone pen or paddock that has a "roof" of netting. Lastly, you notice that the entire bowl has even ridges on the inside of it that were carved at regular intervals that would seem to form seating.

The 2 **sahuagin elites**[D] are not actually fighting but are merely sparring. They are both members of the spire guard and are currently assigned to guard the opening into the spire. As is their wont, they pass the time by sparring.

The two guards are intent on their sparring, so they don't notice the characters as they descend from above unless and until they approach within 20 feet of them. Given their belief in their prowess as members of the spire guard, they fight to the death instead of taking the wiser course of fleeing into the spire in order to raise the alarm.

After the characters deal with these two guards, nothing prevents them from descending through the opening between the two gates.

The platform described above is the royal box. Seven carved stone chairs affixed to the front of the platform are each positioned to maximize the viewing potential of the seated spectator. The middle chair is much more of a throne than the rest and features shark heads as arms of the chair. Nothing else of value or interest is here.

The 20-foot-deep, 40-foot-long, and 10-foot-tall paddock contains 10 **giant sea horses**. These creatures casually mill about this space and take no notice of or interest in the characters. Each of these creatures bears what looks like some sort of bridle. These are the trained mounts used by the sahuagin elite.

The opposed set of metal grating at the very bottom of the door functions as the gates for the spire. These sliding mechanical grates also are important in the operation of the arena above. Unwilling

Contrary to a likely assumption, sahuagin society is complex and deeply structured. That said, this complex and deeply hierarchical society is based on one simple overriding principle. That principle is that the strongest rule. This core precept permeates virtually every stratum of sahuagin society. Thus, the greatest virtues among the sahuagin are self-reliance and obedience to one's superiors. The necessary consequence or corollary to these concepts is that only those that are inadequate fail. This is why virtually every dispute and attempt at social climbing is resolved through a blood duel. These contests do not have to be to the death, but often are. These duels do not necessarily always involve combat. For example, adversaries could agree to a skill challenge such as contests of swimming or hunting prowess. Those are much less common than the traditional blood duel. However, the sahuagin are not simple creatures by any stretch. Just as other intelligent races, they feel love, hate, anger, fear, joy, and sadness. Different from most surface races, these common emotions are filtered through the lenses of specific sahuagin values thereby reinforcing their ordered society and world view. But all that aside, when it comes to the rest of the world and how they view the creatures living in it, it is pretty simple: Meat is meat.

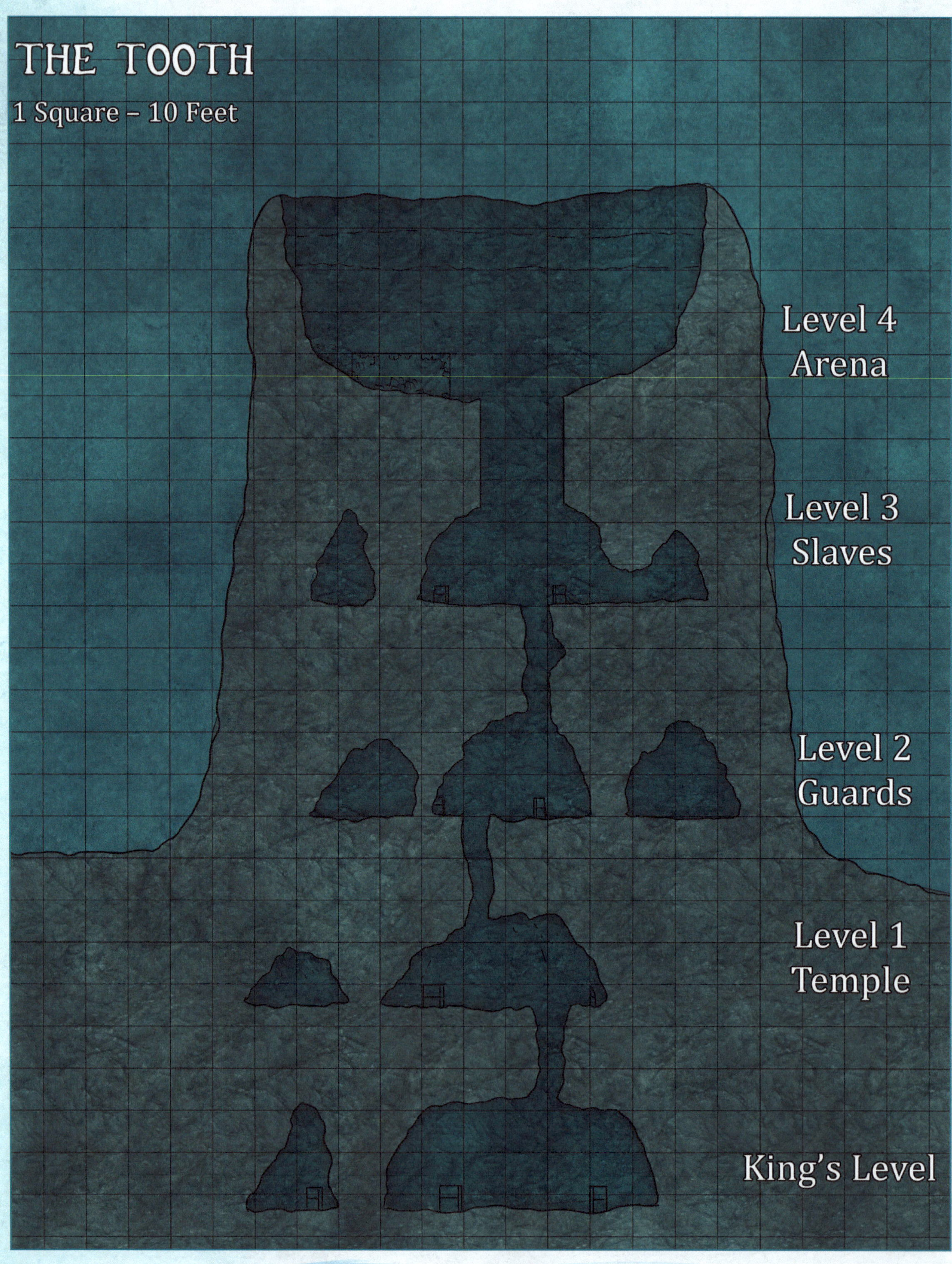

THE TOOTH
1 Square – 10 Feet
Level 4
Arena
Level 3
Slaves
Level 2
Guards
Level 1
Temple
King's Level

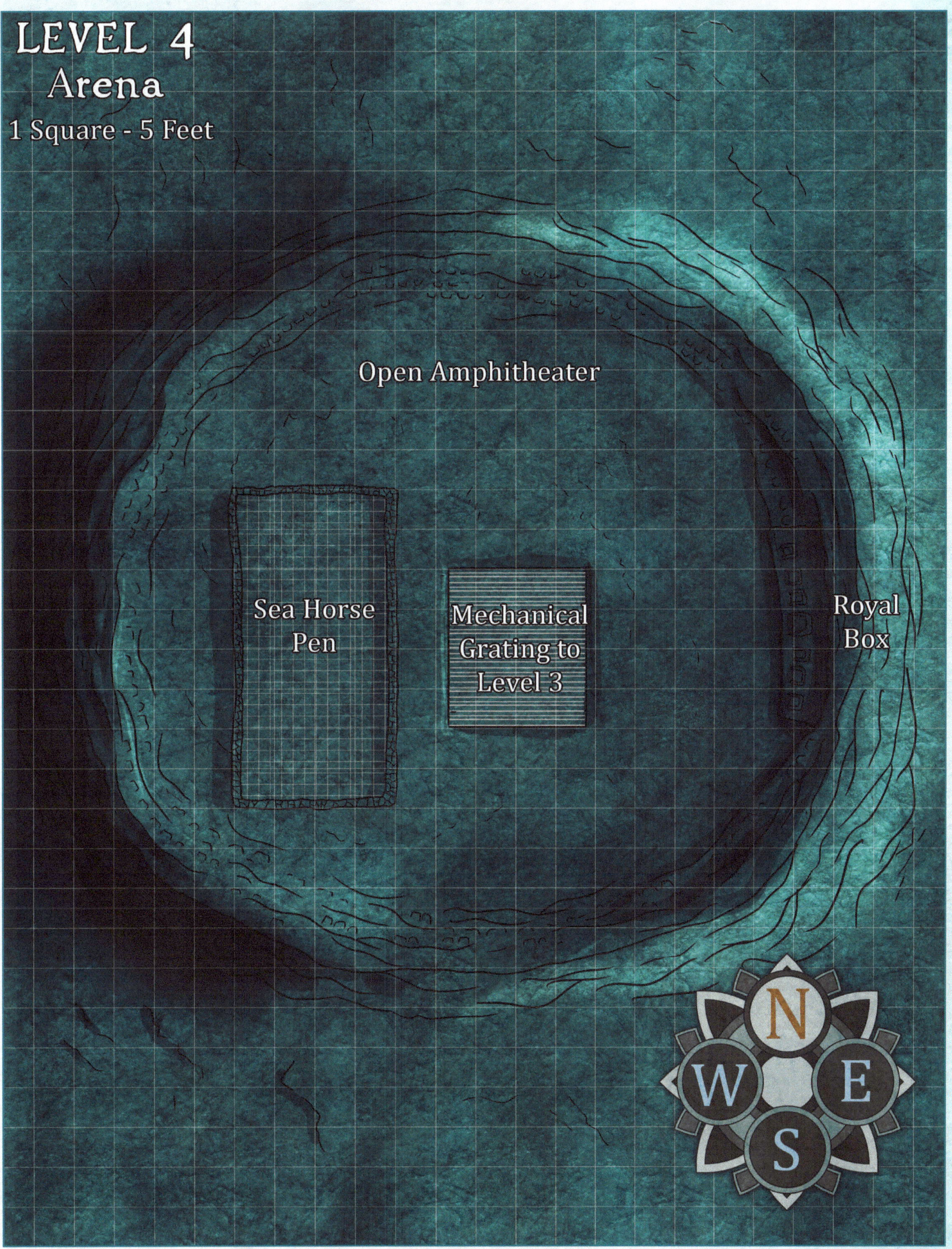

LEVEL 4
Arena
1 Square - 5 Feet
Open Amphitheater
Sea Horse
Pen
Mechanical
Grating to
Level 3
Royal
Box
N
W
E
S

Unless otherwise stated, the floors and ceilings are all rough, unfinished, and uneven. Ceiling heights in the Tooth vary between 10 feet and 15 feet. Lighting is generally dark.

combatants are escorted out of the cell(s) and into the arena staging area immediately underneath the grating. They are then ushered up into the amphitheater to amuse the spectators with their ability to tear their opponents asunder or by having the same done to them.

These horizontal grated gates are controlled with a simple set of mechanical pulleys and chains from underneath in the staging area. Because of the caustic saltwater environment, these grates require constant maintenance including preservation magics cast by the sahuagin priestesses. These metal gates are the pride of King Bachzarisaa as the sahuagin have virtually no ability to forge or manipulate metal. These grates were looted from a sunken cog and retrofitted into the Tooth to function as gates. If the gates are closed, an opening for a Medium-sized creature can be forced with a successful DC 25 Strength check.

As the characters descend through the gates and into Level 3 of the Tooth, please read or paraphrase the following:

> After swimming down past the thick and imposing horizontally aligned gates, you emerge into a roughly circular chamber which is approximately 40 to 50 feet across. The first thing you notice is a hole in the floor that appears to be a passage down. It is approximately 10 feet wide.
>
> Beyond that feature, this naturally formed chamber and its uneven stone floor contains five square-shaped structures that are evenly spaced around the circumference of the room. They look like a type of wall hanging constructed from a variety of pearlescent-hued materials somehow fastened together. They are each about four feet wide and five feet tall.
>
> Finally, you immediately notice a set of dangling chains adjacent to the gates you just passed through. You surmise that these chains are involved in operating the gates.

LEVEL 3: THE PRISON

The characters have found their way to the prison section and slave quarters portion of the Tooth. Two of the chambers radiating from this central hub are housing for slaves while the other three contain specific prisoners detailed below. Any examination of the five structures reveals that they are doors of some sort indicated as such by the bone hinges on the top and bottom edges of the doors. See **A Note on Sahuagin Doors** sidebar for further details. If the characters asked him, this is the area on Kzanto's map where he would have indicated some prisoners were kept.

Two of the three prisoner cells are locked. More accurately, they are barred. Each of the five doors has an external locking mechanism. It is a cleverly designed coral bolt that crosses the mesh point between the top and bottom doors. When the bolt is in the down position, the doors cannot be opened unless forced. A successful DC 15 Intelligence (Investigation) check finds the door's bolt. (Once such a bolt is found, further checks are unnecessary as the characters have figured out how they work at that point.) Characters that don't find the bolt can force the door with a successful DC 25 Strength check.

As to the grates now above the characters, their operation is quite simple. There are two chains. Pulling one down opens the grates

A NOTE ON SAHUAGIN DOORS

The most common building materials for the sahuagin are bone and coral. Unless otherwise stated, all doors in the Tooth are constructed of these materials and are all, in effect, double doors. Unlike terrestrial doors, the seam for a set of double doors is horizontal, not vertical. And instead of the two doors being adjacent to each other like a set of surface double doors, sahuagin doors overlap. Both the top and bottom doors have points or teeth that engage with the opposite door when closed. The reason for this is to resist the gentle currents of water created by virtually any movement in any underwater room. The only way to open these sorts of doors is to pull the two halves outward and toward the opener.

Sahuagin are, of course, adept at opening these doors as they have lived with them for their entire lives. Visitors from the surface are likely to initially struggle with their operation. A successful DC 14 Intelligence check is necessary to figure out how they work. In the alternative, a successful DC 19 Strength check forces such a door open but damages it in the process and makes it impossible to completely close it again until repaired.

NOTE ON SAHUAGIN SENSES

Sahuagin hearing does not work like that of terrestrial creatures. Terrestrial hearing is based on sound waves that are vibrations in the air striking an eardrum and making it vibrate. The sahuagin perceive sound as a function of vibrations that travel through the water that strike their entire body. So while underwater, sahuagin hearing is much more acute than terrestrial hearing.

Sahuagin vision is roughly analogous to surface dwellers' vision.

Finally, the sahuagin sense of smell is very sensitive to blood. They can sense blood in the water from as much as a mile away and can use this enhanced olfactory ability to very effectively track even a lightly wounded creature. Fortunately for adventurers, the scent of blood does not travel nearly as quickly as does sound underwater.

further. Pulling the other closes them. Should the characters seek to disable the grates, the tracks that the grates run in are bendable if the characters have something to pry with and succeed on a DC 30 Strength check. Up to three characters can work together to combine their check results on this check.

There are 2 **sahuagin elite**[D] guards loitering in the passageway between **Levels 3** and **2**. They are supposed to be on the prisoner floor but were bored and migrated down the passage to the next level to watch the sport some of the guards are having torturing a craniform slave. That has all of them rather distracted.

The characters do not see these two sentries unless they move over and look directly down the passageway. The passage to the next level is approximately 30 feet down. The two guards are watching the festivities from where the passageway down opens into the level below.

LEVEL 3
The Prison
1 Square - 5 Feet
3-1
3-2
Mechanism to open/close Gates
3-5
Arena Staging Area
Mechanical Grating Up to Level 4
3-3
3-4
Down to Level 2
N
W
E
S

The torture spectacle taking place on the floor below provides enough cover that the sahuagin below do not hear what the characters are up to on the prisoner level. However, should the characters speak to each other within five feet of the passage down, the two sahuagin sentries at the bottom pick up on the odd speech over the general din caused by the sahuagin sport.

Further, should the characters tarry for more than 30 minutes on the prisoner level, the scent of the blood from the fight with the two sahuagin who were guarding the gate above makes its way down to where the sentries watch. They and the rest of the sahuagin present (for a total of 8 **sahuagin elite**[D]) on the floor below investigate immediately should they sense blood in the water.

The side chambers on Level 3 contain the following:

AREA 3-1: DOMESTIC SLAVE PEN

The door to this chamber is closed but not locked. This is where the sahuagins' slaves are housed. Those slaves are exclusively craniform these days. Some of the craniform are at their duties in the lower levels in the Tooth. However, 6 **craniform**[D] are present currently. They are startled when the door opens and the strange figures of the characters are standing there. Unless someone in the party speaks Aquan, Craniform, or has cast *tongues*, there is no way to communicate with the craniform.

If one of the characters communicates with these unfortunate craniform, they quickly assimilate that the characters are their long-promised saviors and act accordingly. They bow, scrape, and plead with the party to save them. They tell the party of the terrible things done to them by the awful sahuagin and that they deeply miss their brethren. They are desperate to be freed and believe that the characters represent their salvation.

These craniform can describe the areas in **Level 2** and **Level 1** in general terms.

Nothing of value is in this chamber.

AREA 3-2: DOMESTIC SLAVE PEN

This area is similar to **Area 1** and is unlocked as well, but no craniform are currently present. However, a prisoner is chained against the wall. As the characters open the unlocked door, they see what appears to be a sea elf manacled to the wall. This is **Petruska**[D]. She is not a sea elf as she appears. In fact, she is a malenti, a mutant variation of a sahuagin. However, she does her best to convince the party that she is an imprisoned princess from the sea elf city of Azurelume, which is located many leagues northeast of Tzar'Grandula, and is fated to end up on King Bachzarisaa's table.

She makes the following claims:

• She is a princess and is in fact the third daughter of King Brinemere of Azurelume. (King Brinemere is the King of Azurelume, but the rest is false)
• If rescued and returned to Azurelume, the king would handsomely reward her saviors. (False)
• As part of her courtly training, she was trained to be a spy and was captured while attempting to spy on Tzar'Grandula. (She does have those skills, but the rest is false)
• The sea elves are the sworn and most-hated enemies of the sahuagin. (True)
• King Bachzarisaa and the garrisons of Tzar'Grandula would love nothing more than to slaughter each and every sea elf and lay waste to Azurelume. (True)
• She was taken before King Bachzarisaa deep below and into the lowest level of the Tooth before being chained here. (True)
• She likely knows where King Bachzarisaa is holding the sea captain the characters seek. (True)
• The captain is likely in a place called "The Meat Locker." (True)
• The Meat Locker is just two levels down. (False)
• She will lead the party to where it is. (False)
• She wants nothing more than to defy King Bachzarisaa and damage his plans. (False)
• She happily joins the party in exchange for her freedom. (True)
• They are completely aligned in interest. (False)

ROLEPLAYING PETRUSKA

Petruska is very clever and excels at lying. These skills were forced on her in order to help her survive. As a malenti, she suffers an uncomfortable position in sahuagin society. She is universally regarded as being disgusting and weak. At best, malenti are tools to be employed against the hated sea elves. Because the characters represent her best chance at even a slight upgrade in status, she does her absolute best to deceive them. She should be played exactly as she seems without giving any obvious clues suggesting that she might be anything other than what she is attempting to portray. She does her best to present a regal and imperial bearing.

When it comes to encountering other sahuagin before her planned moment of betrayal, she tries to stay toward the back of the characters in combat and fights sahuagin only if she has to. If confronted about her lack of fighting zeal, she states, "I am not a warrior" and "I had others do my fighting for me in the elven court."

Finally, if she is able to maintain the ruse long enough and she gets to the moment of her planned betrayal, she attempts a sneak attack with her assassinate feature on the character she deems the most dangerous. This attack should likely be made with surprise.

Being thoroughly sahuagin despite her appearance, Petruska has absolutely no intention of aiding the party. However, the clever malenti is quick to recognize an opportunity. She is currently very much in disfavor with Enzu, the king's wife and high priestess of Dajobas. This is why she is chained in the slave quarters.

If the characters decide to free Petruska, the manacles can be unlocked with a successful DC 16 Dexterity check with thieves' tools or forced open with a successful DC 16 Strength check.

Petruska does her level best to deceive the characters into allowing her to lead them to their doom below where she promptly betrays the party and, thereby, regains the good graces of her majesty. She begs the characters to arm her. She wants a shortsword but settles for a dagger.

Petruska's plan is ill-conceived and desperate but she is in a tough spot. Leading the party down to Level 2 and then betraying them to the guards there is probably her best move. If the characters believe Petruska and allow her to lead them, she betrays the party as soon as fighting breaks out with the sahuagin elites below. She attempts to assassinate any lightly armored spellcaster in the confusion of melee.

Area 3-3: Arena Slave Pen

The door to this room is not locked. This chamber has one resident: Jathor, a captured female **sea giant**[D]. This wise and proud creature was overwhelmed by a war party of sahuagin and brought back to Tzar'Grandula months ago as a prize for King Bachzarisaa. Enzu, the king's wife and high priestess, fashioned a magical collar to manage Jathor. Unfortunately for Jathor, this collar is a far more effective restraint than any door lock could be.

Enzu holds the control device — a clamshell etched with runes — and activates the collar and summons Jathor to aid her against the party as soon as she is alerted to their presence in the Tooth.

If freed, Jathor immediately attempts to swim away. While appreciative, Jathor does not have it in her to actively help the party rescue the missing sea captain. She is utterly indifferent to the affairs of air-breathers and really to the affairs of anyone.

If the party fails to free Jathor and if Enzu summons her to aid her against the party, the characters are in trouble.

Area 3-4: Arena Slave Pen

The door to this chamber is locked. A successful DC 15 Wisdom (Perception) check alerts the characters that something large is moving on the far side of the door. The source of that movement is a pair of crazed **fanged sea serpents**[D] that the sahuagin have kept for many months in order to participate in arena combats above. As soon as the door to their chamber opens, they attack anything they see and do not cease until slain or incapacitated. The poor creatures have been driven mad by the cruelties heaped on them by the sahuagin.

The repeated charging and bashing of the door by the crazed serpents has greatly weakened the door. Sensing the characters outside the door, the serpents begin to smash at their door in earnest. It takes them three rounds to break free and come for the characters.

Area 3-5: Arena Slave Pen

The door to this chamber is locked. When opened, the party is greeted with an odd sight: A creature shaped like a huge eye floats in the center of the room. This is an **eye of the deep**[D]. Its unblinking gaze locks onto the characters as they open the door. Because it does not recognize the party, it is unsure what to do so it continues to float motionlessly until it is either addressed or attacked. If addressed, it replies in terse sentences. Similar to the other gladiator inhabitants on this level, it was captured and is periodically forced to fight above in the arena. Engaging it in conversation coupled with a successful DC 16 Charisma (Persuasion or Deception) check causes it to leave the character alone as it attempts to escape its imprisonment out the top of the caldera.

However, if the party attacks, it defends itself to the best of its abilities until either slain or incapacitated.

Roleplaying Jathor

Jathor is from the Bathhare Trench many leagues to the west of Tzar'Grandula. Should the party encounter Jathor while she is not being dominated by Enzu (most likely), they find her to be melancholic and stoic. She chafes against her captivity and longs to be free. She answers all the characters' questions freely and as well as she is able. She has not been any deeper into the Tooth than her current position on the slave level. She was exploring far from her home when the sahuagin overwhelmed her. She sulkily points to the silver-hued collar in answer to any sort of "Why are you here?" type questions. She readily explains that Enzu, the high priestess and wife to King Bachzarisaa, placed the collar on her and can command Jathor through it. So far, Enzu has ordered Jathor to fight in the arena above for the amusement of the sahuagin court.

Collar of Giant Control

Wondrous item, Very rare

This rune-etched silver collar automatically expands to fit the neck of any giant-kind. With the collar closed and the control device in hand, the giant suffers the effects of a *dominate monster* spell, excepting the saving throws. While holding the control device, you can command the collared giant to do just about anything other than direct self-harm. Use of the device requires concentration and is of otherwise unlimited use.

The holder of the control device can unlock the collar at will. Otherwise, the collar can be removed in only two ways: unlocked with a successful DC 20 Dexterity check using thieves' tools or with a successful DC 18 *dispel magic* spell attempt. A successful DC 15 Intelligence (Arcana) check informs characters generally of these two removal options.

How Do the Sahuagin Manage the Open Water Arena?

When it is festival day, the Daughters of the Shark and High Priestess Enzu oversee the festivities. They help manage the combatants and make sure that they get to where they are supposed to be with their spells and spell-like abilities. They also take steps to make sure that none of the slave gladiators escapes during the games via means such as Enzu's casting *wall of force* over the top of the arena.

Level 2: The Garrison

Six **sahuagin elite**[D] guards are arrayed in the central landing hub of this level. Two of the six are standing close to the northern edge of the passage up to **Level 3**. These two are facing the commotion located on the northern side of this central chamber. There, the rest of the sahuagin (four of them) are circled around a craniform currently down on what serves as its hands and knees.

They are jeering and poking the unfortunate craniform with their spears as they force it to eat a live scorpionfish. The terrible sahuagin are impressed with the craniforms' ability to seemingly shrug off the poisonous effects of the scorpionfish. They are of course unaware of the poison immunity the craniform enjoy as a result of living for generations adjacent to Crocodile Island. However, the stinging fish still hurts the craniform, as do the spear points.

All six of these sahuagin are distracted by their games, but they are hard to take by surprise given their sensitive hearing.

Five sahuagin doors lead to the five chambers on this level. None of them is locked.

Area 2-1: Sahuagin Barracks

This room contains four sleeping berths, a weapons rack, and four one-foot-tall, two-foot-wide, and one-foot-deep limestone boxes. No sahuagin are present.

The sleeping berths are suspended nets that look more like hammocks than they do traditional terrestrial beds. The weapons rack contains two spears, two tridents, and two javelins of sahuagin manufacture. Their shafts are constructed of porous coral, while the tips are made of either sharpened stone or bone.

The four boxes contain the personal effects of the four sahuagin not present. They are all of simple construction and their respective lids simply lift off. In sahuagin society, no one would think to steal from another. If one sahuagin desired anything possessed by another, it would be settled by a blood duel.

The four boxes contain a variety of detritus, pieces of valueless coral, shells, and pieces of bone, but also contain some more interesting things as follows:

Box 1: A small, soft ball about two inches in diameter. It is a poison gland harvested from some undersea predator. It holds two doses of poison. A creature that ingests a dose of this poison must make a DC 11 Constitution saving throw, taking 10 (3d6) poison damage on a failed save, or half as much damage on a successful one.

Box 2: A dented and heavily tarnished silver cup that has seen better days. Its only value is its weight in silver, which is 5 sp.

Box 3: A glass vial that contains some dark and thick liquid. Any reasonable investigation reveals that it contains oil.

Box 4: A pewter spork. Beyond the conjecture of where a sahuagin would have scavenged such a thing, it has no value.

Area 2-2: Sahuagin Barracks

Same as **Area 2-1**, excepting that this weapons rack contains only one trident and two javelins. Beyond the useless junk, the four limestone boxes in this room contain the following:

Box 1: An old, but whole, wool sock. Any colored dye it once had has long since washed away.

Box 2: A stoppered glass flask contains a luminescent liquid. The substance was harvested from moon jellyfish — DC 16 Wisdom (Nature) to identify — and provides dim light to five feet.

Box 3: A broken but ornate shortsword. All that remains is the pommel, crosspiece, and a few inches of blade. However, the pommel is set with a large transparent red spinel worth 100 gp.

Box 4: Inside is a 15-inch-long metal wand with a small blue crystal affixed to the tip. It is a *wand of magic detection*.

Area 2-3: Occupied Sahuagin Barracks

Like the rest of the doors on this floor, the door to this chamber is unlocked. However, unlike the four other rooms on this level, this chamber is occupied. There are 4 **sahuagin elites**[D] currently asleep in their berths. Fighting outside this room will not wake them as they are used to sleeping through the ruckus that usually takes place in the central hub outside their door. However, they wake immediately if either the door to the room is opened or if any sahuagin blood seeps into their chamber as a result of combat taking place outside of their room. It takes the blood five minutes from the time the first sahuagin wound is sustained in combat immediately outside of this door to seep in and alert the sleeping sahuagin.

Beyond that, the other details of the room are substantially similar to those of **Area 1**, excepting that the weapons rack is full and contains four spears and four tridents. Of final interest are the things in each of the limestone footlockers:

Box 1: A gold ring mounted with a small diamond. It looks like a wedding band favored in many terrestrial cultures and is worth 350 gp.

Box 2: A salvaged glass jar covered with a mesh netting that contains an ornate blue fish with long flowing fins.

Box 3: A rusted and useless curved dagger. The wood-inlaid handles have long since disappeared.

Box 4: A jade cat figurine about 6 inches tall worth 75 gp.

Area 2-4: Sahuagin Barracks

Same as **Area 2-1**, excepting that this weapons rack is empty but for a greataxe that shows no sign of rust or aging. Any inspection reveals the words "Hog's Bane" inscribed on the haft of the axe in Common. It is a *+1 greataxe* with the **Culinary** minor property (after attunement, it constantly whispers favorite recipes to the bearer, most commonly those for roast boar). It was taken long ago off the body of a human sailor. Beyond the useless junk, the four limestone boxes in this room contain the following:

Box 1: A small and stoppered glass vial. This is a vial of *universal solvent*. This vial contains six doses of the useful substance.

Box 2: A finely woven bit of netting that was fashioned into a sack, complete with drawstring, contains an array of severed claws. From what species they were harvested is hard to say.

Box 3: A silver brooch bearing inset matching pink pearls worth 300 gp.

Box 4: A roughly one-foot-by-one-foot square piece of black soapstone that has elven characters inscribed in it. It is part of a sahuagin liturgy and is written in Aquan. If none of the characters speaks Aquan, a DC 17 Intelligence check is necessary to translate it. If the reader speaks Elven, this check is made with advantage. If translated, it reads, "Flesh rends, bones crunch, and blood flows like the tides. The blessed feast on the weak and the faithless. The Red Feast comes anon! Rejoice the voracity of Dajobas the Devourer!"

Area 2-5: Sahuagin Barracks

Same as **Area 2-1**, excepting that this weapons rack contains two spears and two tridents. Beyond the useless junk, the four limestone boxes in this room contain the following:

Box 1: Nothing of interest.

Box 2: A silver belt buckle stylized to look like a mermaid complete with two aquamarine stones serving as her eyes, worth 275 gp.

LEVEL 2
The Garrison
1 Square - 5 Feet
2-2
2-3
Up To
Level 3
2-4
2-1
Down To
Level 1
2-5
N
W
E
S

Box 3: A humanoid skull. It is probably elven based on the size and shape.

Box 4: A gold amulet shaped like a running antlered deer, worth 150 gp.

The passage down to **Level 1** is approximately 40 feet in length.

LEVEL 1: SHRINE TO DAJOBAS

Unlike the upper levels in the Tooth, the passage down from **Level 2** to **1** contains a sahuagin door at the bottom of the passage, effectively in the ceiling of **Level 1**. At all times, directly underneath this door, are 2 **King's Guard sahuagin**[D]. For sahuagin, the King's Guard are the best of the best and do not shirk any aspect of their duties. They are always vigilant and most likely sense the approach of anyone coming down the passage toward them.

The central hub of this level is similar to the two above it but different in a couple of key aspects. While there are five sahuagin doors (situated on the locations indicated on the map), one of them is a different type of door from those the party has previously encountered. Instead of two solid halves coming together at the horizontal junction, the door to the southwest looks more like a gate. It functions the same as the other doors experienced, but it is composed of a lattice of vertical and horizontal struts that have large holes in between the struts whereas the rest of the doors previously encountered were solid. The characters notice the flow of a current in this hub as opposed to the two hubs above. This odd door and the current are explained in **Area 1-1** below.

In addition to these deviations, there is one further distinction that this hub enjoys from the two above it: Two additional doors or baffles cover the mouths of the passage up and the passage down. These doors function the same as the other doors the characters have encountered, but the party notices that they are of heavier construction and each has a heavy-duty locking bar and bolt on the bottom or downward facing side of each door. Neither of these doors is currently locked.

Beyond the two sahuagin guards, this central hub is otherwise empty.

The door on the ceiling that covers the passage up to **Level 2** is closed. As mentioned above, it is lockable, on the down or **Level 1** hub side. Fortunately for the characters, it is not locked. The party can open it as they descend simply by pushing against it and allowing the two parts of the door to part and open before them.

Before opening the door, a successful DC 15 Wisdom (Perception) check alerts the party to movement beyond the door. The sahuagin King's Guard almost certainly sense the movement of the characters coming down the passage toward them, but they are not alarmed as movement up and down the passages of the Tooth is far from uncommon. These two King's Guard sahuagin act as a checkpoint to make sure that anyone coming down to **Level 1** of the Tooth has a legitimate reason to be there.

These two guards quickly assimilate that the characters are a threat and rush to the attack. These four-armed brutes are the finest sahuagin warriors alive. They believe that they can easily dispatch any interlopers and so rush to attack in a frenzy rather than attempting to raise the alarm. They both fight to the death or incapacitation.

Finally, a successful DC 12 Wisdom (Perception) check reveals that the source of the current in this hub is through the strange grated door to the southwest (**Area 1-1**).

AREA 1-1: KING'S MUSSEL BED

The appetites of King Bachzarisaa the Insatiable are legendary among the sahuagin of Tzar'Grandula. While the king aspires to eat fresh humanoid every meal and as successful as his hunters are, that is just not possible given the depths of his appetites.

So as a partial solution, the king has ordered the cultivation of a carefully curated mussel bed here inside the Tooth. Many types of mussels are grown here, including blue mussels, horse mussels, zebra mussels, and box mussels.

As filter feeders, a consistent current is key to the health of mussels as they feed on plankton and other microscopic sea creatures that are free-floating in seawater. King Bachzarisaa's adherents engineered around this problem and it makes for quite a sight.

It is a simple matter for the characters to peer through the gaps in this door to see at least some of the details of the chamber beyond. If any of the characters decide to examine the door and the room beyond, please read or paraphrase the following:

Despite the gaps in the door, this door functions just like all of the other sahuagin doors the party has encountered.

The source of the pulsating current that provides sustenance to the mussel beds is a chained **sea cow**[D] that displaces large amounts of water with its flippers as it "treads water" in place. Its caretaker and the overseer of this mussel farm is a **sea troll**[D] that is in the process of feeding the sea cow some kelp as the characters approach. Finally, 2 **sahuagin elites**[D] stand as guards — very bored guards — at the far end of the chamber.

The sea troll and sahuagin guards ignore anything that happens outside of this chamber. However, if the characters enter the mussel chamber, the sea troll and the sahuagin attack immediately seeking to protect their charge, these mussel beds. The sea troll and sahuagin fight until they are slain or otherwise incapacitated.

AREA 1-2: CHAMBERS OF THE DAUGHTERS OF THE SHARK

The door to this chamber is unlocked. This is the private chamber of the Daughters of the Shark, the highest level of clergy of the Shark God Dajobas short of the high priestess herself.

There are 2 **Daughters of the Shark**[D] present. They are currently at rest relaxing in their berths. They aggressively attack as soon as they

DAJOBAS, THE SHARK GOD AND DEVOURER OF WORLDS

Servitors of Dajobas yearn for the release of the terrible Dajobas, the scourge of the seas, currently imprisoned in the deep and sunless chasms of the undersea. Adherents strive to bring forth the Red Feast, a slaughter so devastating that the seas of the world run red with spilled blood. This rapture will draw Dajobas from the depths and once more to the world of sunlight where he will feed ceaselessly on the unbelievers in the waves as well as on those on the shores of the world. There, the sun worshipers who foolishly believed they were safe from the devastation and glory of Dajobas' gory maw as they splashed in the shallows will suffer the apocalypse of his raging hunger and will despair.

LEVEL 1
Shrine to Dajobas
1 Square - 5 Feet
1-3
1-4
1-2
Down To
King's Level
Up To
Level 2
1-5
1-1
N
W
E
S

realize the characters are present. They gleefully fight the invading infidels to death or incapacitation.

This cavern houses 5 total Daughters. Two of the three Daughters are at ritual in the Fane of the Shark God (**Area 1-3**) and the final Daughter is in the Kitchen (**Area 1-4**) overseeing the preparation of the king's meal.

Beyond the net-like sleeping berths, each daughter has a small chest for her personal possessions. These five chests vary slightly in size but are all crafted of coral with bone clasps. The hinges are made of some unknown thick hide. Chests two and five are trapped as noted below. In addition to mundane or uninteresting personal possessions, they contain the following:

Chest 1: A bloated human hand and forearm. A successful DC 14 Wisdom (Medicine) check informs the characters that it was recently acquired, likely within the week, and that the upper ends of the ulna and radius where they would meet the elbow have been recently chewed upon.

Chest 2 (Trapped): Inside is a *necklace of prayer beads* cut off the head of an unfortunate ship's cleric some time ago.

SIMPLE PARALYSIS TRAP

Trigger. Anyone opening the chest other than the owner triggers the carefully carved runes on the lip of the chest's lid.

Effect. Opening the chest results in a flash that affects every creature within 5 feet. Any in range must succeed on a DC 15 Constitution saving throw or be paralyzed for 1 minute. An affected creature can repeat the saving throw at the end of its turn, ending the effect on itself on a success.

Countermeasures. A successful DC 18 Wisdom (Perception) or Intelligence (Investigation) reveals the arcane carvings. *Detect magic* indicates the presence of Enchantment magic. A successful DC 17 Intelligence (Arcana) check reveals the same. *Dispel magic* suppresses the effect for one hour. Should a character try to physically disarm the trap, he or she must come up with a logical plan for doing so and must succeed on a DC 15 Dexterity (Sleight of Hand) check. Failure triggers the trap.

Chest 3: A fine silver tiara of high craftsmanship. It features two stylized dolphins that seem to be swimming away from each other and is inlaid generously with mother of pearl, worth 2,500 gp.

Chest 4: Among the detritus in this chest is a vial containing three doses of *potion of invisibility*. Oddly, the vial looks empty but when picked up, it quickly becomes apparent that it is filled with liquid.

Chest 5 (Trapped): This chest contains a series of gruesome trophies, including a necklace of what look like elven ears; a small box filled with a variety of humanoid thumbs; and a bracelet of humanoid teeth.

COMPLEX COMPULSION TRAP

Trigger. A creature that is not a devotee or worshiper of Dajobas who opens the chest triggers the effect.

Effect. The creature opening the chest is targeted by powerful magic and must succeed on a DC 18 Wisdom saving throw or become charmed by that magic. While charmed in this way, the creature is compelled to worship and serve Dajobas. Specifically, the creature is compelled to move immediately to the Fane of the Shark God (**Area 1-3**) and genuflect before the altar therein. Considering what is going on in the fane presently, a character who does this is likely in trouble.

A repeat save is possible after either the creature genuflects before the altar in **Area 1-3** or is attacked by an enemy. Otherwise, the affected creature moves at normal speed to fulfill its compulsion. If other characters try to physically intervene by holding back the affected character, the affected character tries to break free via an opposed strength contest.

Countermeasures. A *detect magic* spell indicates the presence of enchantment magic inside the chest. *Dispel magic* cast on the chest before the chest is opened suppresses the effect for one hour. *Dispel*

magic cast with a successful DC 15 Spell Check on an affected character breaks the compulsion.

Notes: For the full effect, either via a passed note or through a quick side conference away from the rest of the party, consider giving the charmed characters some Dajobas devotional sayings that can be muttered as they make their way in an almost zombie-like fashion to the fane as commanded. Some examples are: "Glory to the sanguine feast!" "I ache with hunger! The hunger to serve." "The devourer comes! Praise to he who consumes all!"

AREA 1-3: FANE OF THE SHARK GOD

The door to this part of the Tooth is unlocked. Unlike just about every other cavern in the Tooth, this door opens to a passageway before opening to the chamber proper. After the characters open the door and enter the passage beyond, please read or paraphrase the following:

The images are of course all in homage to Dajobas. If a character is under the compulsion from the chest trap in **Area 3**, they touch the reliefs reverently, muttering praise to Dajobas as they move forward.

A successful DC 15 Intelligence (Religion or History) check informs the characters that all these images are in tribute to Dajobas, the Shark God and Devourer of Worlds.

Beyond lies the Fane of the Shark God, the sahuagin temple of Dajobas and the locus of the Devourer's power in the region. As the characters enter the fane, they interrupt the remaining 2 **Daughters of the Shark**[D] and 2 **sahuagin priestesses**[D] in the middle of a profane ritual.

On the orders of the High Priestess Enzu herself, these priestesses just finished ritualistically sacrificing one of the remaining live captives from the *Zephyr's* crew. The next step is then to serve this just sacrificed, and therefore fresh, body to King Bachzarisaa.

At this point, there are three remaining crew members of the *Zephyr* alive and kept in the Meat Locker (**Area K-2b**): Elisa Brand; the *Zephyr's* first mate, Nora Snape; and one rank-and-file sailor named Nesbit. The plan is to sacrifice all three of the remaining prisoners in an orgiastic and profane feast in a few days. High Priestess Enzu believes that this sanguine feast may be enough to inflame Dajobas into breaking free from his bonds and initiating the true Red Feast.

Because of the recent bloodletting, the entire fane is suffused with blood. All the priestesses are in an ecstatic state of blood frenzy as the characters enter. Finally, as soon as the party enters the passageway to the fane, the priestesses are aware of their approach.

As the characters enter the temple, please read or paraphrase the following:

Any non-sahuagin who enters the Fane of the Shark God is a shocking profanity and so the collected priestesses zealously fight until dead or incapacitated.

The priestesses each bear a sacrificial dagger made of coral and bone. Each has a stylized shark on its haft. They are otherwise normal daggers. The priestesses don't carry anything else of value.

Area 1-4: Kitchen

The door to the chamber is unlocked. Presently, 4 **craniform**[D] slaves supervised by a **Daughter of the Shark**[D] wait for this priestess' sisters to enter with the remains of their grisly ritual from the fane (**Area 1-3**). The sahuagin priestess is shocked by the appearance of the characters and leaps to the attack. The craniform are surprised and confused by the appearance of the characters and cower in the farthest reaches of the room.

While everyone who accepted the Sea Mother's Blessing can understand Aquan, they cannot actually speak to the craniform unless some magical means are employed. Under no circumstance are the craniform hostile or aggressive.

All of King Bachzarisaa's meals are prepared here under the oversight of the Daughters of the Shark. Enzu, the king's wife, is a fanatical follower of Dajobas. She has infected King Bachzarisaa with her zeal and convinced him that if each meal, especially those featuring the flesh of enemies, is sanctified by a ritual to Dajobas, the Shark God's power will flow into the king and increase his personal power and strength.

This cavern contains a series of low stone tables. The king's meals are prepared on these tables. There are also piles of shallow netting baskets with a variety of different netting patterns. These are serving trays, and the variety of different netting types are designed to accommodate different types of food.

The craniform can describe portions of the lower level where the king and his wife await their meal. This includes the passage down to that level, the guards waiting at the bottom of that level, and the throne room in which they are to serve the king and the high priestess. In the normal course, the craniform carry the king's meal down to the King's Level on the netting trays found in this room. They then serve him his meal in the throne room (**Area K-2**) while being supervised by one of the Daughters of the Shark. If the characters can communicate with the craniform, they willingly accept any instructions given.

Area 1-5: Guest Chambers

A **sequana genie**[D] from the elemental plane of water is currently visiting the court of King Bachzarisaa. Her name is Gamaa the Brackish. She is in Tzar'Grandula to investigate the troubling rumors that King Bachzarisaa and his consort, Enzu, the high priestess of Dajobas, are actively attempting to free the dread Shark God from his undersea prison. While such talk and sentiment are common among

single-minded creatures such as the sahuagin, the powers that be from the Palace of Prisms (the seat of rulership for the Great Durbar of the Sequana and dominant power on the Elemental Plane of Water) want to make sure that this ambitious sahuagin king and his fanatical wife have not actually found a way to free the terrible Shark God.

King Bachzarisaa is tolerating Gamaa's visit because he really has no choice. She is a powerful adversary, and he is not foolish enough to provoke the Palace of Prisms.

Could Gamaa swoop in at a critical moment to save the party? Well, that depends on how the characters treat with her. She will certainly not hinder the party in any way unless they foolishly decide to attack or insult her.

The baffle door on the floor of this level is not locked. The passage leads down to the **King's Level**.

THE KING'S LEVEL

The characters should be at least 9th level to have a chance of surviving this level of the Tooth and living through a confrontation with King Bachzarisaa and his consort.

The waterfilled passage from **Level 1** down to the **King's Level** is about 50 feet. Like the top of this passage, it is sealed with a sahuagin double baffle door. This door at the bottom of the passage and on the ceiling of the level below is 15 feet above the floor of the level below.

At all times, 2 **King's Guard sahuagin**[D] are stationed here. They immediately attack any non-authorized creature, sahuagin or otherwise, that comes through the door on the ceiling.

Like the levels above, the chambers of this level radiate off a central hub. This level features three doors. The doors to **Areas K-1** and K-3 are identical. However, the door to **Area K-2** is twice the size of normal sahuagin doors and is covered with Aquan runes (see **Area K-2** for details).

AREA K-1: KING'S GUARD BARRACKS

The door to this chamber is unlocked. Three off duty and resting **King's Guard sahuagin**[D] are in this cavern. While unconcerned about any disturbance they sense outside of their barracks, they immediately leap to the attack if the door to their chamber is opened by anyone other than a member of the King's Guard.

A weapons rack is against the south wall. It contains three spears, two tridents, and five javelins of sahuagin manufacture. The shafts of these weapons are constructed of porous coral, while the tips are of either sharpened stone or bone. One spear is from the surface world. Despite the caustic environment, the metal tip remains rust free and the wooden shaft remains true. It is a *+2 spear* taken during a raid years ago.

A total of 10 berths are in these barracks. Instead of a footlocker or box approach, each member of the King's Guard keeps his or her meager personal possessions in a netting sack attached to their respective berth. In addition to mundane things, they contain the following:

Sack 1: A large and unfinished agate worth 250 gp, but twice that amount if finished by a competent gemologist.

Sack 2: A rusty keyring containing five rusted skeleton keys that open unknown locks.

Sack 3: A collection of four sea elf skulls.

Sack 4: A large clamshell. *Detect magic* picks up Evocation magic from inside the shell. If opened, the opener is greeted with bright light. The shell contains a smooth, one-inch diameter stone that was the beneficiary of a *light* spell made permanent.

Sack 5: A heavily frayed and barely held together coin purse containing 65 pp.

Sack 6: A set of 7 jade polyhedral dice. Value 100 gp.

Sack 7: A battered pair of eyeglasses with only one of the crystal lenses remaining. *Detect magic* reveals that they are magical and are, in fact, *eyes* (now eye) *of minute seeing*. Their purpose is divined either through attunement or via an *identify* spell. The one lens still works on its own, but the user gets a headache if used continuously

for more than one minute. This headache imposes disadvantage on all checks and saving throws based either on Intelligence or Wisdom. Any magical healing cures the headache, but absent that, the headache abates on its own after one hour of not using the magical lens.

Sack 8: A set of three long bone shards that have been purposefully carved. A successful DC 16 Wisdom (Nature or Healing) check reveals that they are humanoid femur bones that have been fashioned into eating utensils.

Sack 9: A stone idol to Dajobas. It is 10 inches tall and looks like a sahuagin with a shark's head. Someone can recognize it for what it is following a successful DC 17 Intelligence (Religion) check.

Sack 10: A completely rust-free and ornate gauntlet. It does radiate magic if subjected to a *detect magic* spell. After either attunement or an *identify* spell, it is revealed to be one gauntlet from a set of *gauntlets of ogre power*.

Unfortunately, the matching gauntlet of this set was lost long ago. And while only one can be used at a time, they were designed to be used as a pair. If a character dons and attempts to use the single gauntlet, that action or attack is performed at Strength 19. However, because the magic powering it is not balanced by its lost twin, the user must make a DC 12 Dexterity saving throw or become overbalanced to the side bearing the gauntlet and fall prone.

AREA K-2: THRONE ROOM

The door to this room is not locked, but it is trapped (see sidebar **Trial of the Shark God**). The Aquan runes around the larger door to this part of the complex is a partial liturgy to Dajobas that Enzu modified and reads as follows:

> Rejoice those gluttonous for blood! Beyond lies the sanctum of the coming Red Feast. Only those of the keenest hunger and purest zealotry in Dajobas, the Devourer of Worlds, may pass unharmed. Surrender to your voracious appetite and declare your faith or suffer the pain of your apostasy.

If someone in the party can read Aquan, read this aloud to the character and provide them **Player Handout 6: Aquan Liturgy**. If not, the runes remain indecipherable.

The High Priestess Enzu crafted these Aquan runes to provide another layer of protection for herself and her king while compelling yet further devotion to her dark master, Dajobas the Devourer. These

TRIAL OF THE SHARK GOD

Trigger. The *Trial of the Shark God* is a spell-like effect that is triggered by any denier or disbeliever in Dajobas. Any creature that touches the door without first verbalizing some sort of devotion to Dajobas triggers the *trial*.

Effect. When triggered, the trial erupts with magical energy in a 20-foot-radius half sphere centered on the door and radiating out into the central hub of this level. Each creature in the area must make a DC 18 Dexterity saving throw. A creature takes 36 (8d8) lightning damage on a failed saving throw, or half as much damage on a successful one.

Countermeasures. To touch the door without triggering the *bane*, the opener must mutter some form of devotion to Dajobas. It can be as simple as "I serve you, Dajobas." The engravings powering the trap can be noted and understood with a successful DC 18 Intelligence (Arcana) check.

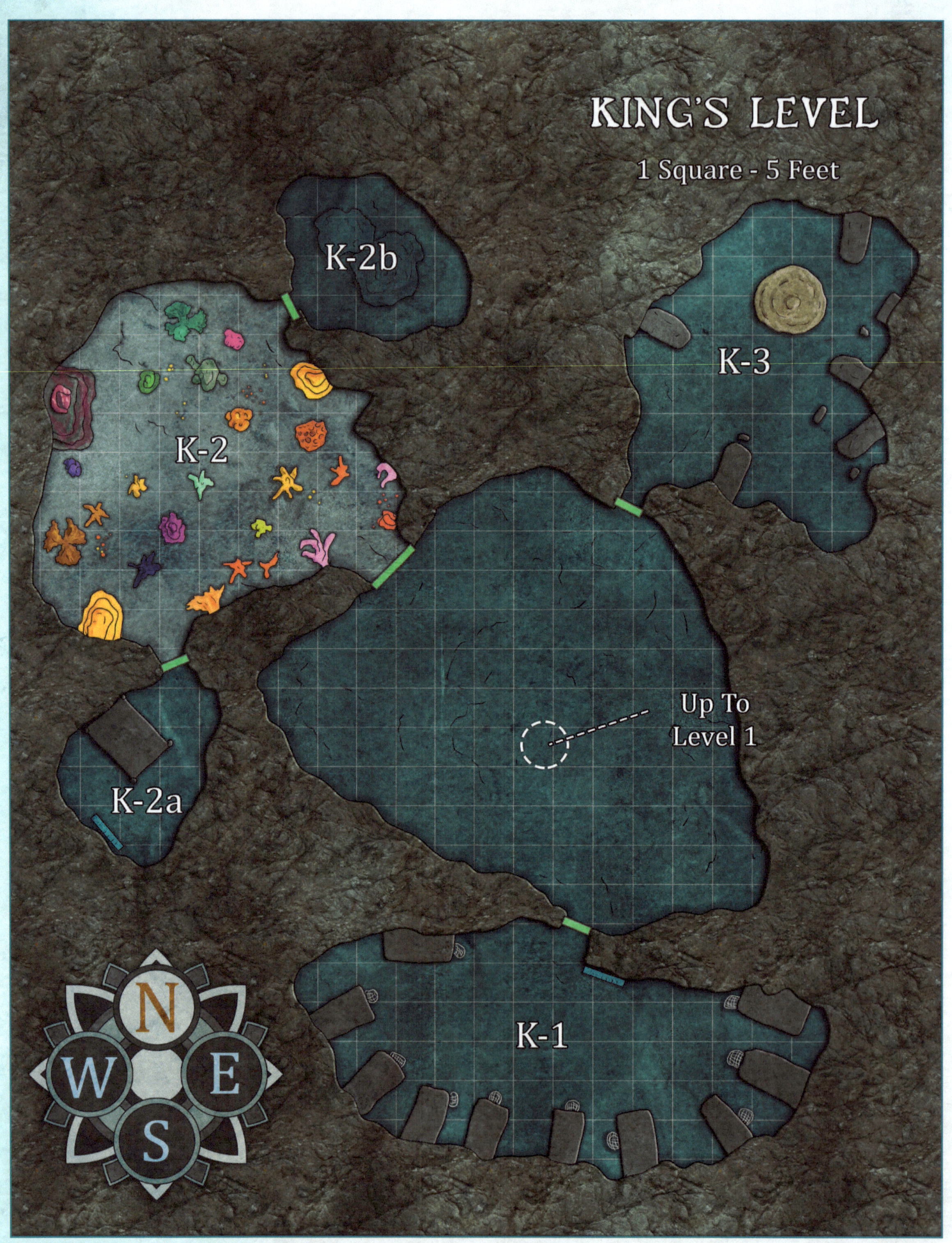

KING'S LEVEL
1 Square - 5 Feet
K-2b
K-3
K-2
K-2a
Up To
Level 1
K-1
N
W
E
S

runes form the *Trial of the Shark God*. If the characters are able to translate the runes, a successful DC 16 Intelligence (Religion) check informs the successful character of all that is contained in the **Dajobas, the Shark God and Devourer of Worlds** sidebar and a successful DC 18 Intelligence (Arcana) check confirms that the runes contain some potential destructive effect. Finally, A *detect magic* spell indicates the presence of Abjuration magic on the door. *Dispel magic* suppresses the effect for one hour.

Once past the doors, please read or paraphrase the following:

As you move past the menacing doors and into the massive chamber beyond, you cannot help but be impressed by the breathtaking beauty arrayed before you. It is as if you have stepped into another realm entirely. Gone is the uniformly drab, dark, and profoundly utilitarian sahuagin sea cavern complex. Replacing it is an undersea world of unimaginable beauty and astonishing whimsy. Unlike the rest of the sahuagin stronghold, this cavern is almost bright with every mote of light seemingly reflecting off myriad shimmering surfaces.

Spectacular and purposefully sculpted coral gardens sweep ahead of you and feature an array of colors and textures that seem simply otherworldly and impossible. Brightly-hued fish, shrimp, and crabs dart and cavort throughout as if they are all moving to some unheard music.

Looking more closely, you see many other small creatures living on these reefs. Many of them glow with their own light. Included are innumerable species of urchins, starfish, and sponges. You cannot help but notice that the corals are generously inset with pearls of every size and color imaginable. Lastly, you see that the coral reefs and shoals create a gently winding path through the surrounding opulence to the far side of this dazzling undersea exhibition.

In all, it feels as if you have stepped into an underwater fairy tale. That is until you spot what awaits you at the far end of the chamber. The wonderous gardens and fantastic corals all lead to an assemblage of figures on the other end of the cavern, three standing and one seated, atop a three-stepped dais.

Of this cluster of figures, the two creatures at the very top seize your immediate attention. Seated on a shimmering throne that seems to have been carved out of some sort of colossal and striated crystal is the largest sahuagin you have ever seen. Leaning forward slightly in its impressive throne while clutching an 8-foot-long, gleaming trident in one of its four claws, you see that its hide is dark charcoal gray. Even at this distance of 75 feet or so, you would guess that the creature must weigh in excess of 400 pounds. And unlike any other sahuagin you have ever seen, it seems to be wearing shell armor of some sort. It bears a rune-covered breastplate apparently fashioned out of a huge clamshell.

Not to be outdone, however, is the creature standing to the left of the seated sahuagin. This sahuagin is much slighter in stature but not in any way less impressive. Unlike the three

This is **King Bachzarisaa the Insatiable**[D], **High Priestess Enzu of Dajobas**[D], and 2 **King's Guard sahuagin**[D].

King Bachzarisaa's initial demeanor is one of amusement. However, High Priestess Enzu barely restrains herself from lashing out. King Bachzarisaa allows the party to approach and even speaks with them. That said, there is only one outcome acceptable to the king and his consort: the characters' deaths followed by the king and his consort consuming them in an orgiastic tribute to their shark god.

This grand chamber is 90 feet deep and 50 feet wide. The natural cavern ceiling averages 30 feet in height. Due to all the bioluminescent creatures and the reflective surfaces, the entire throne room is brightly lit.

King Bachzarisaa is interested in knowing if the characters are a lone group or are the vanguard of a full invasion force. Some good roleplaying or good checks by the characters should be rewarded with the characters taking the king and his guards by surprise. Not

Enzu, though, as she is single-minded in her vigilance. For example, the characters could pretend to be emissaries from the craven surface world. Or they could pretend to be devotees of Dajobas on a pilgrimage to witness his Aquan avatar (King Bachzarisaa). However, the moment any of the characters display any overt sign of hostilities or do anything tactical such as spreading out, the intelligent king orders the attack.

Tactics: Enzu becomes aware of the characters' presence as they work on the door to the throne room, if not before then. As she has time to prepare, she casts *mage armor* and *globe of invulnerability* on herself by the time the characters enter the throne room. Enzu also has already sought to activate the *collar of giant control*[B] to summon Jathor (**Area 3-3**). If the characters failed to free Jathor of the collar, she arrives five rounds after the characters enter the throne room. If they released Jathor, nothing happens when Enzu attempts to activate the collar's control device.

Due to the general luminescence from all of the reflective surfaces, it is difficult to pick up the faint shimmer of the *globe* Enzu cast. However, the characters can identify the faint shimmer around the king and Enzu with a successful DC 20 Wisdom (Perception) check.

As soon as hostilities commence, the two King's Guard sahuagins move forward to engage whatever party members are closest to the royal couple. The king joins the melee shortly thereafter but waits until at least the second round of melee combat. He engages the most formidable-looking fighter in a frenzy and relies on his overwhelming strength and his favorite combination of claw/claw/bite/trident.

Enzu attacks the most dangerous-looking spellcaster with the *bite of Dajobas* from her staff and then follows by summoning sharks via

Roleplaying King Bachzarisaa

The ancient king has ruled Tzar'Grandula for hundreds of years. He has survived countless challenges to his authority and now rules in complete confidence in the fact that he is the master of his realm. The more than 600-year-old king is famous for his legendary appetites. His consort, Enzu, believes that the king's insatiable hunger clearly marks him as a favorite of Dajobas. He is more than just a little curious about the sudden appearance of the characters. To the extent that King Bachzarisaa is willing to treat with the characters, it is in a high-handed and vastly superior manner.

Finally, decades of focused worship of Dajobas overseen by the zealous Enzu has made King Bachzarisaa an extremist. He believes he has the power to release the Great Devourer from its prison in the depths. King Bachzarisaa is convinced of his destiny in this respect and has little time or interest in hearing the wishes of mortal surface dwellers. The characters are simply meat to King Bachzarisaa.

Common Sayings

- "The shark does not negotiate with the cuttlefish."
- "Meat is meat."

her staff as well as casting whatever spells she deems most effective. When any character directs an attack against Enzu that would normally inflict damage but is instead absorbed by her ward, consider allowing that character to attempt a DC 15 Wisdom (Perception) check with a success enabling that character to notice a momentary flash that surrounds Enzu from her arcane ward.

The sahuagin all fight until dead or incapacitated. No quarter is asked, and certainly none is given. The king and high priestess are inflamed by the strength of their faith in Dajobas and their belief that they are destined to trigger the Red Feast and the end of the civilized world. Finally, the king would prefer to take a few of the characters alive in order to restock his Meat Locker (**Area K-2b**).

Pearls of just about every conceivable variety are embedded in the ornamental corals all over this chamber. If they spend the time searching, the characters find opaque, lustrous white, lavender, yellow, and pink pearl varieties that vary in size and average 100 gp in value. Hundreds of pearls are in this chamber, so the number the party finds really is just a function of how much time they spend harvesting them. Each character can find and remove 20 pearls for each hour spent searching; they can take up to a maximum of 200 total pearls.

The throne is carved out of a massive piece of fluorite. Its layered colors of greens, pinks, and oranges make for an impressive sight. It weighs several tons and is of inestimable value.

When the characters have an opportunity to explore the throne room, they discover sahuagin doors leading into smaller side chambers, one to the south and one to the north.

This door is unlocked. Given the opulence of the throne room, this small chamber is almost startlingly plain. Instead of the usual netted sleeping berths common throughout the Tooth, this room features a structure that looks more like a terrestrial bed. It has four posts forming the corners of a large stone rectangle. Nets stretched across the body of the rectangle create the surface of the bed.

On the far southern wall is a large weapons rack. It contains a variety of sahuagin weapons including spears, tridents, and javelins. Several terrestrial weapons are also on the rack, the fruit of hundreds of years of raiding. The rack contains a *+1 longsword*, a *+2 longbow*, a *+1 warhammer*, and a *+1 flail*.

The other notable feature in the room is a great stone chest at the foot of the bed. It is unlocked and not trapped; no sahuagin would dare attempt to steal from King Bachzarisaa. Contained in the chest are the king's favorite pieces of tribute and plunder. The characters find: three different carved idols of Dajobas made of jade, lapis lazuli, and onyx (100 gp, 150 gp, and 75 gp); a fine netted sack of 15 polished fire agates (50 gp each); 632 gp coins of a variety of mintings; 210 pp; a small netted pouch of 5 opaque pure pearls (500 gp each); a platinum crown featuring a stylized stag in mid-leap on its brow, but marred by a deep cut on one side (1,000 gp; 1,500 gp if repaired); a gold ring set with a large, deep-green colored emerald (2,000 gp); a loose ruby the size of a chicken's egg (4,000 gp); 3 *potions of superior healing*; a *ring of spell storing*; a *ring of greater protection*[B]; a *wand of web*; and, an *elemental gem*.

STAFF OF DAJOBAS

Staff, artifact (requires attunement by an evil creature)

Made from coral as hard as iron and bearing Aquan runes, the staff is topped with a magically enlarged shark head with its jaws agape. Any creature of a non-evil alignment that tries to attune to the staff must make a DC 17 Constitution saving throw. On a successful save, the creature takes 8d6 necrotic damage. On a failed save, the creature dies.

MINOR ABILITIES

While attuned to this staff, you gain a +3 bonus to attack and damage rolls made with it. The staff deals an extra 2d12 necrotic damage on a hit.

While attuned to the staff, you can't be charmed or frightened and your swim speed increases by 20 feet. If you do not already have a swim speed, you have a swim speed of 20 feet.

Further, while attuned to the staff and due to its caustic aqueous nature, all holy water within 10 feet of it is destroyed, and magic potions within 10 feet of it are rendered nonmagical.

While attuned to the staff, you are filled with an unabating hunger and must eat and drink six times the normal amount each day.

Finally, while attuned to the staff, you gain a +3 bonus to Armor Class while holding it.

MAJOR ABILITIES

Bite of Dajobas. While you are holding the staff, as an action you can call forth the *bite of Dajobas*. After selecting a target that you can see within 60 feet, a spectral head of a huge shark appears and attempts to bite the target at +10 to hit, doing 45 (10d8) piercing damage on a successful hit.

Call Sharks. While you are holding the staff, you can use an action to conjure sharks, calling forth up to 2 **giant sharks**. The sharks magically appear in unoccupied spaces within 300 feet of you and obey your commands until they are destroyed or until dawn of the next day, when they disappear. Once you use this property of the staff, you can't use it again until the next dawn.

Sentience. The *staff of Dajobas* is a sentient, chaotic evil item with an Intelligence of 16, a Wisdom of 12, and a Charisma of 16. It has hearing and darkvision out to a range of 120 feet.

The staff communicates telepathically with its wielder and can speak, read, and understand Aquan.

Personality. The staff's purpose is to help satisfy Dajobas's desire to consume everything in the multiverse. The staff is cold, cruel, nihilistic, and bereft of humor. The staff fills you with an unrelenting hunger (see above) that forces you to concentrate on the subject of your next meal to the exclusion of just about anything else.

SEA KING'S TRIDENT

Trident, very rare (requires attunement)

While attuned to this trident, you gain a +3 bonus to attack and damage rolls made with it. On a hit, the trident deals 2d8 piercing damage and an additional 2d8 thunder damage and the target is pushed 10 feet away from you. You have a swim speed of 40 feet while bearing this trident. Finally, this trident has one additional minor property:

Narcissistic. While bearing this trident you have an excessive interest in yourself and your physical appearance and feel that you are the best at everything. You have an unending need for admiration and suffer from a lack of empathy for other people.

Area K-2b: The Meat Locker

The door to this chamber is unlocked. When the characters open this door, they are confronted by quite a sight. When they enter, please read or paraphrase the following:

> As you enter this otherwise unadorned stone cavern, you are confronted with what looks like two large inflated balloons. You see that the two, whatever they are, are attached to each other. One is slightly larger than the other. The skin or surface of the two objects is diaphanous, so you can at least make out what they contain. The smaller one closest to you is empty. However, the second one contains a slight supine figure. Looking closer, you see that it is a human female matching the description of Captain Elisa Brand. You can hardly believe what you are seeing. As you peer intently, you can make out the very faint rise and fall of her chest. She is alive! But she is definitely unconscious. After recovering from the shock of finally seeing the object of your seemingly endless quest, you notice that the big balloon-like things are approximately eight feet in diameter and that they both have some sort of tentacles draping from the sides of them.

Elisa Brand is unconscious, rendered so by the poison of the now-dead creature within which she lies. A successful DC 16 Intelligence (Nature) check reveals that these balloon-like things are huge jellyfish that have somehow been inflated with air. A successful DC 14 Wisdom (Perception) check finds a stone peg jutting out of the far northern wall. On it are five linked metal bracelets that each bear Aquan runes on the separate silver links. A *detect magic* spell reveals Transmutation magic. A successful DC 18 Intelligence (Arcana) check informs the characters that these bracelets are designed to protect terrestrials from the effects of water pressure. Finally, a successful DC 18 Wisdom (Perception) check reveals a glint of silver metal on Elisa Brand's right wrist — one of these bracelets. This check is made with advantage if the characters have already found and divined the purpose of the other bracelets hanging on the far side of the room.

The second jellyfish is used as an airlock of sorts and allows the sahuagin to install and remove alive but unconscious humanoid victims from the Meat Locker. The priestesses cut the membranes of the two jellyfish open as needed and then repair them via a *mending* spell. Periodically, these membranes are taken to the surface of the sea to re-inflate them.

A successful DC 20 Intelligence check informs the characters how all this works. Award advantage on this check to any of the characters who have an engineering background or are doing a good job using logic to figure out what is going on here.

The question then remains: How to safely extract Elisa Brand from her prison and safely get her to the water's surface. By now, the characters should have some sort of mechanism for underwater breathing beyond their Sea Mother's Blessing. A good plan is a must for seeing Elisa Brand safely out of the dangerous sahuagin city.

AREA K-3: NURSERY, INCUBATOR, CONSORTS

The door to this chamber is unlocked. The 5 female **Sinnar sahuagin**[D] are the current consorts of King Bachzarisaa. Their 10 **sahuagin young**[D] are presently in the nursery. As is the king's routine, a new set of consorts rotates into service every few months or so. Each set of females produces two hatches of young, with only the strongest few of each hatch surviving to adolescence. Most prized are the mutated, four-armed offspring that may eventually join the King's Guard. However, being birthed with four arms guarantees nothing. These hatchlings must survive the gauntlet of sahuagin youth just like any other.

The five females are supervising the young "at play." These young sahuagin each have short spears and are busily attacking each other. The central feature of the room is a large circular limestone incubator. These females laid their second batch of eggs into the incubator weeks ago. The young sahuagin fighting in the room currently are the surviving few of these females' first hatch. The incubator containing the second hatch will not be opened for several more weeks.

Sleeping berths and other valueless personal items are scattered about the room.

The incubator is made from sandstone. It is circular with a diameter of approximately eight feet. A DC 18 Strength check is needed to successfully remove the heavy stone lid. Several characters can work together to try to open the lid given its size.

Inside are 25 or so sahuagin hatchlings. At this early stage, they look like big toothy bullfrogs. It takes them several minutes to realize that the ceiling has been removed from their prison. In the meantime, they fight each other, and the characters even see a couple of the nasty little things munching on the corpse of one of their fellows. At this stage of development, the sahuagin hatchlings are not fed. They are thereby forced to feed on each other to ensure that only the strong survive incubation.

The five females immediately attack any intruders, and the sahuagin young quickly join in. As with all sahuagin, they won't surrender and fight until dead or incapacitated.

CONCLUSION

It takes a well-conceived plan to get the weakened Elisa Brand out of Tzar'Grandula. Trying to leave through the city proper is suicide. The most reasonable plan is likely to leave the same way they came. If the sequana genie Gamaa the Brackish is still present, she is not displeased to hear of the passing of King Bachzarisaa and the zealous Enzu. She might very well be willing to help the characters escape the city.

The *Bounty* and *Zephyr* are still at anchor wherever the characters left them. The crew is very glad to see the characters and the returned Captain Brand. Even Captain Timothy is grudgingly pleased.

The journey home west, back across the Sinnar Ocean, can be as eventful as you like. For example, spreading the crew of the *Bounty* between two ships likely makes the return journey more difficult. Should they return to Bridgeport in one piece, Jaxon Brand is most delighted by the successful rescue and return of his daughter. He owes each character 1,000 gp and happily pays it.

So ends Sea King's Malice.

Bridgeport

Population: 32,679
Alignment: Neutral
Rulers: Baron Goron Ulien
Government: Oligarchy
Race Breakdown: human 80%, halfling 10%, dwarf 5%, other 5%
Languages: Common, Elven, Gnome, Dwarven, Halfling
Religion: Regional, Moderate
Technology Level: Medieval

Modest fortifications and stone buildings hover over the rocky shoreline, protecting the piers and docks that are the lifeblood of Bridgeport. Most of the shoreline stretching from Falconmere Peninsula up to the Worntooth Peaks can't support the large structures needed to form a good harbor as the shoreline varies from high and rocky to soft and swampy. Bridgeport is the closest safe port for large merchant vessels arriving through the Strait of Praeis and, of course, the last safe port before departing the Crescent Sea, providing it with very heavy shipping and merchant traffic that the city does its best to support and encourage.

History and People

Like many of the areas nearby, Bridgeport was once under the control of the Kingdom of Foere but that control fell away when Foere turned its focus on the Eastern Provinces. Olduvar's open revolt against the crown and the simple presence of Brookmere help keep Bridgeport independent. Most of the citizens are human residents of Foerdewaith descent but there is also a significant population of halfling craftsman and dwarves that migrated here from Brookmere years ago. A healthy mix of other races resides here as well; Bridgeport sees enough merchant traffic through its harbor that occasionally visitors decide to stop here and take up residence.

The foundations here are deep and ancient. As one of the few areas able to support a sizeable harbor along this stretch of coastline, there has been a city of some type here for thousands of years. Warfare, piracy, and even massive storms have changed the shape and form of the city over time, as well as its residents. This location is ideal for traders and merchants, so even in the face of catastrophe the city is always rebuilt. The present structures have been standing for several centuries but the flooded catacombs beneath the city are from a distant, unrecorded past.

Religion

All religions are welcome in Bridgeport as the city leaders do not want to alienate any merchants or traders. The Temple District is inland from the Trademoot and contains many temples, some grand and others quite humble. The leading among these are temples to Sefagreth (trade), Quell (the sea), and Belon (trade). A temple to Muir is smaller and has fewer devotees. The Green Father is also worshipped here with a well-maintained temple and altar.

Trade and Commerce

Trade is the major lifeblood of Bridgeport, whether it is agricultural goods traveling to the port to be transported out or goods from the ships docking here meant to be sent inland, most of the city is devoted to attracting and keeping merchant traffic going through. After agriculture, fishing and shipbuilding and repair are the next-largest contributors to the city's coffers, with the various smaller guilds following closely behind.

While shipping and trade are certainly the primary concerns of Bridgeport, farming runs a not-so-distant second. The entire region is known for its large plantations. These farms fan out inland around Bridgeport and line the trade way to Brookmere. The semi-tropical climate, the fertile ground, and easy access to distant and eager markets make this region an agricultural hotbed.

While there are farms that raise livestock, the vast majority of the plantations in the region produce cash crops, with the most significant ones being allspice, figs, cotton, gold melon, pineapple, maize, millet, olives, oranges, and turnips.

Another of Bridgeport's primary features is that it boasts one of the few true shipyards of the Crescent Sea. Shipwrights here are capable of building ships of almost any size and capability, and the shipyard can also perform repairs on damaged boats. The one drawback to the shipyard here is that it is small enough that only one major ship can be built at a time, and each ship takes a considerable amount of construction time.

Three major trade houses are located in Bridgeport. They are Risen Star, The Tamil Group, and Zephyr Assimilated. These three concerns, and others, are responsible for shipping the local agricultural products abroad as well as inland. They then return with a vast array of goods from far-flung points in the Lost Lands to sell locally in Bridgeport or the surrounding cities.

Of these three major mercantile houses, Zephyr Assimilated is the biggest and most widely known. Zephyr trades and ships all over the Lost Lands and frequents every major port of call. If you want something reliably shipped, pay Zephyr. They enjoy an excellent reputation for honest and reliable dealings.

Because of these other strong economic sectors, there is a robust guild presence in Bridgeport as well. Many of the guilds focus on the peripheral aspects of the seafaring trades. Leading guilds are the Sailmakers Loft, Shipwrights, Galley's Hands, Victuallers, Ropers, Tanners, Wheelwrights, Drawers, Chandler, and Spicers, among dozens of other smaller guilds.

Many other important businesses in Bridgeport play important roles in day-to-day life there. Tallard's Festhall is one of them. In addition to being a casino and a brothel, it is the base of operations of the Tallard family, the most significant and influential organized crime operation in Bridgeport. Tallard's is essentially the thieves' guild. If there is an unsavory task that needs doing, for the right number of coins spent at Tallard's, that task will be done.

Another seminal business in Bridgeport is the Rising Sun Coinhouse. Most of the major businesses and concessions in Bridgeport have accounts at the Rising Sun. A note or marker from the Rising Sun is accepted as legal tender in all the major cities in the Lost Lands.

The busiest part of the city is the Trademoot. Close to the docks, the Trademoot is a combination open-air market and auction arena. The booths are filled with locals selling their wares and produce, and the open-air auction house is where all manner of things are sold. Most of the influential guilds and finest shops in Bridgeport surround the Trademoot.

Loyalty and Diplomacy

Bridgeport has a mutual defense treaty with the Free City of Brookmere, but, in truth, it would expect any attack against it to come from the sea, making the treaty of little benefit. Trade agreements with the City-State of Castorhage, Brookmere, the Kingdom of North Heath, and even distant Reme help maintain trade traffic through the city. There are no present agreements with the Free States of Taicho, but there is considerable trade traffic with merchant vessels from the far side of the Crescent Sea.

GOVERNMENT

Bridgeport is a barony, but not exactly in the classic sense. While the baron is the nominal ruler of Bridgeport, he is advised by a council of city leaders called "The Seven." The Seven are the heads of powerful and influential families residing in Bridgeport. Most of the members of The Seven are either from one of the major merchant houses or are plantation owners, the two biggest industries in Bridgeport (trade and farming). So the baron is more like a mayor, working with the advice and consent of The Seven, than a baron in the traditional sense.

The baron serves an indefinite term, one basically determined by the confidence and support of The Seven. This means the baron is forced to consider his supporters in all the decisions he makes. Baron Ulien has made it his goal to become as important as possible to the livelihood of the Free City of Brookmere, as he believes it can only enhance and protect Bridgeport's status. Lax laws and reasonable tariffs ensure that a great deal of trade runs through the city, but without the support of a larger city or nation-state, Baron Ulien and others of the city's elite believe their chances of growing larger are limited.

Laws here are enforced by a well-armed and organized militia, but these laws are designed to encourage trade and visitors, not turn them away. Import laws with respect to drugs and other items are equally friendly. There is a single court system in town managed by judges picked by the mayor, usually with the approval of various city leaders. Corruption in the courts is common; wealthy patrons have little to fear in the court system.

MILITARY

The militia here is officially under the control of Colonel Girese Longcoat, who commands the guardsmen of the city. Bridgewater has a small but effective navy that patrols the waters just outside the harbor and periodically makes rounds to watch over active fishermen and whalers. Captain Coral White oversees the navy which is made up of one galley and three longships. While the militia here is not very large, they are well-trained, making their defensive positions formidable in the event of an attack. Most of the work of the militia comes in the form of acting as guardsmen policing the city for violent crimes.

MAJOR THREATS

Baron Ulien and the city leaders believe that Bridgeport's major threat is its dependence on trade. So they are making a concerted effort to encourage more skilled craftsmen to come to the city and hope to encourage the proliferation of its already robust agricultural sector.

NOTABLE INNS

The Blushing Cabin Boy, The Wagon Wheel, and The Sprite's Trist.

NOTABLE SHOPS

Judicious Passage, Seafarer's Sundries, Ash's Implements, and Ace Armaments.

TZAR'GRANDULA, THE CITY OF FEASTS

Population: Unknown
Alignment: Lawful Evil
Rulers: King Bachzarisaa the Insatiable
Government: Dictatorship
Race Breakdown: Sahuagin
Languages: Sahuagin, Aquan
Religion: Extreme, Radical
Technology Level: Unknown

Tzar'Grandula — which means "City of Feasts" in sahuagin — lies on a seafloor basin in the southern Sinnar Ocean. It sits at a depth of approximately 500 feet under the surface of the sea. The primary geological aspects include a set of low "hills" that encircle the city and a series of long dormant calderas from a quiescent fault line. These peaks form a rough line through the heart of the city and over the ages have gradually been partially hollowed out to become the primary residences of the king, his court, as well as for other powerful sahuagin. The central tower known as "The Tooth" stands at the very center of the city. This tower is surrounded by ornamental coral gardens and clam beds.

Beyond the existence of a ring of watch towers that encircle the city, little else is known about Tzar'Grandula. Any population number would be a guess at best. There are certainly hundreds of sahuagin that reside there, but more exact information simply does not exist. The scant amount known about the sahuagin city was gleaned from captured sahuagin raiders before they were summarily executed.

APPENDIX B: GLOSSARY OF MAGIC ITEMS

All the magic items that can be found in the adventure are listed below alphabetically. Those that are not in the Fifth Edition SRD are marked with an asterisk and described afterwards.

Item	Location	Chapter
+1 flail	Area K-2a on the King's Level of the Tooth	C. 5
+1 greataxe	Weapons rack in Area 2-4 on Level 2 of the Tooth	C. 5
+1 longsword	Area K-2a on the King's Level of the Tooth	C. 5
+1 saber	Area 6, Discovery	C. 3
+1 warhammer	Area K-2a on the King's Level of the Tooth	C. 5
+2 breastplate	Area K-2 on the King's Level of the Tooth	C. 5
+2 longbow	Area K-2 on the King's Level of the Tooth	C. 5
+2 Spear	Area K-1 on the King's Level of the Tooth	C. 5
*Amulet of Stoneskin**	Area K-2 on the King's Level of the Tooth	C. 5
*Collar of giant control**	Area 3-3 on Level 3 of the Tooth (Control device carried by Enzu, Area K-2 on the King's Level of the Tooth)	C. 5
Elemental gem	Area K-2a on the King's Level of the Tooth	C. 5
Eyes (eye) of minute seeing	Sack 7 in Area K-1 on the King's Level of the Tooth	C. 5
*Handaxe of lightning**	Captain Garth Blackbeard's cave	C. 4
Necklace of adaptation	Area 6, Discovery	C. 3
Necklace of prayer beads	Chest 2 in Area 1-2 on Level 1 of the Tooth	C. 5
Potion of invisibility	Chest 4 in Area 1-2 on Level 1 of the Tooth	C. 5
Potion of superior healing	Area 6, Discovery	C. 3
Potion of superior healing	Area K-2a on the King's Level of the Tooth	C. 5
Potion of water breathing	Area 6, Discovery	C. 3
*Ring of greater protection**	Area K-2a on the King's Level of the Tooth	C. 5
Ring of spell storing	Area K-2a on the King's Level of the Tooth	C. 5
*Ring of water breathing**	Captain Garth Blackbeard's cave	C. 4
*Sea King's Trident**	Area K-2 on the King's Level of the Tooth	C. 5

Item	Location	Chapter
Spellbook	Area 5, Discovery	C. 3
*Staff of Dajobas**	Area K-2 on the King's Level of the Tooth	C. 5
Wand of magic detection	Box 4 in Area 2-2 on Level 2 of the Tooth	C. 5
Wand of web	Area K-2a on the King's Level of the Tooth	C. 5

AMULET OF STONESKIN

Wondrous item, very rare (requires attunement)

While wearing this amulet, you have resistance to non-magical bludgeoning, piercing, and slashing damage.

HANDAXE OF LIGHTNING

Handaxe, very rare (requires attunement)

You gain a +2 bonus to attack and damage rolls made with this weapon. When you hit with an attack with this weapon, the target takes an additional 1d6 lightning damage. Further, the weapon bears the additional minor property:

Aqueous: While you are attuned to this item, you attack underwater without the normal underwater melee penalty and you have advantage on Strength (Athletics) checks to swim.

RING OF WATER BREATHING

Ring, uncommon (requires attunement)

While wearing this ring you can breathe normally underwater.

RING OF PROTECTION

Wondrous item, rarity varies (requires attunement)

While wearing this ring, you gain a bonus to your AC and saving throws. The amount of the bonus depends on the ring's rarity.

Ring of...	Rarity	Bonus
Protection	rare	+1
Greater protection	very rare	+2
Superior protection	legendary	+3

COLLAR OF GIANT CONTROL

Wondrous item, Very rare

This rune-etched silver collar automatically expands to fit the neck of any giant-kind. With the collar closed and the control device in hand, the giant suffers the effects of a *dominate monster* spell, excepting the saving throws. While holding the control device, you can command the collared giant to do just about anything other than direct self-harm. Use of the device requires concentration and is of otherwise unlimited use.

The holder of the control device can unlock the collar at will. Otherwise, the collar can be removed in only two ways: unlocked with a successful DC 20 Dexterity check using thieves' tools or with a successful DC 18 *dispel magic* spell attempt. A successful DC 15

Intelligence (Arcana) check informs characters generally of these two removal options.

SEA KING'S TRIDENT

Trident, very rare (requires attunement)

While attuned to this trident, you gain a +3 bonus to attack and damage rolls made with it. On a hit, the trident deals 2d8 piercing damage and an additional 2d8 thunder damage and the target is pushed 10 feet away from you. You have a swim speed of 40 feet while bearing this trident. Finally, this trident has one additional minor property:

Narcissistic. While bearing this trident you have an excessive interest in yourself and your physical appearance and feel that you are the best at everything. You have an unending need for admiration and suffer from a lack of empathy for other people.

STAFF OF DAJOBAS

Staff, artifact (requires attunement by an evil creature)

Made from coral as hard as iron and bearing Aquan runes, the staff is topped with a magically enlarged shark head with its jaws agape. Any creature of a non-evil alignment that tries to attune to the staff must make a DC 17 Constitution saving throw. On a successful save, the creature takes 8d6 necrotic damage. On a failed save, the creature dies.

MINOR ABILITIES

While attuned to this staff, you gain a +3 bonus to attack and damage rolls made with it. The staff deals an extra 2d12 necrotic damage on a hit.

While attuned to the staff, you can't be charmed or frightened and your swim speed increases by 20 feet. If you do not already have a swim speed, you have a swim speed of 20 feet.

Further, while attuned to the staff and due to its caustic aqueous nature, all holy water within 10 feet of it is destroyed, and magic potions within 10 feet of it are rendered nonmagical.

While attuned to the staff, you are filled with an unabating hunger and must eat and drink six times the normal amount each day.

Finally, while attuned to the staff, you gain a +3 bonus to Armor Class while holding it.

MAJOR ABILITIES

Bite of Dajobas. While you are holding the staff, as an action you can call forth the *bite of Dajobas*. After selecting a target that you can see within 60 feet, a spectral head of a huge shark appears and attempts to bite the target at +10 to hit, doing 45 (10d8) piercing damage on a successful hit.

Call Sharks. While you are holding the staff, you can use an action to conjure sharks, calling forth up to 2 **giant sharks**. The sharks magically appear in unoccupied spaces within 300 feet of you and obey your commands until they are destroyed or until dawn of the next day, when they disappear. Once you use this property of the staff, you can't use it again until the next dawn.

Sentience. The *staff of Dajobas* is a sentient, chaotic evil item with an Intelligence of 16, a Wisdom of 12, and a Charisma of 16. It has hearing and darkvision out to a range of 120 feet.

The staff communicates telepathically with its wielder and can speak, read, and understand Aquan.

Personality. The staff's purpose is to help satisfy Dajobas's desire to consume everything in the multiverse. The staff is cold, cruel, nihilistic, and bereft of humor. The staff fills you with an unrelenting hunger (see above) that forces you to concentrate on the subject of your next meal to the exclusion of just about anything else.

APPENDIX C: NAUTICAL TERMS

Aft The back part of a ship or boat.

Azimuth Compass An azimuth compass is a nautical instrument that is used to measure the magnetic azimuth, which is the angle of the arc on the horizon between the direction of the sun or some other chosen celestial object and magnetic north.

Barrelman A barrelman is a sailor stationed in the barrel of the foremast or crow's nest of a ship to serve as a navigational aid. In many early ships, the crow's nest was a barrel or basket that was lashed to the tallest mast. It later became a specially-designed platform that had a protective railing.

Binnacle A binnacle is a waist-high case or stand found on the deck of a ship. It is generally mounted in front of the helmsman and is where navigational instruments are placed for easy and quick reference and helps protect the delicate instruments.

Bosun The officer who is responsible for the sails, ropes, rigging, and boats on a ship. The bosun issues commands to the crew of a ship via a pipe.

Bow The front part of a ship.

Bull Ensign A senior ensign who assumes additional responsibilities above and beyond other ensigns.

Cable A measure of length or distance that is equivalent to 120 fathoms.

Carpenter An officer who is responsible for the hull, masts, spars, and boats of a vessel. The carpenter is also responsible for all of the woodwork aboard a ship.

Clipper A very fast sailing ship with three or more masts, a square rig, a long, low hull, and a sharply raked stem.

Cog A large cargo ship with multiple masts.

Conning Officer An officer on a naval vessel who is responsible for giving instructions to the helmsman on which course to steer. The officer is said to *"have the conn"* while performing this duty.

Deck The outside, top part of a ship upon which sailors walk, fight, and perform other activities.

Dinghy A small boat, usually a rowboat, that a larger vessel often carries or tows as a ship's boat.

Ensign An ensign is the lowest-ranking officer on a ship.

Fathom A nautical unit of measurement. One fathom is equal to one yard.

Forecastle The front part of a ship.

Foremast A three-masted ship's forwardmost mast.

Galley A ship's kitchen.

Gunwale The upper edge of the side of a boat or ship.

Helmsman An officer in charge of steering a ship.

Hold The area of a ship where cargo is transported.

League Nautical unit of measurement. One league is equal to 3.45 miles.

Main Mast A three-masted ship's centermost mast.

Mast A tall, vertical pole found on a ship. Horizontal yards hang from it to supports the ship's sails.

Mizzenmast A three-masted ship's rearmost mast.

Pilot A ship's navigator.

Port When you are facing forward on a ship, port is to your left.

Porthole A small window found on the side of a ship.

Portolan Chart Portolan charts are navigational maps based on compass directions. They are used to estimate distances observed by pilots at sea.

Purser An officer who buys and sells all stores on a ship, including victuals, rum, and tobacco.

Spar A thick and strong pole on a boat used to support something — often the sails.

Starboard When you are facing forward on a ship, starboard is to your right.

Stern The rear part of a ship.

This appendix has a brief section of named NPCs followed by a larger sections of general creatures found in this adventure but not in the Fifth Edition SRD.

Named NPCs

High Priestess Enzu, the King of the Sinnar sahuagin, Bachzarisaa, and the cunning prisoner Petruska have their stats listed in this section.

Enzu,
High Priestess of Dajobas

Medium humanoid (sahuagin), lawful evil

Armor Class 17 (natural armor and *staff of Dajobas*) (20 with *mage armor*)
Hit Points 97 (13d8 + 39)
Speed 30 ft., swim 40 ft.

STR	DEX	CON	INT	WIS	CHA
12 (+1)	14 (+2)	16 (+3)	18 (+4)	15 (+2)	14 (+2)

Skills Arcana +8, History +8, Perception +6, Religion +8
Damage Resistances bludgeoning, piercing, and slashing from nonmagical attacks
Senses darkvision 120 ft., passive Perception 16
Languages Sahuagin, Aquan
Challenge 9 (5,000 XP)

Limited Amphibiousness. Enzu can breathe air and water but begins to suffocate if not submerged at least once every 4 hours.
Blood Frenzy. Enzu has advantage on melee attack rolls against any creature that doesn't have all its hit points.
Saltwater Sensitivity. While completely submerged in saltwater, Enzu has advantage on Wisdom (Perception) checks that rely on hearing.
Shark Telepathy. Enzu can magically command any shark within 120 feet of her, using a limited telepathy.
Spellcasting. Enzu is a 13th-level spellcaster. Her spellcasting ability is Intelligence (spell save DC 16, +8 to hit with spell attacks). Enzu has the following wizard spells prepared:
Cantrips (at will): *blade ward, dancing lights, mending, message, ray of frost*
1st level (4 slots): *alarm*, mage armor*, magic missile, shield**
2nd level (3 slots): *arcane lock*, invisibility*
3rd level (3 slots): *counterspell*, dispel magic*, lightning bolt*
4th level (3 slots): *banishment*, stoneskin**
5th level (2 slots): *cone of cold, wall of force*
6th level (1 slot): *flesh to stone, globe of invulnerability**
7th level (1 slot): *symbol*, teleport*
*Abjuration spell of 1st level or higher
Arcane Ward. Enzu has a magical ward that has 30 hit points.

Whenever she takes damage, the ward takes the damage instead. If the ward is reduced to 0 hit points, Enzu takes any remaining damage. When she casts an abjuration spell of 1st level or higher, the ward regains a number of hit points equal to twice the level of the spell.
Carried possessions: Control device for the *collar of giant control*[B] and the *staff of Dajobas*[B].

Actions

Staff of Dajobas. Melee Weapon Attack: +7 to hit, reach 5 ft., one target. *Hit:* 7 (1d6 + 4) bludgeoning damage plus 13 (2d12) necrotic damage.
Bite of Dajobas (from staff). A spectral head of a Huge shark attacks a target that she can see within 60 feet of her. The attack is made at +10 to hit and does 45 (10d8) necrotic damage on a successful hit.
Call Sharks (from staff, 1/day). Enzu summons 2 **giant sharks**. The sharks magically appear in unoccupied spaces within 300 feet of her and obey her commands until they are destroyed.

King Bachzarisaa the Insatiable

Large humanoid (sahuagin), lawful evil

Armor Class 18 (*+2 breastplate*)
Hit Points 142 (15d10 + 60)
Speed 30 ft., swim 50 ft.

STR	DEX	CON	INT	WIS	CHA
20 (+5)	16 (+3)	18 (+4)	14 (+2)	13 (+1)	17 (+3)

Saving Throws Dex +6, Con +7, Int +5, Wis +4
Skills Perception +5
Damage Resistances bludgeoning, piercing, and slashing from nonmagical attacks
Senses darkvision 120 ft., passive Perception 15
Languages Sahuagin, Aquan
Challenge 9 (5,000 XP)

Blood Frenzy. King Bachzarisaa has advantage on melee attack rolls against any creature that doesn't have all its hit points.

Limited Amphibiousness. King Bachzarisaa can breathe air and water but begins to suffocate if not submerged at least once every 4 hours.

Magic Resistance. King Bachzarisaa has advantage on saving throws against spells and other magical effects.

Saltwater Sensitivity. While completely submerged in saltwater, King Bachzarisaa has advantage on Wisdom (Perception) checks that rely on hearing.

Shark Telepathy. King Bachzarisaa can magically command any shark within 120 feet of him, using a limited telepathy.

Carried possessions: *Amulet of Stoneskin*[B], *+2 breastplate* and *Sea King's Trident*[B]

Actions

Multiattack. King Bachzarisaa makes one Bite attack and four Claw attacks; or he makes one Bite attack, two Claw attacks, and one Trident attack.

Bite. *Melee Weapon Attack:* +9 to hit, reach 5 ft., one target. *Hit:* 10 (2d4 + 5) piercing damage.

Claws. *Melee Weapon Attack:* +9 to hit, reach 5 ft., one target. *Hit:* 12 (2d6 + 5) slashing damage.

Sea King's Trident. *Melee or Ranged Weapon Attack:* +12 to hit, reach 5 ft. or range 20/60 ft., one creature. *Hit:* 16 (2d8 + 8) piercing damage plus 8 (2d8) thunder damage and target is pushed back 10 feet.

Petruska

Medium humanoid (sahuagin [malenti]), lawful evil

Armor Class 16 (natural armor)
Hit Points 84 (13d8 + 26)
Speed 30 ft., swim 40 ft.

STR	DEX	CON	INT	WIS	CHA
11 (+0)	18 (+4)	14 (+2)	11 (+0)	10 (+0)	16 (+4)

Saving Throws Dex +7, Int +3
Skills Acrobatics +7, Athletics +3, Deception +7, Perception +3, Sleight of Hand +7, Stealth +7
Senses darkvision 120 ft., passive Perception 13
Languages Aquan, Common, Elven, Sahuagin,
Challenge 5 (1,800 XP)

Blood Frenzy. Petruska has advantage on melee attack rolls against any creature that doesn't have all its hit points.

Limited Amphibiousness. Petruska can breathe air and water but begins to suffocate if not submerged at least once every 4 hours.

Shark Telepathy. Petruska can magically command any shark within 120 feet of her, using a limited telepathy.

Cunning Action. On each of her turns, Petruska can use a bonus action to take the Dash, Disengage, or Hide action.

Evasion. If Petruska is subjected to an effect that allows her to make a Dexterity saving throw to take only half damage, Petruska instead takes no damage if she succeeds on the saving throw, and only half damage if she fails.

Sneak Attack (1/turn). Petruska deals an extra 14 (4d6) damage when she hits a target with a weapon attack and has advantage on the attack roll, or when the target is within 5 feet of an ally of Petruska that isn't incapacitated and she doesn't have disadvantage on the attack roll.

Assassinate. Petruska has advantage on attack rolls against any creature that hasn't taken a turn in the combat yet. In addition, any hit Petruska scores against a creature that is surprised is a critical hit.

Actions

Multiattack. Petruska makes three attacks with any finesse weapon*.

****Example — Dagger.*** *Melee Weapon Attack:* +7 to hit, reach 5 ft., one target. *Hit:* 6 (1d4 + 4) piercing damage.

Reactions

Uncanny Dodge. Petruska halves the damage that she takes from an attack that hits her. She must be able to see the attacker.

General Creatures

Please note that the Sea Giant and Volcano Giant are both listed under Giant while the Giant Anemone, the Giant Fly, and the Giant Sloth are listed under Anemone, Fly, and Sloth, respectively. The Red Bulette and the Sea Troll are also listed under the more generic Bulette and Troll.

Allosaurus

A quintessential hunter, the allosaurus is a dinosaur of great size, strength, and speed. Very few types of prey have the speed necessary to escape it over open ground. After pouncing on its target, it pulls the prey down with its wicked claws.

Allosaurus

Large beast, unaligned

Armor Class 13 (natural armor)
Hit Points 51 (6d10 + 18)
Speed 60 ft.

STR	DEX	CON	INT	WIS	CHA
19 (+4)	13 (+1)	17 (+3)	2 (−4)	12 (+1)	5 (−3)

Skills Perception +5
Senses passive Perception 15
Languages —
Challenge 2 (450 XP)

Pounce. If the allosaurus moves at least 30 feet straight toward a creature and then hits it with a claw attack on the same turn, that target must succeed on a DC 13 Strength saving throw or be knocked prone. If the target is prone, the allosaurus can make one bite attack against it as a bonus action.

Actions

Bite. *Melee Weapon Attack:* +6 to hit, reach 5 ft., one target. *Hit:* 15 (2d10 + 4) piercing damage.
Claw. *Melee Weapon Attack:* +6 to hit, reach 5 ft., one target. *Hit:* 8 (1d8 + 4) slashing damage.

Anemone, Giant

Anemones are predatory marine animals. Sea anemones come in a range of sizes, but the giant ones are the most dangerous to humanoids. They are found in a variety of marine environments including being attached via a single polyp to a hard surface by its base, living in soft sediment, and floating near the surface of the water. The polyp has a columnar trunk topped by an oral disc with a ring of tentacles and a central mouth. The tentacles can be retracted inside the body cavity or expanded to catch passing prey. In addition to their poisonous tentacles, they can exude a poisonous cloud that makes the waters around them highly toxic.

Giant Anemone

Medium Beast, unaligned

Armor Class 15 (natural armor)
Hit Points 84 (8d12 + 32)
Speed 5 ft.

STR	DEX	CON	INT	WIS	CHA
17(+3)	10 (+0)	19 (+4)	1 (−5)	10 (+0)	6 (−2)

Damage Immunities Poison
Conditional Immunities Blinded, Deafened, Poisoned
Senses blindsight 60 ft., passive Perception 10
Languages —
Challenge 5 (2,300 XP)

Retraction. When the giant anemone takes damage, as a reaction it can retract its vulnerable flesh into its stone-like base. While retracted the anemone has three-quarters cover (granting it AC 20) and gains resistance to all damage except psychic damage. While retracted it can only use its poison cloud. The anemone can extend its tentacles as a bonus action.

Underwater Camouflage. The anemone has advantage on Dexterity (Stealth) checks made while underwater.

Actions

Multiattack. The giant anemone makes two Tentacle attacks.

Tentacles. *Melee Weapon Attack:* +5 to hit, reach 10ft., one target. *Hit:* 18 (4d8) poison damage, and the target must succeed on a DC 14 Constitution saving throw or be poisoned for 1 minute. Until the poisoned condition ends, the target is paralyzed. The target can repeat the saving throw at the end of each of its turns, ending the effects of the poison on a success. The target is grappled (escape DC 13) if it is a Medium or smaller creature and the anemone doesn't have two or more other creatures grappled.

Poison Cloud (recharge 6). The anemone exudes poison gas in a 20 ft. radius cloud. The poison spreads around corners. When a creature first enters the cloud or if it begins its turn there, it must make a DC 14 Constitution saving throw, taking 27 (6d8) poison damage on a failed save, or half as much damage on a successful one. The cloud dissipates naturally after 10 minutes.

Blood Orchid

This beast has three downward curving "petals" of flesh with dark, pebbly outer hides and pallid whitish undersides. The petals converge at the blood orchid's center and end with split tips. On its underside at the center dangle a swarm of writhing pallid tentacles: sixteen manipulator arms and eight thinner tendrils with red eyes at the ends. At the center of these tentacles is a sphincter-shaped mouth at the end of a flexible trunk one foot long and six inches in diameter. At the apex of the creature, there is another cluster of eye tendrils.

Blood orchids are territorial, xenophobic, and possessive. They rarely form alliances with other creatures as their alien mindset keeps them from forming any common ground. They regard other races as aberrant and not to be trusted, even other lawful creatures.

Communication by blood orchids is through a means of empathy/telepathy. They have no sense of hearing, which helps render them immune to sonic effects. The blood orchid can close its outer petals downward and rest on the ground, where it resembles a rocky nodule or fungus of some kind.

Blood orchids occasionally develop sorcerous talents and transform into savants. When their abilities have reached a certain level, they can evolve into a grand savant. Normally each colony of blood orchids is led by a single grand savant, and another cannot evolve while one is present. Typically, a blood orchid savant ready to become a grand savant leaves the colony with a few followers and sets out to establish a new brood elsewhere.

Blood Orchid

Large aberration, lawful evil

Armor Class 14 (natural armor)
Hit Points 76 (9d10 + 27)
Speed 5 ft., fly 30 ft.

STR	DEX	CON	INT	WIS	CHA
15 (+2)	12 (+1)	16 (+3)	11 (+0)	12 (+1)	13 (+1)

Skills Stealth +4
Damage Resistances acid, cold, lightning, fire
Damage Immunities thunder
Senses darkvision 60 ft., passive Perception 11
Languages telepathy 120 ft.
Challenge 5 (1,800 XP)

Hyper-Awareness. A blood orchid cannot be surprised.
Telepathic Bond. Blood orchids have a telepathic link to other
blood orchids that are within 120 feet.

Actions

Multiattack. The blood orchid uses Blood Drain and makes up
to three Tentacle attacks.
Tentacle. Melee Weapon Attack: +5 to hit, reach 5 ft., one target.
Hit: 11 (2d8 + 2) bludgeoning damage and the target must
succeed on a DC 13 Constitution saving throw or be poisoned
for 1 hour. The target is also grappled (escape DC 11). While
grappled this way, the creature is restrained. Until the grapple
ends, the blood orchid can't use this tentacle on another target.
The blood orchid has three tentacles with which it can attack.
Blood Drain. The blood orchid feeds on a creature it is
grappling. The creature must succeed on a DC 13 Constitution
saving throw or its hit point maximum is reduced by 5 (1d10).
This reduction lasts until the creature finishes a long rest. The
target dies if this effect reduces its hit point maximum to 0.

Bog Beast

This creature appears as a large, shaggy, fur-covered humanoid with clawed hands and feet. Two, long, upright tusks protrude from its mouth. Its eyes are dull brown and its fur is brownish-yellow.

Bog beasts make their homes in bogs and swamps and feed on creatures that dwell there. They are avid hunters and a bog beast's hunting area usually covers a large expanse of ground several miles around its lair.

A bog beast stands over 9 feet tall and weighs around 1,100 pounds. It makes its lair amid overgrown swamplands and attacks just about any creature that travels too close to its lair. They seem to be able to communicate with one another through a series of guttural grunts and growls but do not speak any known language.

Bog beasts attack with their claws and always fight to the death. A creature killed by a bog beast is dragged back to its lair, where it is devoured.

Bog Beast

Large monstrosity, neutral

Armor Class 13 (natural armor)
Hit Points 76 (8d10 + 32)
Speed 30 ft.

STR	DEX	CON	INT	WIS	CHA
20 (+5)	11 (+0)	18 (+4)	5 (−3)	12 (+1)	9 (−1)

Skills Perception +5, Survival +5
Senses darkvision 60 ft., passive Perception 15
Languages —
Challenge 3 (700 XP)

Keen Smell. The bog beast has advantage on Wisdom (Perception) checks that rely on smell.

Actions

Multiattack. The bog beast makes two attacks with its Claws.

Claws. *Melee Weapon Attack:* +7 to hit, reach 10 ft., one target. *Hit:* 12 (2d6 + 5) slashing damage. If the target is a creature, it must succeed on a DC 14 Constitution saving throw against disease or become poisoned until the disease is cured. Every 24 hours that elapse, the target must repeat the saving throw, reducing its hit point maximum by 5 (1d10) on a failure. The disease is cured on a success. The target dies if the disease reduces its hit point maximum to 0. This reduction of the target's hit point maximum lasts until the disease is cured.

Bulette, Red

The red bulette spends the majority of its time underground, feeding on the rare minerals and rocks found there. With a skin temperature that varies between 500°–1200° F, the red bulette moves through bedrock and earth by swimming through it at its full movement rate. While not necessarily carnivorous, they are attracted to all refined metals and will happily swallow a warrior for the metal content of its weapons and armor. Red bulettes like rare metals (refined or raw ore) best of all. This makes the mere sighting of one in the wild a real and present threat to any local treasure vaults or royal economies.

Red Bulette

Huge monstrosity, unaligned

Armor Class 18 (natural armor)
Hit Points 135 (10d12 + 70)
Speed 40 ft., burrow 80 ft.

STR	DEX	CON	INT	WIS	CHA
20 (+5)	12 (+1)	24 (+7)	3 (−4)	10 (+0)	5 (−3)

Saving Throws Dex +6, Con +11, Wis +4
Skills Perception +4
Damage Immunities fire
Senses blindsight 60 ft., darkvision 60 ft., passive Perception 14
Languages —
Challenge 12 (8,400 XP)

Metalsense. The red bulette is aware of all metals within 60 feet of it.

Mineral Rich. If a red bulette is killed, its planar connection is immediately severed. Over the course of 4 to 6 hours, its body cools to the ambient temperature of the environment. While the vast majority of its body cools into a basalt-like stone, its digestive track solidifies into roughly 1,000 pounds of an alloy admixture of every mineral substance it has consumed. Depending upon its recent feeding habits, this substance is the equivalent of metal-rich ore of many types in combination, and can be smelted back down into standard and precious metals by experts knowledgeable in such methods. Additionally, a few diamonds can be found in what was the red bulette's gizzard.

Planar Connection. Because their arcane natures link red bulettes to the Elemental Plane of Fire, they also simultaneously exist there as insubstantial and barely visible shadows of themselves.

Tunneler. The bulette can burrow through solid rock at its burrow speed leaving a 10-foot-diameter tunnel in its wake.

Vanishing Act. Red bulettes avoid overland movement, preferring to swim through earth and bedrock. If confronted above ground, they reflexively increase their body temperatures enough to melt their way down into the ground and vanish. If threatened by a much larger creature, they simply dive underground and "swim" away. However, if they are threatened by any creature that wears or is carrying refined metals, they instinctively return and attempt to ambush with a bite/swallow attack from underground.

Actions

Bite. Melee Weapon Attack: +9 to hit, reach 5 ft., one target. Hit: 31 (4d12 + 5) piercing damage plus 7 (2d6) fire damage, and the target is grappled (escape DC 15). Until this grapple ends, the target is restrained, and the bulette can't bite another target.

Swallow. The bulette makes one bite attack against a Medium or smaller target it is grappling. If the attack hits, the target is also swallowed, and the grapple ends. While swallowed, the target is blinded and restrained, it has total cover against attacks and other effects outside the bulette, and it takes 21 (6d6) fire damage at the start of each of the bulette's turns. A bulette can have three Medium or smaller creatures swallowed at the same time.

Death from Below (recharge 5–6). If the bulette burrows at least 20 feet as part of its movement, it can then use this action to surface from underground in a space that contains one or more creatures. Each of those creatures must succeed on a DC 16 Strength or Dexterity saving throw (target's choice) or be knocked prone and splashed with globules of molten rock, taking 18 (2d12 + 5) bludgeoning damage plus 14 (4d6) fire damage. On a successful save, the creature takes only half damage, isn't knocked prone, and is pushed 5 feet out of the bulette's space into an unoccupied space of the creature's choice. If no unoccupied space is within range, the creature falls prone in the bulette's space.

CRANIFORM

This medium-sized creature is a bipedal cancriform humanoid. They bear a carapace of chitinous composition, eyestalks, antennae, and a pair of mandibles set to either side of a complementary set of horizontally-aligned maxillae that constitute the creatures' mouths. Extending outward from the neck of each creature is a set of short but large chitinous arms, each of which terminate in a seemingly oversized claw. Below these larger claws is another set of arms. These extend from either side of the upper torso, not unlike how arms extend from shoulders in more familiar humanoids. This second set of smaller chitinous arms each end with a smaller pincer. The creatures' torsos and legs are covered by the same chitinous exoskeleton and extend to cover their clawed feet. Females and males are hard to tell apart, but males are slightly smaller than females.

Craniform inhabit tropical coastal waters where they usually create permanent colonies. These timid and reclusive creatures are very rare and stay well away from other humanoid settlements. Craniform typically live in coastal caves, but some communities excavate more expansive subterranean underwater burrows beneath the waterline and back up and under the shoreline. Craniform speak their own language, a series of clicks and hisses, as well as Aquan. Craniform society is as complex as most terrestrial societies. Craniform are led temporally and spiritually by a group of priestesses who oversee most of their important functions, rituals, and endeavors.

Craniform are communal creatures but mate for life. Their offspring are few and therefore precious to them. Craniform live off the bounty of the sea. They feel a deep connection to the sea and their fellow sea creatures. So while Craniform hunt other sea creatures, they do so respectfully, making sure to not wipe out a given population of fish or crustaceans through over hunting. Craniform are deeply reverential of their deity, the Sea Mother, goddess of all sea creatures, and see themselves as the Sea Mother's chosen stewards of the sea. While little is known of the magics of the reclusive Craniform and their priestesses, it is believed that they can confer the ability to breathe underwater to surface dwellers through a ritual venerating the Sea Mother called the Sea Mother's Blessing.

CRANIFORM

Medium humanoid (craniform), lawful good

Armor Class 13 (natural armor)
Hit Points 37 (5d10 + 10)
Speed 30 ft., swim 40 ft.

STR	DEX	CON	INT	WIS	CHA
16 (+3)	11 (+0)	15 (+2)	10 (+0)	10 (+0)	10 (+0)

Skills Perception +4
Senses darkvision 60 ft., passive Perception 14
Languages Craniform, Aquan
Challenge 2 (450 XP)

Limited Amphibiousness. The craniform can breathe air and water but begins to suffocate if not submerged at least once every 4 hours.

Actions

Multiattack. The craniform makes two Pincer attacks or one Pincer attack and one Spear attack.

Pincer. *Melee Weapon Attack:* +5 to hit, reach 5 ft., one target. *Hit:* 10 (2d6 + 3) slashing damage. The target is grappled (escape DC 13) if it is a Large or smaller creature and the craniform doesn't have another creature grappled already. The target is restrained until the grapple ends.

Spear. *Melee Weapon Attack:* +5 to hit, reach 5 ft. or range 20/60 ft., one target. *Hit:* 7 (1d8 +3) piercing damage.

Craniform Priestess

Blessed by the Sea Mother herself, the craniform priestess is called to the Sea Mother's service in a vision. This vision reveals the Sea Mother's true form: a massive sea turtle. Craniform priestesses are referred to as "gifted" among fellow craniforms.

Craniform priestesses serve an integral role in craniform communities. They are the spiritual advisors, healers, and ritual officiants, and also the leaders of their respective communities. Every major decision that affects a craniform colony must first be approved by the priestesses.

Craniform Priestess

Medium humanoid (craniform), lawful good

Armor Class 13 (natural armor)
Hit Points 37 (5d10 + 10)
Speed 30 ft., swim 40 ft.

STR	DEX	CON	INT	WIS	CHA
16 (+3)	11 (+0)	15 (+2)	10 (+0)	14 (+2)	10 (+0)

Skills Perception +4
Senses darkvision 60 ft., passive Perception 14
Languages Craniform, Aquan
Challenge 3 (700 XP)

Limited Amphibiousness. The craniform priestess can breathe air and water but begins to suffocate if not submerged at least once every 4 hours.

Spellcasting. The craniform priestess is a 6th-level spellcaster. Her spellcasting ability is Wisdom (spell save DC 12, +4 to hit with spell attacks). She has the following cleric spells prepared:

Cantrips (at will): *guidance, thaumaturgy*
1st level (4 slots): *bless, detect magic, guiding bolt*
2nd level (3 slots): *hold person, spiritual weapon* (trident)
3rd level (3 slots): *mass healing word, tongues*

Actions

Multiattack. The craniform priestess makes two Pincer attacks or one Pincer attack and one Spear attack.

Pincer. *Melee Weapon Attack:* +5 to hit, reach 5 ft., one target. *Hit:* 10 (2d6 + 3) slashing damage. The target is grappled (escape DC 13) if it is a Large or smaller creature and the craniform priestess doesn't have another creature grappled already. The target is restrained until the grapple ends.

Spear. *Melee Weapon Attack:* +5 to hit, reach 5 ft. or range 20/60 ft., one target. *Hit:* 7 (1d8 +3) piercing damage.

Deathwatch Beetle

This creature appears as a giant beetle with a dark-green carapace and wing casings. Its body is covered in leaves and sticks. Its mandibles are silver, and its legs are black.

The deathwatch beetle makes its lair in forests and uses a mixture of saliva and earth to stick rubbish (leaves and twigs, for instance) to itself in order to attack by surprise.

The deathwatch beetle begins combat using its death rattle ability. Any creatures that survive are bitten by the beetle's mandibles and devoured.

Deathwatch Beetle

Medium beast, unaligned

Armor Class 14 (natural armor)
Hit Points 75 (10d8 + 30)
Speed 30 ft.

STR	DEX	CON	INT	WIS	CHA
20 (+5)	10 (+0)	16 (+3)	1 (−5)	10 (+0)	9 (−1)

Damage Immunities necrotic
Senses darkvision 60 ft., passive Perception 10
Languages —
Challenge 5 (1,800 XP)

Actions

Bite. *Melee Weapon Attack:* +8 to hit, reach 5 ft., one target. *Hit:* 12 (2d6 + 5) piercing damage.

Death Rattle (recharge 5–6). The deathwatch beetle emits a clicking noise with a resonance frequency that affects creatures within 30 feet of it. Creatures in this area must make a DC 13 Constitution saving throw, taking 10 (3d6) thunder damage on a failed save, or half as much damage on a successful one.

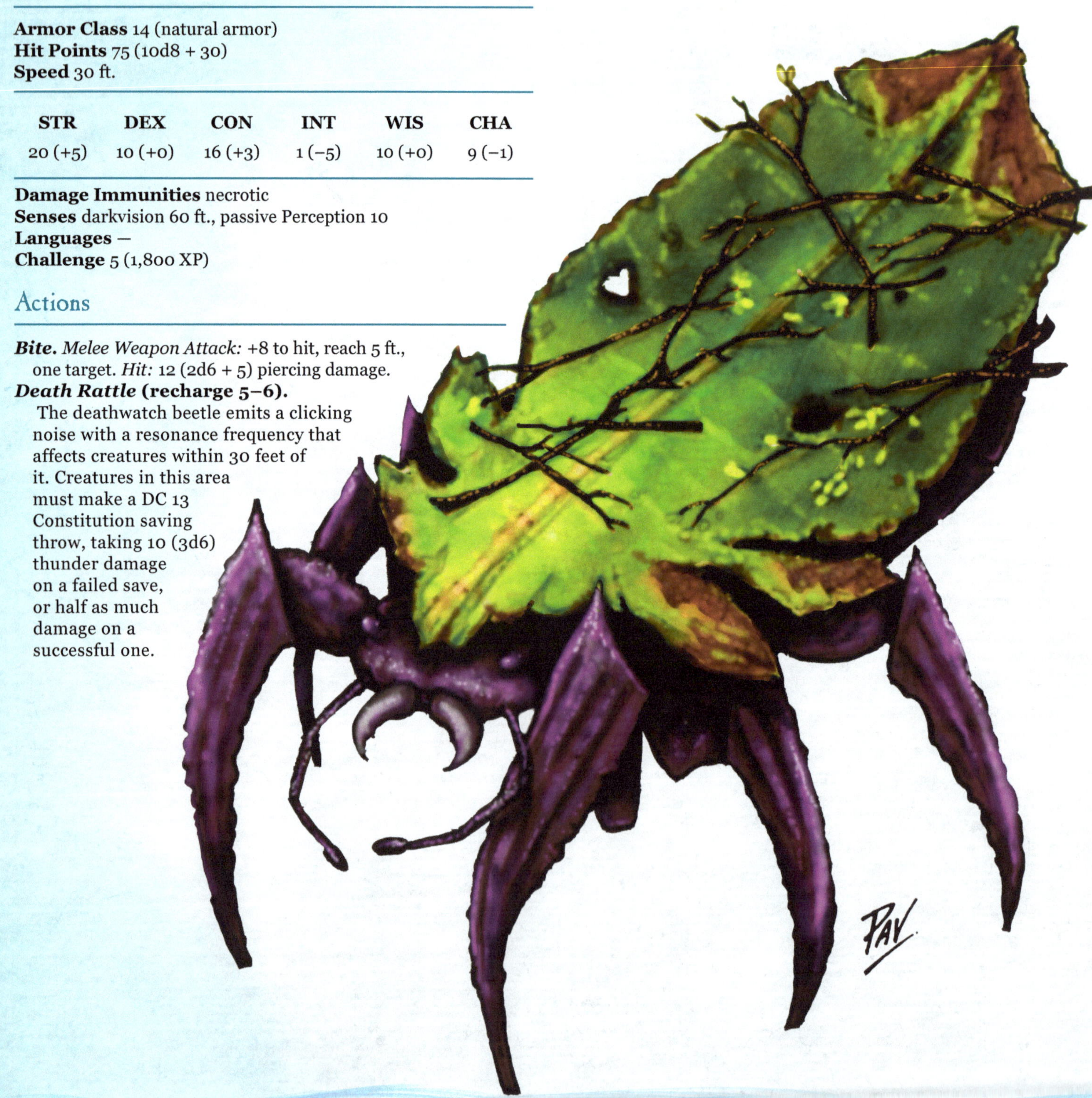

Eye of the Deep

This creature is a 5-foot-wide orb dominated by a central eye and large serrated mouth. Hundreds of small seaweed-like bristles hang from the bottom of its body. Two large crab-like pincers protrude from its body, and two long, thin eyestalks sprout from the top of its orb.

Eyes of the deep are found only in the deepest parts of the ocean, though on occasion one moves too close to the shoreline and ends up beached on the sands. An eye of the deep stranded in this manner dies in 2d4 minutes unless placed back into the water.

An eye of the deep floats slowly through the oceans searching for its prey. It attacks using its eye rays; then it grasps an opponent with its pincers and subjects the victim to its bite attack. An eye of the deep's pincers are considered to be primary attacks.

Eye of the Deep

Medium aberration, lawful evil

Armor Class 14 (natural armor)
Hit Points 117 (18d8 + 36)
Speed 5 ft., swim 20 ft.

STR	DEX	CON	INT	WIS	CHA
14 (+2)	10 (+0)	14 (+2)	12 (+1)	13 (+1)	13 (+1)

Skills Perception +4
Senses darkvision 60 ft., passive Perception 14
Languages Aquan, Common, Deep Speech
Challenge 5 (1,800 XP)

Amphibious. The eye of the deep can breathe in both air and water.

Flyby. The eye of the deep doesn't provoke an opportunity attack when it swims out of an enemy's reach.

Hyper-Awareness. An eye of the deep's eyestalks allow it to see in all directions at once. It cannot be surprised.

Stun Cone. An eye of the deep's central eye produces a cone extending straight ahead from its front to a range of 30 feet. At the start of each of its turns, the eye of the deep decides which way the cone faces and whether the cone is active. All creatures in this area must succeed on a DC 15 Constitution saving throw or be stunned for 1 minute. A creature can repeat the saving throw at the end of each of its turns, ending the effect on itself on a success.

Actions

Multiattack. The eye of the deep makes one Bite attack and two with its Pincers.

Bite. *Melee Weapon Attack:* +5 to hit, reach 5 ft., one target. *Hit:* 12 (3d6 + 2) piercing damage.

Pincers. *Melee Weapon Attack:* +5 to hit, reach 5 ft., one target. *Hit:* 15 (3d8 + 2) bludgeoning damage. The target is grappled (escape DC 12) if the eye of the deep isn't already grappling a creature, and the target is restrained until the grapple ends.

Eye Rays. Each of the creature's eyestalks can produce a magical ray once per round. The creature can aim both of its eye rays in any direction and they have a range of 150 feet.

Paralytic Ray. Using its left eye, the eye of the deep unleashes a powerful paralytic beam. The target must make a DC 15 Wisdom saving throw or be paralyzed for 1 minute. A creature can repeat the saving throw at the end of each of its turns, ending the effect on itself on a success.

Enfeeblement Ray. Using its right eye, the eye of the deep unleashes a powerful ray of enfeeblement. The target must make a DC 15 Wisdom saving throw or deal half damage with all attacks that use Strength for 1 minute. A creature can repeat the saving throw at the end of each of its turns, ending the effect on itself on a success.

Major Image. The eye of the deep concentrates its eye rays together to project a major image illusion. The illusion is generated at any point within range and in the eye of the deep's line of sight. Seeing through the illusion requires a successful DC 15 Intelligence (Investigation) check.

Fanged Sea Serpent

This serpent is 12 to 15 feet long and 5 feet thick. Its body scales are thickened and hardened, which slows it somewhat in water but provides good protection. The serpent's most outstanding features, however, are the rows of long, sharp teeth that fill its mouth. It has large, lidless red eyes with white pupils.

The fanged sea serpent is a vicious predator of the seas feared for its tendency to travel in packs and swarm over creatures much larger than itself. Fanged sea serpents are nomadic, traveling with ocean currents. They prefer to hunt in groups, which they can surround and attack from all sides. Fanged sea serpents have been known to attack their own kind, but only when starving.

Fanged sea serpents on their own usually live on large fish and avoid confronting intelligent opposition unless they believe their victims to be helpless. However, when they are in groups, they become much more aggressive, and attack creatures much larger than themselves. They prefer to use swarm tactics, surrounding their target and attacking simultaneously from all directions; in the water, where they can also attack from above and below, few marine creatures can stand up to a prolonged assault.

Fanged Sea Serpent

Large dragon, neutral evil

Armor Class 15 (natural armor)
Hit Points 93 (11d10 + 33)
Speed 0 ft., swim 40 ft.

STR	DEX	CON	INT	WIS	CHA
18 (+4)	13 (+1)	16 (+3)	5 (−3)	11 (+0)	6 (−2)

Skills Athletics +7, Perception +3
Damage Immunities poison
Condition Immunities poisoned, prone
Senses darkvision 60 ft., passive Perception 13
Languages Aquan, Draconic
Challenge 5 (1,800 XP)

Amphibious. The fanged serpent can breathe air and water.

Actions

Bite. *Melee Weapon Attack:* +7 to hit, reach 5 ft., one target. *Hit:* 10 (1d12 + 4) piercing damage plus 7 (2d6) poison damage, and the target is grappled (escape DC 15). Until this grapple ends, the target is restrained, and the sea serpent cannot grapple another target. While the fanged serpent has a creature grappled in its bite, it cannot bite a different creature, and has advantage on bite attacks against the grappled creature.

Roll. One target that the fanged serpent has grappled takes 21 (6d6) slashing damage as the fanged serpent rolls quickly. After this damage is dealt, the target is no longer grappled.

Fly, Giant

Bristling with coarse hairs, this enormous fly's legs twitch just before it launches into the air on buzzing wings. This human-sized insect has large, red, globular eyes, a body covered in hairy bristles, and two rapidly vibrating translucent wings.

Giant flies are larger relatives of normal flies. Like their lesser cousins, they are most often found in areas of garbage, litter, and refuse. A giant fly resembles a normal fly and can grow to a length of 12 feet, though most average about 6 feet long.

Giant flies attack by biting their opponents.

Giant Fly

Medium beast, unaligned

Armor Class 13
Hit Points 22 (3d8 + 9)
Speed 30 ft., fly 60 ft.

STR	DEX	CON	INT	WIS	CHA
12 (+1)	17 (+3)	16 (+3)	2 (−4)	7 (−2)	2 (−4)

Skills Perception +2
Senses darkvision 60 ft., passive Perception 12
Languages —
Challenge 1/2 (100 XP)
Keen Smell. The giant fly has advantage on Wisdom (Perception) checks that rely on smell.

Actions

Bite. *Melee Weapon Attack:* +5 to hit, reach 10 ft., one target. *Hit:* 10 (2d6 + 3) piercing damage. If the target is a creature it must succeed on a DC 13 Constitution saving throw or be diseased until the condition is cured. While the creature is diseased it is poisoned. Every 24 hours that elapse, the target must repeat the saving throw, reducing its hit point maximum by 5 (1d10) on a failure. The disease is cured on a success. The target dies if the disease reduces its hit point maximum to 0. This reduction to the target's hit point maximum lasts until the disease is cured.

GENIE, SEQUANA

Denizens of the Palace of Prisms (the seat of rulership for the Great Durbar of the Sequana and dominant power on the Elemental Plane of Water), sequana are among the most wondrous of genie-kind. Large and piscine, sequana are an amazing sight to behold, particularly when clad in the finely-stitched vests and colorful pantaloons they favor. As sequana care not for the affairs of terrestrials, land dwellers rarely encounter them.

SEQUANA GENIE

Large elemental, neutral

Armor Class 17 (natural armor)
Hit Points 229 (17d10 + 136)
Speed 30 ft., fly 60 ft., swim 90 ft.

STR	DEX	CON	INT	WIS	CHA
22 (+6)	12 (+1)	26 (+8)	18 (+4)	17 (+3)	18 (+4)

Saving Throws Dex +5, Wis +7, Cha +8
Damage Resistances Acid, Cold, Lightning
Senses blindsight 30 ft., darkvision 120 ft., passive Perception 13
Languages Aquan
Challenge 11 (7,200 XP)

Amphibious. The sequana genie can breathe air and water.

Innate Spellcasting. The sequana genie's innate spellcasting ability is Charisma (spell save DC 16, +8 to hit with spell attacks). It can innately cast the following spells, requiring no material components:

At will: *create or destroy water, detect evil and good, detect magic, fog cloud, purify food and drink*
3/day each: *tongues, water breathing, water walk*
1/day each: *conjure elemental* (water elemental only), *control water, gaseous form, invisibility, plane shift*

Actions

Multiattack. The sequana genie makes two Trident attacks.

Trident. *Melee or Ranged Weapon Attack:* +10 to hit, reach 5 ft. or range 20/60 ft., one target. *Hit:* 13 (2d6 + 6) piercing damage, or 15 (2d8 + 6) piercing damage if used with two hands to make a melee attack.

Water Jet. The sequana genie magically shoots water in a 60-ft. line that is 5 ft. wide. Each creature in that line must make a DC 16 Dexterity saving throw. On a failure, a target takes 21 (6d6) bludgeoning damage and, if it is Huge or smaller, is pushed up to 20 ft. away from the sequana genie and knocked prone. On a success, a target takes half the bludgeoning damage, but is neither pushed nor knocked prone.

Giant, Sea

This huge being has bluish green skin and eyes that reflect light like two silvery moons. Rippling with muscle, this creature rises from the depths with a crash of waves on rocks.

Sea giants are the reclusive cousins of storm giants. They are most often found in the deepest depths of the seas where they make their dwelling in the cones of long-dead undersea volcanoes.

Sea giants have a druid-like power over the forces of the seas and are a living embodiment of its bounty and destructive wrath.

Sea giants seldom come into contact with surface-dwellers but have been known on rare occasions to exact bounties from coastal cities to ensure the safety of their navies and merchant vessels. Sea giants are most commonly encountered within a few hundred miles of their lair, tending to their domain and battling off incursions of sahuagin, aboleth, krakens and other such destructive forces of the undersea.

An adult male sea giant stands 10 feet tall and weighs about 6,000 pounds. Females are slightly shorter and lighter. Both have sea-green skin, dark-green or black hair, and silver eyes. Sea giants adorn themselves in loose flowing robes of white, blue, or green. Many wear wreaths of coral in their hair.

When battling at the surface of the seas, sea giants hurl rocks at great length against opposing ranged attackers, usually including crews of siege engines. When battling against surface ships their tactic is to disguise themselves by creating rough waters with their *control water* ability. They then hammer the hull with their mighty fists until it is holed, without ever revealing themselves to the crew. Once holed, they tear the hull apart and drown the crew.

When fighting beneath the waves they use their crushing pressure special ability to increase the water pressure around themselves in an effort to destroy interlopers and trespassers.

Sea Giant

Large giant, chaotic neutral

Armor Class 17 (natural armor)
Hit Points 178 (17d10 + 85)
Speed 40 ft., swim 30 ft.

STR	DEX	CON	INT	WIS	CHA
29 (+9)	14 (+2)	20 (+5)	17 (+3)	18 (+4)	19 (+4)

Saving Throws Con +9
Skills Acrobatics +6, Athletics +13, Intimidation +8, Perception +8, Stealth +6
Senses darkvision 120 ft., passive Perception 18
Languages Aquan, Common, Giant
Challenge 9 (5,000 XP)

Amphibious. The sea giant can breathe air and water.

Innate Spellcasting. The sea giant's innate spellcasting ability is Charisma (spell save DC 16, +8 to hit with spell attacks). It can innately cast the following spells, requiring no material components:

At will: *create or destroy water, detect magic*
5/day: *control water*
3/day: *control weather*

Actions

Multiattack. The sea giant makes two slam attacks.
Slam. *Melee Weapon Attack:* +13 to hit, reach 10 ft., one target. *Hit:* 18 (2d8 + 9) bludgeoning damage.
Rock. *Ranged Weapon Attack:* +13 to hit, range 60/240 ft., one target. *Hit:* 27 (4d8 + 9) bludgeoning damage.
Crushing Pressure (recharge 5–6). The sea giant chooses an area of water no larger than a 50-foot cube within 30 ft. of it. The water pressure within the space magically increases, and creatures within the area treat it as difficult terrain. In addition, any creature who enters or begins its turn within the area must make a DC 18 Constitution saving throw, taking 18 (4d8) bludgeoning damage on a failed saving throw, or half as much damage on a successful one. The area remains affected by this magic for 1 minute, until the sea giant dismisses it as an action, or until the sea giant dies.

Giant, Volcano

This 18-foot-tall, barrel-chested giant has leathery, reddish-brown skin and haunting amber eyes. The creature is tough and wiry, with the strength and texture of copper.

Volcano giants make their homes in the many twisting caves and subterranean rooms of volcanic cones, enlarging and reinforcing them for comfort and convenience.

Clothing for a volcano giant usually consists of little more than a simple wrap of fire lizard skin. Volcano giants wears ornaments made of bone, shell, and obsidian, and their general culture and society is similar to that of humanoid civilizations on tropical islands. Such island societies often get along well with local tribes of volcano giants, engaging in trade and peacefully coexisting. Should a tribe of volcano giants form an allegiance with a human tribe, the giants warn the humans of possible eruptions of their volcano to allow them time to escape the destruction.

Although volcano giants can be described as good-natured and peaceful people, their demeanor can change quickly. At a real or imagined affront, a volcano giant can erupt with a passion that is rivaled only by the fire and fury of the volcano in which it lives.

Volcano giants feel that their shadow is actually their soul, and do not tolerate any creature that dares to trod upon it. Volcano giants usually use gargantuan longspears in combat. They are fierce and brave warriors, not backing down from any adversary. Many choose to open combat with their breath weapon so as to soften up their foes before attacking.

Volcano Giant

Huge giant, chaotic neutral

Armor Class 19 (natural armor)
Hit Points 187 (15d12 + 90)
Speed 40 ft.

STR	DEX	CON	INT	WIS	CHA
29 (+9)	15 (+2)	22 (+6)	16 (+3)	18 (+4)	18 (+4)

Saving Throws Con +11
Skills Acrobatics +7, Intimidation +9, Nature +8, Perception +9
Damage Vulnerabilities cold
Damage Immunities fire
Senses passive Perception 19
Languages Giant, Ignan
Challenge 13 (10,000 XP)

Heated Body. The volcano giant's attacks deal an additional 7 (2d6) fire damage (included in the attacks below).

Actions

Multiattack. The volcano giant makes one one-handed Spear attack and one Slam attack, or two Slam attacks.

Spear. *Melee or Ranged Weapon Attack:* +14 to hit, reach 10 ft. or range 40/120 ft., one target. *Hit:* 23 (4d6 + 9) piercing damage plus 7 (2d6) fire damage, or 27 (4d8 + 9) piercing damage plus 7 (2d6) fire damage if used with two hands to make a melee attack.

Slam. *Melee Weapon Attack:* +14 to hit, reach 15 ft., one target. *Hit:* 19 (3d6 + 9) bludgeoning damage plus 7 (2d6) fire damage.

Rock. *Ranged Weapon Attack:* +14 to hit, range 60/240 ft., one target. *Hit:* 27 (4d8 + 9) bludgeoning damage plus 7 (2d6) fire damage.

Sulfuric Breath (recharge 5–6). The volcano giant exhales a cloud of warm sulfuric gas in a 30-foot cone. All creatures in the area must succeed on a DC 19 Constitution saving throw or take 35 (10d6) acid damage and be poisoned for 1 minute.

Lacedon

Lacedons are an aquatic type of ghoul. Similar to ghouls in all other respects, they are distinguished by their natural ability to swim as well as they can walk. They are found only in water, usually prowling near unseen reefs and other dangerous locations where boats and ships are at risk of sinking.

Lacedon

Medium undead, chaotic evil

Armor Class 12
Hit Points 22 (5d8)
Speed 30 ft., swim 40 ft.

STR	DEX	CON	INT	WIS	CHA
13 (+1)	15 (+2)	10 (+0)	7 (−2)	10 (+0)	6 (−2)

Damage Immunities Poison
Condition Immunities Charmed, Exhaustion, Poisoned
Senses darkvision 60 ft., passive Perception 10
Languages Common
Challenge 1 (200 XP)

Limited Amphibiousness. The lacedon can breathe air and water but begins to suffocate if not submerged in the sea at least once a day for 1 minute.

Actions

Bite. *Melee Weapon Attack:* +2 to hit, reach 5 ft., one creature. *Hit:* 9 (2d6 + 2) piercing damage.

Claws. *Melee Weapon Attack:* +4 to hit, reach 5 ft., one target. *Hit:* 7 (2d4 + 2) slashing damage. If the target is a creature other than an elf or undead, it must succeed on a DC 10 Constitution saving throw or be paralyzed for 1 minute. The target can repeat the saving throw at the end of each of its turns, ending the effect on itself on a success.

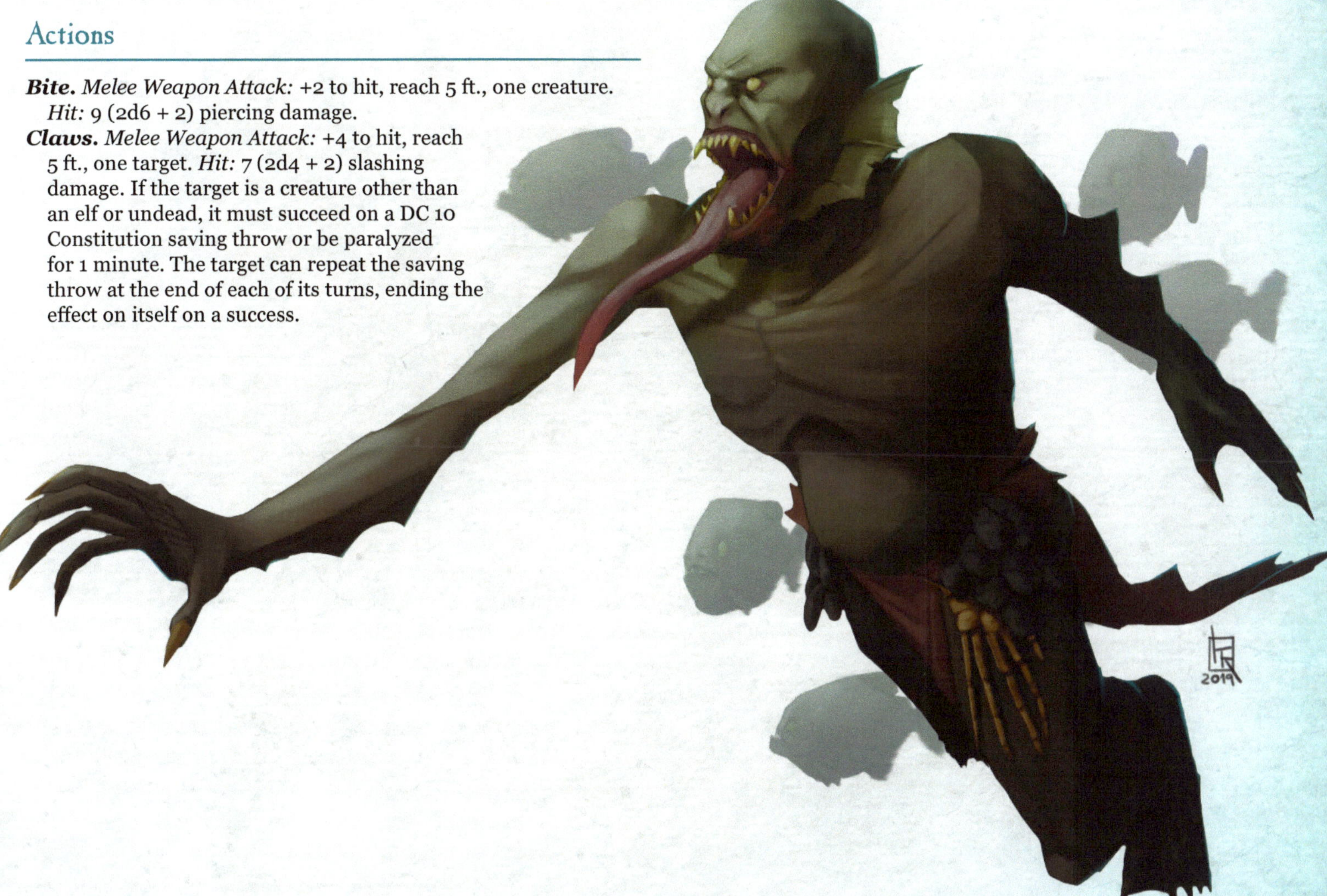

MOBAT

This creature appears as a large brown bat with razor-sharp fangs and green glowing eyes.

The mobat has a wingspan of approximately 15 feet. It is a nocturnal creature, cruising silently through the night sky in its never-ending quest for food. A mobat, like any species of normal bat, has huge ears and an upturned snout. Mobats are omnivores and often include warm-blooded prey in their diet.

A mobat attacks by biting its opponent using its razor-sharp fangs. Surviving prey is subjected to the mobat's stunning screech attack.

MOBAT

Large monstrosity, neutral

Armor Class 14 (natural armor)
Hit Points 51 (6d10 + 18)
Speed 20 ft., fly 40 ft.

STR	DEX	CON	INT	WIS	CHA
17 (+3)	15 (+2)	16 (+3)	6 (−2)	13 (+1)	6 (−2)

Skills Perception +3
Senses blindsight 60 ft., passive Perception 13
Languages —
Challenge 1 (200 XP)

Echolocation. The mobat can't use its blindsight while deafened.

Flyby. The mobat doesn't provoke an opportunity attack when it flies out of an enemy's reach.

Keen Hearing. The mobat has advantage on Wisdom (Perception) checks that rely on hearing.

Actions

Bite. *Melee Weapon Attack:* +5 to hit, reach 5 ft., one target. *Hit:* 13 (3d6 + 3) piercing damage.

Stunning Screech (recharge 5–6). The mobat emits a piercing screech. All creatures within 30 feet of it that can hear it must make a DC 12 Constitution saving throw or be stunned for 1 minute. A stunned target can repeat the saving throw at the end of each of its turns, ending the effect on itself on a success.

Prehistoric Honey Badger

The prehistoric honey badger is no mere oversized weasel. Its thick skin and powerful jaws makes it a terrifying creature to contend with, and its fearlessness makes it more dangerous than many humanoids.

The prehistoric honey badger stands two feet at the shoulder and is over five feet long, weighing over 100 pounds. Strictly a carnivore, the fearless prehistoric honey badger will hunt venomous or poisonous creatures, or humanoids, and even chase off larger creatures to steal their kills. Its jaws are capable of tearing through fresh meat like a cleaver and crushing through bone without trouble.

Prehistoric honey badgers make their homes in dry grasslands and in moist forests. They dig burrows with their strong claws, where they lair alone, only nearing another honey badger to mate during the fall months. A honey badger's cubs are born in late winter, and after 6–8 weeks with the female honey badger, the cubs are left to fend for themselves.

Prehistoric Honey Badger

Medium beast, unaligned

Armor Class 14 (natural armor)
Hit Points 51 (6d8 + 24)
Speed 30 ft., burrow 30 ft.

STR	DEX	CON	INT	WIS	CHA
20 (+5)	12 (+1)	18 (+4)	7 (−2)	11 (+0)	5 (−3)

Skills Survival +2
Damage Resistances poison; bludgeoning, piercing, and slashing from nonmagical weapons
Condition Immunities frightened
Senses darkvision 60 ft., passive Perception 10
Languages —
Challenge 4 (1,100 XP)

Keen Hearing and Smell. The prehistoric honey badger has advantage on Wisdom (Perception) checks based on hearing or smell.

Relentless (recharges after a short or long rest). If the badger takes 14 damage or less that would reduce it to 0 hit points, it is reduced to 1 hit point instead.

Actions

Multiattack. The prehistoric honey badger makes one Bite attack and one Crunch attack.

Bite. *Melee Weapon Attack:* +7 to hit, reach 5 ft., one target. *Hit:* 16 (2d10 + 5) piercing damage, and the target must succeed on a DC 15 Strength saving throw or be grappled (escape DC 15).

Crunch. *Melee Weapon Attack:* +7 to hit, reach 5 ft., one grappled creature. *Hit:* The target suffers from broken bones and must make a DC 15 Constitution saving throw at the beginning of each of its turns. On a failed saving throw, the target cannot take any actions or reactions during that turn. If the target receives magical healing or takes a long rest, the effect ends.

SABER-TOOTH JAGUAR

This hulking predator has two enlarged serrated canines jutting from its lower jaw, a thick neck, and robustly muscled forelimbs and shoulders. It has spotted fur that allows it to hide in tall grasses and ambush prey.

The saber-tooth jaguar is a large predator, standing 4 feet at the shoulder, 7 feet long, and weighing over 400 pounds. It is different from other large felines in that its main upper canine teeth are large, curved, and serrated, which it uses in combination with its thickly muscled neck to deliver devastating slashing bites. Its forelimbs are also well-developed and longer than other feline creatures, with sharp claws.

The saber-tooth jaguar's fur is covered in rosettes, small dark spots that function as camouflage in the dappled light of its forest habitat. The jaguar is an apex predator and is not preyed on in the wild. The feline is a strict carnivore, and often aims for the head of its prey, biting into the skull to deliver a fatal blow to the brain.

SABER-TOOTH JAGUAR

Large beast, unaligned

Armor Class 13
Hit Points 76 (9d10 + 27)
Speed 40 ft., climb 30 ft.

STR	DEX	CON	INT	WIS	CHA
20 (+5)	16 (+3)	16 (+3)	3 (−4)	12 (+1)	8 (−1)

Skills Perception +3, Stealth +7
Senses passive Perception 13
Languages —
Challenge 4 (1,100 XP)

Keen Smell. The jaguar has advantage on Wisdom (Perception) checks that rely on smell.

Pounce. If the jaguar moves at least 20 feet straight toward a creature and then hits it with a claw attack on the same turn, that target must succeed on a DC 15 Strength saving throw or be knocked prone. If the target is prone, the jaguar can make one bite attack against it as a bonus action.

Surprise Attack. If the saber-tooth jaguar surprises a creature and hits it with an attack during the first round of combat, the target takes an extra 10 (3d6) damage from the attack.

Actions

Bite. *Melee Weapon Attack:* +7 to hit, reach 5 ft., one target. *Hit:* 27 (4d10 + 5) piercing damage.

Claw. *Melee Weapon Attack:* +7 to hit, reach 5 ft., one target. *Hit:* 12 (2d6 + 5) slashing damage.

SAHUAGIN, DAUGHTER OF THE SHARK

The sword arm of the dread shark god Dajobas, these especially cruel and powerful sahuagin priestesses are focused on one singular goal: freeing their terrible god from the sunless rifts of the undersea and returning this nightmare creature to the world of the living. To accomplish this, they seek to launch the Red Feast, a slaughter so devastating and massive that the seas will run red with blood. The Red Feast alone is a ritual powerful enough to return Dajobas to the shores of the world.

Daughters of the Shark are only the most powerful and fanatical of sahuagin priestesses. Their cruelty is legendary, and few non-sahuagin survive an encounter with one of these creatures to tell the tale. Fortunately for terrestrials and intelligent humanoids of the seas and oceans, there are not as many Daughters when compared with the legions of normal sahuagin priestesses. As a result, they are a preciously guarded resource usually found in the depths serving as the primary advisor or consort of sahuagin royalty.

DAUGHTER OF THE SHARK SAHUAGIN

Medium humanoid (sahuagin), lawful evil

Armor Class 12 (natural armor)
Hit Points 75 (10d8 + 30)
Speed 30 ft., swim 40 ft.

STR	DEX	CON	INT	WIS	CHA
12 (+1)	10 (+0)	16 (+3)	10 (+0)	15 (+2)	14 (+2)

Skills Perception +5, Religion +3
Damage Resistances bludgeoning, piercing, and slashing from nonmagical attacks
Senses darkvision 120 ft., passive Perception 15
Languages Sahuagin, Aquan
Challenge 5 (1,800 XP)

Limited Amphibiousness. The daughter of the shark sahuagin can breathe air and water but begins to suffocate if not submerged at least once every 4 hours.

Blood Frenzy. The daughter of the shark sahuagin has advantage on melee attack rolls against any creature that doesn't have all its hit points.

Saltwater Sensitivity. While completely submerged in saltwater, the daughter of the shark has advantage on Wisdom (Perception) checks that rely on hearing.

Shark Telepathy. The daughter of the shark sahuagin can magically command any shark within 120 feet of her, using a limited telepathy.

Innate Spellcasting. The daughter of the shark sahuagin's spellcasting ability is Wisdom (spell save DC 13, +5 to hit with spell attacks). She can innately cast the following spells, requiring no material components:

At will: *command, create or destroy water*
3/day each: *control water, darkness, hold person, water walk*
1/day each: *lightning bolt, dispel magic*

Actions

Multiattack. The sahuagin makes one Bite attack and one attack with her Claws.

Bite. *Melee Weapon Attack:* +3 to hit, reach 5 ft., one target. *Hit:* 3 (1d4 + 1) piercing damage.

Claws. *Melee Weapon Attack:* +3 to hit, reach 5 ft., one target. *Hit:* 3 (1d4 + 1) slashing damage.

Touch of the Shark (recharge 5–6). *Melee Spell Attack:* +5 to hit, reach 5 ft., one creature. *Hit:* 27 (5d10) piercing damage.

Sahuagin Elite

Strength — and more specifically, strength displayed as prowess in battle — is the highest of sahuagin virtues. Only the best sahuagin warriors ascend to the ranks of elites. These sahuagin fighters are larger, stronger, and more skilled than rank-and-file sahuagin. Elites often lead raiding parties or sahuagin war bands as well as serve as personal guards of other powerful and/or noble sahuagin.

Sahuagin Elite

Medium humanoid (sahuagin), lawful evil

Armor Class 16 (breastplate)
Hit Points 65 (10d8 + 20)
Speed 30 ft., swim 50 ft.

STR	DEX	CON	INT	WIS	CHA
17 (+3)	14 (+2)	14 (+2)	11 (+0)	12 (+1)	11 (+0)

Skills Intimidation +2, Perception + 3, Stealth +6, Survival +3
Senses darkvision 120 ft., passive Perception 13
Languages Sahuagin, Aquan
Challenge 3 (700 XP)

Blood Frenzy. The sahuagin elite has advantage on melee attack rolls against any creature that doesn't have all its hit points.

Limited Amphibiousness. The sahuagin elite can breathe air and water but begins to suffocate if not submerged at least once every 4 hours.

Saltwater Sensitivity. While completely submerged in saltwater, the sahuagin elite has advantage on Wisdom (Perception) checks that rely on hearing.

Shark Telepathy. The sahuagin elite can magically command any shark within 120 feet of it, using a limited telepathy.

Actions

Multiattack. The sahuagin elite makes one Bite attack and one with its Claws or Trident.

Bite. *Melee Weapon Attack:* +5 to hit, reach 5 ft., one target. *Hit:* 8 (2d4 + 3) piercing damage.

Claws. *Melee Weapon Attack:* +5 to hit, reach 5 ft., one target. *Hit:* 10 (2d6 + 3) slashing damage.

Trident. *Melee or Ranged Weapon Attack:* +5 to hit, reach 5 ft. or range 20/60 ft., one target. *Hit:* 10 (2d6 + 3) piercing damage, or 12 (2d8 + 3) piercing damage if used with two hands to make a melee attack.

Sahuagin, King's Guard

As their name implies, these few and rare sahuagin are almost universally reserved for service to sahuagin royalty. These massive four-armed brutes are picked from the best of the best. Larger and stronger than any other sahuagin fighters, they are a terror to behold. Because leadership in sahuagin society is merit-based with the merit metric being strength in arms, King's Guard sahuagin usually end up becoming royalty themselves by deposing their former leader through a traditional sahuagin challenge.

King's Guard Sahuagin

Large humanoid (sahuagin), lawful evil

Armor Class 16 (breastplate)
Hit Points 76 (9d10 + 27)
Speed 30 ft., swim 50 ft.

STR	DEX	CON	INT	WIS	CHA
19 (+4)	15 (+2)	16 (+3)	14 (+2)	13 (+1)	17 (+3)

Saving Throws Dex +5, Con +6, Int +5, Wis +4
Skills Perception +4
Senses darkvision 120 ft., passive Perception 17
Languages Sahuagin, Aquan
Challenge 5 (1,800 XP)

Blood Frenzy. The king's guard has advantage on melee attack rolls against any creature that doesn't have all its hit points.

Limited Amphibiousness. The king's guard sahuagin can breathe air and water but begins to suffocate if not submerged at least once every 4 hours.

Saltwater Sensitivity. While completely submerged in saltwater, the king's guard sahuagin has advantage on Wisdom (Perception) checks that rely on hearing.

Shark Telepathy. The king's guard sahuagin can magically command any shark within 120 feet of it, using a limited telepathy.

Actions

Multiattack. The king's guard sahuagin makes one Bite attack and four Claw attacks; or the guard makes one Bite attack, two Claw attacks, and one Trident attack.

Bite. *Melee Weapon Attack:* +7 to hit, reach 5 ft., one target. *Hit:* 9 (2d4 + 4) piercing damage.

Claws. *Melee Weapon Attack:* +7 to hit, reach 5 ft., one target. *Hit:* 11 (2d6 + 4) slashing damage.

Trident. *Melee or Ranged Weapon Attack:* +7 to hit, reach 5 ft. or range 20/60 ft., one target. *Hit:* 13 (2d8 + 4) piercing damage.

Sahuagin Priestess

Sahuagin worship the shark god Dajobas. Only female sahuagin are allowed to channel their god's power; therefore, sahuagin priestesses hold positions of prestige and power in sahuagin cites.

Sahuagin Preistess

Medium humanoid (sahuagin), lawful evil

Armor Class 12 (natural armor)
Hit Points 33 (6d8 + 6)
Speed 30 ft., swim 40 ft.

STR	DEX	CON	INT	WIS	CHA
13 (+1)	11 (+0)	12 (+1)	12 (+1)	14 (+2)	13 (+1)

Skills Perception +6, Religion +3
Senses darkvision 120 ft., passive Perception 16
Languages Sahuagin, Aquan
Challenge 2 (450 XP)

Blood Frenzy. The sahuagin priestess has advantage on melee attack rolls against any creature that doesn't have all its hit points.

Limited Amphibiousness. The sahuagin priestess can breathe air and water but begins to suffocate if not submerged at least once every 4 hours.

Saltwater Sensitivity. While completely submerged in saltwater, the sahuagin priestess has advantage on Wisdom (Perception) checks that rely on hearing.

Shark Telepathy. The sahuagin priestess can magically command any shark within 120 feet of her, using a limited telepathy.

Spellcasting. The sahuagin priestess is a 6th-level spellcaster. Her spellcasting ability is Wisdom (spell save DC 12, +4 to hit with spell attacks). She has the following cleric spells prepared:

Cantrips (at will): *guidance, thaumaturgy*
1st level (4 slots): *bless, detect magic, guiding bolt*
2nd level (3 slots): *hold person, spiritual weapon* (trident)
3rd level (3 slots): *mass healing word, tongues*

Actions

Multiattack. The sahuagin makes one Bite attack and one with her Claws.

Bite. *Melee Weapon Attack:* +3 to hit, reach 5 ft., one target. *Hit:* 3 (1d4 + 1) piercing damage.

Claws. *Melee Weapon Attack:* +3 to hit, reach 5 ft., one target. *Hit:* 3 (1d4 + 1) slashing damage.

SAHUAGIN, SINNAR

Among sailors, very few things evoke the same instant unease and disquiet that the mere mention of sahuagin or the "sea devils" does. This scaly humanoid is the self-proclaimed ruler of the seas. Their arms and legs end in webbed claws, and their piscine heads feature a toothy maw. Sahuagin raiders terrorize the depths, the shallows, and the shorelines of the Sinnar. The primary rival to the sahuagin claim of control of the Sinnar are the sea elves, their mortal enemies. Wars between the two races have raged for centuries along the coasts and seas of the Lost Lands, disrupting maritime trade and drawing other races into the bloody conflict.

SINNAR SAHUAGIN

Medium humanoid (sahuagin), lawful evil

Armor Class 12 (natural armor)
Hit Points 22 (4d8 + 4)
Speed 30 ft., swim 40 ft.

STR	DEX	CON	INT	WIS	CHA
13 (+1)	11 (+0)	12 (+1)	12 (+1)	13 (+1)	9 (−1)

Senses darkvision 120 ft., passive Perception 11
Languages Sahuagin, Aquan
Challenge 1/2 (100 XP)

Blood Frenzy. The Sinnar sahuagin has advantage on melee attack rolls against any creature that doesn't have all its hit points.

Limited Amphibiousness. The Sinnar sahuagin can breathe air and water but begins to suffocate if not submerged at least once every 4 hours.

Saltwater Sensitivity. While completely submerged in saltwater, the Sinnar sahuagin has advantage on Wisdom (Perception) checks that rely on hearing.

Shark Telepathy. The Sinnar sahuagin can magically command any shark within 120 feet of it, using a limited telepathy.

Actions

Multiattack. The Sinnar sahuagin makes one Bite attack and one Claw or Spear attack.

Bite. *Melee Weapon Attack:* +3 to hit, reach 5 ft., one target. *Hit:* 3 (1d4 + 1) piercing damage.

Claw. *Melee Weapon Attack:* +3 to hit, reach 5 ft., one target. *Hit:* 3 (1d4 + 1) slashing damage.

Spear. *Melee or Ranged Weapon Attack:* +3 to hit, reach 5 ft. or range 20/60 ft., one target. *Hit:* 4 (1d6 + 1) piercing damage, or 5 (1d8 + 1) piercing damage if used with two hands to make a melee attack.

Sahuagin, Young

These youthful sahuagin are smaller and less deadly than their parents, but still fierce fighters, having bested their weaker littermates to survive.

Sahuagin, Young

Small humanoid (sahuagin), lawful evil

Armor Class 12
Hit Points 5 (2d6 - 2)
Speed 30 ft., swim 40 ft.

STR	DEX	CON	INT	WIS	CHA
7 (−2)	15 (+2)	9 (−1)	8 (−1)	7 (−2)	8 (−1)

Senses darkvision 60 ft.
Languages Sahuagin, Aquan
Challenge 1/8 (25 XP)

Limited Amphibiousness. The sahuagin young can breathe air and water but begins to suffocate if not submerged at least once every 4 hours.

Saltwater Sensitivity. While completely submerged in saltwater, the sahuagin young has advantage on Wisdom (Perception) checks that rely on hearing.

Actions

Spear. *Melee Weapon Attack:* +4 to hit, reach 5 ft., one target. *Hit:* 4 (1d4 + 2) piercing damage.

Bite. *Melee Weapon Attack:* +4 to hit, reach 5 ft., one target. *Hit:* 4 (1d4 + 2) piercing damage.

Sea Cow

Sea cows are large, fully aquatic, mostly herbivorous marine mammals. They have paddle-like flippers and are slow, peaceful plant-eaters similar to cows on land. They often graze on water plants in tropical seas.

Sea Cow

Large beast, unaligned

Armor Class 11
Hit Points 52 (8d10 + 8)
Speed 10 ft., swim 60 ft.

STR	DEX	CON	INT	WIS	CHA
17 (+3)	13 (+1)	13 (+1)	4 (−3)	10 (+0)	4 (−3)

Skills Perception +4, Stealth +5
Senses darkvision 60 ft., passive Perception 14
Languages —
Challenge 1 (200 XP)

Hold Breath. While out of water, the sea cow can hold its breath for 1 hour.
Water Breathing. The sea cow can breathe only underwater.

Actions

Slam. *Melee Weapon Attack:* +5 to hit, reach 5 ft., one target. *Hit:* 7 (1d8 + 3) bludgeoning damage.

Sloth, Giant

This massive sloth is brownish-black, and its fur has a greenish tint to it. Its eyes are white.

Giant sloths grow up to be 10 feet long and weigh up to 450 pounds. The fur of a giant sloth is stained green by algae.

A giant sloth attacks by biting and rending its opponent with its claws.

Giant Sloth

Huge beast, neutral

Armor Class 15 (natural armor)
Hit Points 76 (8d12 + 24)
Speed 15 ft., climb 30 ft.

STR	DEX	CON	INT	WIS	CHA
22 (+6)	10 (+0)	17 (+3)	2 (−4)	12 (+1)	5 (−3)

Skills Athletics +9
Senses passive Perception 11
Languages —
Challenge 5 (1,800 XP)

Keen Scent. The giant sloth has advantage on Wisdom (Perception) checks based on scent.

Actions

Multiattack. The giant sloth makes one Bite attack and two Claw attacks.

Bite. *Melee Weapon Attack:* +9 to hit, reach 5 ft., one target. *Hit:* 15 (2d8 + 6) piercing damage.

Claw. *Melee Weapon Attack:* +9 to hit, reach 10 ft., one target. *Hit:* 17 (2d10 + 6) slashing damage, and the target must make a DC 17 Strength saving throw or be knocked prone.

Spell Parrot

The bird appears to be an entirely ordinary parrot. When it speaks, however, it utters the words of a magical spell, and arcane energy begins to swirl around it.

Spell parrots are an exceedingly rare and unexplained phenomenon. They look, think, and act primarily like parrots, despite high intelligence for an animal. No one knows why they are able to do what they do though it is clear that the ability they possess is as likely to be a burden as a boon to them. When spell parrots first hear and mimic a spellcaster, they rarely seem to understand or expect the results of their mimicry. Older wild spell parrots have usually learned how to utilize their strange and unpredictable powers but rarely will do so unless threatened.

Spell parrots can be tamed as pets, but since they occur spontaneously (within any of the larger parrot species), it is difficult to discover one young enough to socialize it properly. Careful training by someone with exceptional animal handling skills can result in a spell parrot that only mimics spells at a signal from its humanoid handler. However, they can be cantankerous creatures, and moody, with questionable senses of humor, and even the best-trained spell parrot may choose to disobey its handler.

Like mundane parrots, spell parrots often live a little longer than humans, and while they cannot become fluent in humanoid languages, they can memorize small vocabularies and engage in rudimentary verbal communication. Talking to a well-trained spell parrot is similar in clarity, depth, grammar, and logic to communication with a small toddler.

Spell Parrot

Tiny monstrosity, unaligned

Armor Class 12
Hit Points 3 (2d4 − 2)
Speed 10 ft., fly 50 ft.

STR	DEX	CON	INT	WIS	CHA
2 (−4)	14 (+2)	8 (−1)	2 (−4)	12 (+1)	6 (−2)

Skills Perception +3
Senses passive Perception 13
Languages —
Challenge 3 (700 XP)

Spell Mimicry. Whenever the spell parrot hears a cantrip or a 1st- through 5th-level spell that has a verbal component being cast, it can attempt to mimic the casting of that spell on its next turn. The spell parrot ignores any somatic or material component that the spell requires. When the spell parrot attempts to mimic the spell, roll a d6. If the spell is a cantrip or 1st-level spell, the casting succeeds if the result is a 3–6. If the spell is 2nd level or higher, the casting succeeds on the result of a 5 or 6. Once the spell parrot mimics a spell, it forgets the spell. The spell parrot uses the original caster's spell save DC and spell attack bonus, and the spell must have a valid target for the spell parrot to use as the target of the mimicked spell.

Actions

Bite. *Melee Weapon Attack:* +4 to hit, reach 5 ft., one target. *Hit:* 1 piercing damage.

Swarm of Poisonous Frogs

Each frog in the hopping army bears black stripes on its hind legs and sickly, yellowish eyes.

Poisonous frog swarms are composed of small, fierce, poisonous frogs. The swarm moves collectively, hopping or jumping toward their prey.

Single poisonous frogs mate during the second half of the year. The male attracts a female through a series of unique mating calls consisting of strange guttural sounds. When a female answers the call, she lays a clutch of 1d6 eggs in a damp, dark area covered with leaves. The male fertilizes the eggs and protects them during their incubation period. Two weeks later the eggs hatch and the male carries the tadpoles to the water on its back. Tadpoles reach maturity in two to three months.

A single poisonous frog is a small dark-green frog with black bands or stripes on its hind legs. These stripes function as a warning to predators that the frog is poisonous. The skin of a poisonous frog is very smooth to the touch. The middle digit on each of its extremities is slightly shorter than the others.

Poisonous frog swarms attack by engulfing their prey and subjecting it to the frog's deadly poison. Creatures that begin their turn in a poisonous frog's space suffer swarm and poison damage.

Swarm of Poisonous Frogs

Medium swarm of Tiny beasts, unaligned

Armor Class 13 (natural armor)
Hit Points 59 (17d8 − 17)
Speed 20 ft., swim 20 ft.

STR	DEX	CON	INT	WIS	CHA
1 (−5)	13 (+1)	8 (−1)	1 (−5)	8 (−1)	3 (−4)

Skills Perception +1, Stealth +3
Damage Immunities poison
Condition Immunities poisoned
Senses passive Perception 11
Languages —
Challenge 1 (200 XP)

Amphibious. The swarm can breathe air and water.
Keen Smell. The swarm has advantage on Wisdom (Perception) checks that rely on smell.
Standing Leap. The swarm's long jump is up to 10 feet and its high jump is up to 5 feet, with or without a running start.
Swarm. The swarm can occupy another creature's space and vice versa, and the swarm can move through any opening large enough for a poisonous frog. The swarm can't regain hit points or gain temporary hit points.

Actions

Bite. *Melee Weapon Attack:* +3 to hit, reach 0 ft., one target. *Hit:* 11 (3d6 + 1) piercing damage, and the target must succeed on a DC 12 Constitution saving throw or be poisoned for 1 hour.

Troll, Sea

Sea Trolls live near the large bodies of water of the world. Due to mutations, sea trolls have become viable hunters on land and in the water. Those that have mostly piscine diets have even taken on some of the physical traits of their prey (see **Piscine Mutations** under **Actions**).

Due to their extended time in water, sea trolls have adapted to have a heightened sense of hearing instead of smell similar to echo location. Their bodies have become more resistant to fire as well. However, their bodies have developed a vulnerability to thunder damage, so much so that it arrests the regenerative properties of their flesh.

Sea Troll

Large giant, chaotic evil

Armor Class 16 (natural armor)
Hit Points 94 (9d10 + 45)
Speed 30 ft., swim 30 ft.

STR	DEX	CON	INT	WIS	CHA
18 (+4)	14 (+2)	20 (+5)	7 (−2)	9 (−1)	5 (−3)

Skills Perception +2
Senses darkvision 60 ft., passive Perception 12
Languages Giant
Challenge 7 (2,900 XP)

Keen Hearing. The sea troll has advantage on Wisdom (Perception) checks that rely on hearing.

Regeneration. The t sea roll regains 10 hit points at the start of its turn. If the troll takes acid or thunder damage, this trait doesn't function at the start of the troll's next turn. The troll dies only if it starts its turn with 0 hit points and doesn't regenerate.

Limited Amphibiousness. The sea troll can breathe air and water but begins to suffocate if not submerged in the sea at least once a day for 1 minute.

Actions

Multiattack. The troll makes one Piscine Mutation attack and two Claw attacks.

Claw. *Melee Weapon Attack:* +7 to hit, reach 5 ft., one target. *Hit:* 11 (2d6 + 4) slashing damage.

Piscine Mutations. The sea troll has one or more of the following attack options, provided it has the appropriate anatomy:

Bite. *Melee Weapon Attack:* +7 to hit, reach 5 ft., one target. *Hit:* 11 (2d6 + 4) piercing damage.

Poison Quills. *Melee Weapon Attack:* +7 to hit, reach 5 ft., one creature. *Hit:* 8 (1d8 + 4) poison damage, and the target must succeed on a DC 12 Constitution saving throw or be poisoned for 1 minute. The target can repeat the saving throw at the end of each of its turns, ending the effect on itself on a success.

Tentacle. *Melee Weapon Attack:* +7 to hit, reach 10 ft., one target. *Hit:* 8 (1d8 + 4) bludgeoning damage, and the target is grappled (escape DC 16) if it is a Medium or smaller creature.

WERESHARK

In either humanoid or hybrid form, weresharks have burly builds with little to no hair covering their bodies, and a mouth full of large, sharp, teeth. Their cruel and bloodthirsty nature is a matter of legend. Weresharks, like most lycanthropes, are ostracized by most humanoid communities. However, this is not true among the sahuagin. The sahuagin view the lycanthropic curse as a gift or blessing from their terrible shark god Dajobas.

WERESHARK

Medium humanoid (sahuagin), chaotic evil

Armor Class 12 in sahuagin form, 13 in shark and hybrid form
Hit Points 171 (18d8 + 90)
Speed 30 ft., swim 40 ft. Usable only in hybrid or shark form

STR	DEX	CON	INT	WIS	CHA
20 (+5)	10 (+0)	21 (+5)	11 (+0)	12 (+1)	12 (+1)

Skills Perception +7
Damage Immunities Bludgeoning, Piercing, and Slashing from nonmagical attacks that aren't silvered
Senses blindsight 40 ft. (usable only in water while in hybrid or shark form), passive Perception 17
Languages Aquan, Sahuagin (cannot speak in shark form)
Challenge 6 (2,300 XP)

Shapechanger. The wereshark can use its action to polymorph into a Large shark-humanoid hybrid or into a Large shark, or back into its true form of a sahuagin. Its statistics, other than its size and AC, are the same in each form. Any equipment it is wearing or carrying isn't transformed. It reverts to its true form if it dies.

Keen Smell. The wereshark has advantage on Wisdom (Perception) checks that rely on smell.

Blood Frenzy. The wereshark has advantage on melee attack rolls against any creature that doesn't have all its hit points.

Water Breathing. The wereshark can breathe only underwater while in shark form.

Limited Amphibiousness. In either hybrid or sahuagin form, it can breathe air and water but begins to suffocate if not submerged at least once every 4 hours.
.

Actions

Multiattack. In shark form, the wereshark makes two Bite attacks. In sahuagin form, it makes one Claw attack and one Bite attack. In hybrid form, it can attack like a shark or a sahuagin.

Bite (shark or hybrid form only). *Melee Weapon Attack:* +8 to hit, reach 5 ft., one target. *Hit:* 17 (3d10 + 5) piercing damage.

Claws (hybrid or sahuagin form only). *Melee Weapon Attack:* +8 to hit, reach 5 ft., one target. *Hit:* 12 (2d6 + 5) slashing damage.

APPENDIX E: THE SHIP REGISTRY

This appendix contains stat blocks for the *Bounty*, the *Discovery*, and the *Zephyr*, the three ships found in the adventure.

THE BOUNTY

Two-Masted Schooner, Gargantuan vehicle (20 ft. by 60 ft.)

Armor Class 17
Hit Points 400 (Threshold 20)
Speed 5 knots average, 10 knots max (oars 1 knot)

STR	DEX	CON	INT	WIS	CHA
20 (+5)	7 (−2)	17 (+3)	0 (−5)	0 (−5)	0 (−5)

Capacity 65 crew, 10 passengers
Hull Reinforced wood construction
Max Cargo 8 tons
Movement The *Bounty* moves either with its oars or its sails.

Foredeck Staterooms of the characters. The foremast is located here.
Main Deck Largest deck between fore and aft. The main storage hold is below this deck and is the lowest deck. The main mast is located here.
Aft Deck Staterooms are found here, including those of the captain and ship's officers. This is the highest deck and is where the helm is located.
Forecastle Crew quarters
Main Hold Storage
Aft Hold Galley
Crew 50 sailors (use **bandit** stats) and 11 officers: bosun, bull ensign, carpenter, conning officer, ensign (x2), helmsman, purser, pilot (use **bandit captain** stats for all except one ensign who is an **acolyte**); Captain Timothy Brand (use **bandit captain** stats); and First Mate Jace Westhoff (use **veteran** stats).

The Discovery

Three-Masted Cog, Gargantuan vehicle (25 ft. by 80 ft.)

Armor Class 16
Hit Points 500 (Threshold 15)
Speed 4 knots average, 9 knots max (oars 1 knot)

STR	DEX	CON	INT	WIS	CHA
24 (+7)	4 (−3)	20 (+5)	0 (−5)	0 (−5)	0 (−5)

Capacity 80 crew, 50 passengers

Hull Reinforced wood construction
Max Cargo 75 tons
Movement The *Discovery* moves either with its oars or its sails.
Foredeck Passenger staterooms. The foremast is located here.
Main Deck Largest deck between fore and aft. The main storage hold is below this deck and is the lowest deck. The main mast is located here. There are four hatches accessing the hold below.
Aft Deck Officers' staterooms are found here, including those of the captain and ship's officers. This is the highest deck and is where the helm is located. The mizzenmast is located here.
Forecastle Crew quarters
Main Hold Storage
Aft Hold Galley

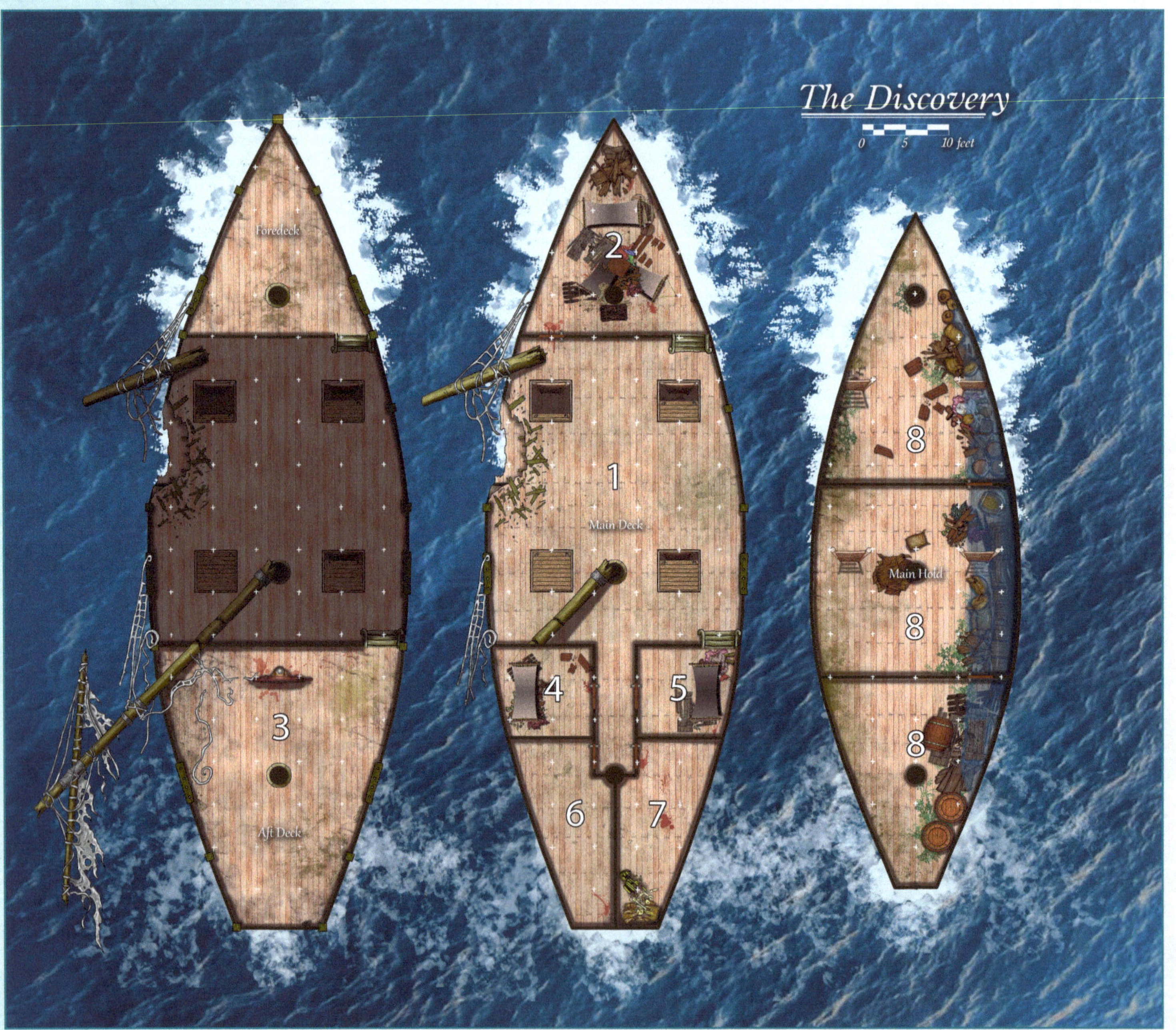

THE ZEPHYR

Three-Masted Clipper, Gargantuan vehicle (20 ft. by 100 ft.)

Armor Class 17
Hit Points 450 (Threshold 15)
Speed 6 knots average, 12 knots max (oars 1 knot)

STR	DEX	CON	INT	WIS	CHA
20 (+5)	7 (−2)	20 (+5)	0 (−5)	0 (−5)	0 (−5)

Capacity 90 crew, 20 passengers

Hull Reinforced wood construction
Max Cargo 8 tons
Movement The *Zephry* moves either with its oars or its sails.
Foredeck Passenger staterooms. The foremast is located here.
Main Deck Largest deck between fore and aft. The main storage hold is below this deck and is the lowest deck. The main mast is located here.
Aft Deck Officers' staterooms are found here, including those of the captain and ship's officers. This is the highest deck and is where the helm is located. The mizzenmast is located here.
Forecastle Crew quarters
Main Hold Storage
Aft Hold Galley

Essays of Brilliance, Wisdom, and Profundity

by Sir Captain Timothy Brand.

Essay #6: Sir Captain Timothy's Guide to Dealing with Ingrates, Commoners, and the Unwashed

Despite being crushingly busy and even with the grave import of the myriad of my daily duties, I still have somehow found time to compose these essays for the benefit of my fellow citizens of Bridgeport. Such is the depth of my civic virtue and the extent of my genuine desire to improve the lives of those around me.

Today's lesson is an important one: Dealing with those who are beneath you.

I understand that this can be a touchy subject for some. But too often I see members of high society, some of them almost of a stature to be considered my peers, coddle their servants. It is an outrage! Citizens of Bridgeport, household servants are not pets to be spoiled. No. Those of the lower caste should be dealt with severely and strictly, as their lowly status demands.

Just the other night I was at a society dinner when I witnessed the hostess and lady of the house, who shall remain nameless, not only allow a household servant to address her as if it were an equal, but also then share a laugh over some doubtless bawdy and tasteless jibe. I was shocked! Outrageous! This sort of conduct only encourages the hoi polloi to assume airs and allow them to mistakenly believe that they can address their betters in any manner in which they please. This cannot stand!

Consider me old fashioned, but servants should rarely, if ever, be allowed to speak in our presence. Impudence and impertinence of any nature, including speaking out of turn, must be met with immediate, harsh, and severe punishment. Proper relations with the unwashed require an absolute zero tolerance policy. While I understand that it is no longer considered fashionable to beat one's servants, I for one strongly believe that corporal punishment is a key element in running a proper household.

Servants are servants for a reason. Mollycoddling the vulgus spells nothing but trouble for us, their betters. Please consider this a clarion call for proper master/servant relations. Allow me to once again grant some exemplary guidance while continuing to provide a shining example of proper conduct and decorum. I strongly suggest that everyone of proper society retain a servant whose sole duty is to punish your other servants. You do not want to sully your own hands in striking one of these curs. As tempting as it is to beat your help, such conduct is beneath you. Please take my suggestion under serious consideration. Hire a servant to beat your servants for you.

As always, you are welcome for this sagacity.

Yours in fidelity, Sir Captain Timothy Brand.

Handout 2: Captain Zeb Quindal's Journal (Excerpt)

Ocros 2nd

A most unusual encounter today. We spotted the ZA Zephyr out of Bridgeport today. It was great to see Elisa Brand so unexpectedly. I haven't seen her since the last time she was my first mate when she was still learning the trade. It was delightful to see that she was as fierce and energetic as ever.

After she and her officers were rowed over, we hosted them all for dinner. She was most excited to tell me about a previously uncharted island that they were headed for. In fact, she barely mentioned the serious repairs the Zephyr had to perform on the open water to their rudder. But in any event, I have never heard of this mystery island myself. She called it 'Crocodile Island' and even shared its believed location with me.

She apparently learned of this island from Jasper Cronko. It is folly to trust anything that old sea dog has to say, but Elisa is a fine sea captain and I trust her judgement. And it seemed that she has the backing of her crew. She believes this small island out in the middle of the Sinnar is full of precious gems of some sort that are just lying around to picked up. I will believe it when I see it. I certainly wish her well with this. Her family are old friends and an unexpected boon could not happen to a nicer family.

Handout 3: Crocodile Island

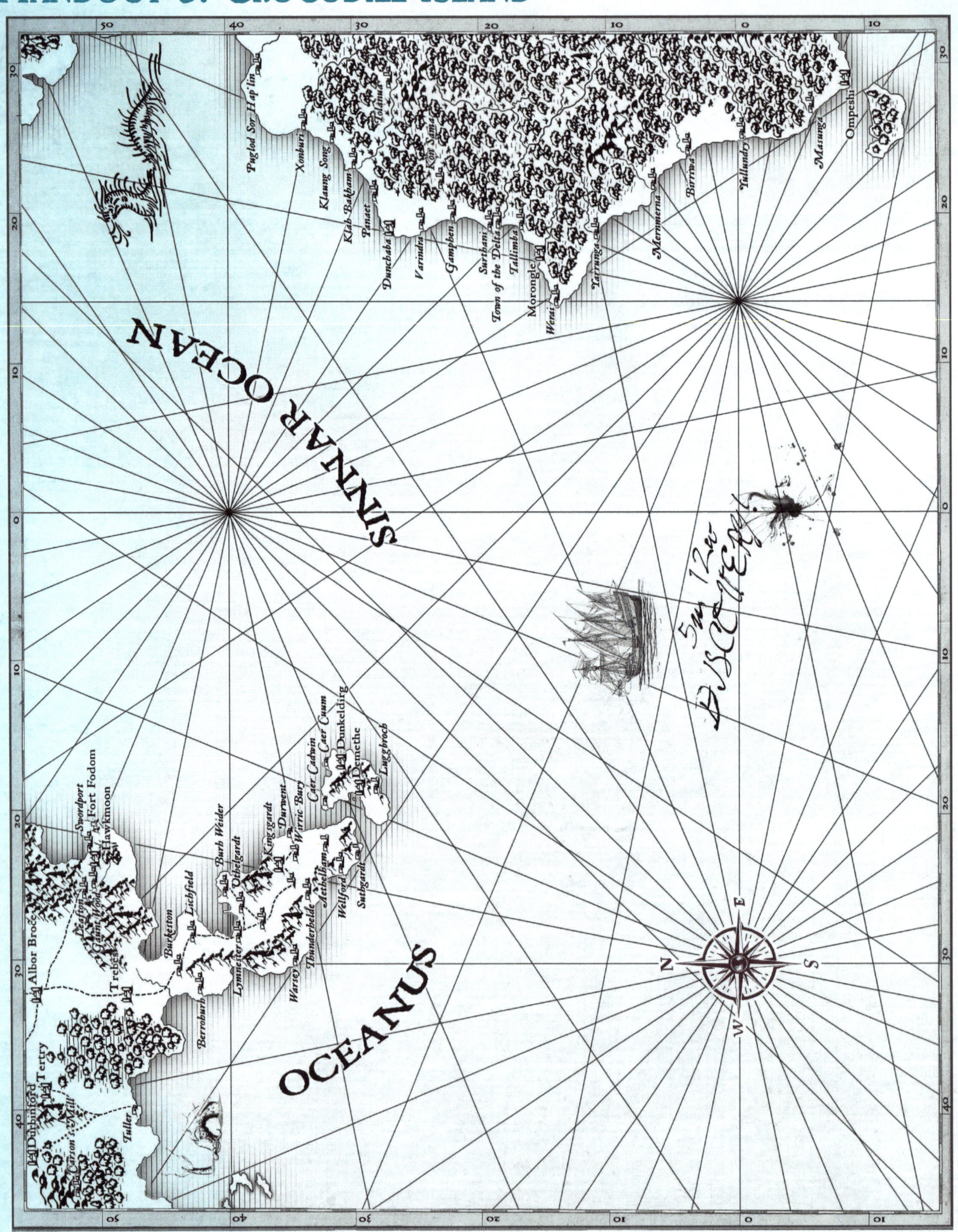

Winterfyll 15th

Depart Bridgeport for Warsley and then onto San Casco City I have a fine crew and a hold full of cotton and local produce We should be able to turn a solid coin in Warsley and in turn take on much grain and copper ore at Warsley, both of which are much sought after in San Casco Here is to another successful expedition!

Yule 8th

Without event, arrived at Warsley and started the process of selling our goods and buying new ones for our run to San Casco. Ran into that old drunk Jasper Cronks at The Tangled Rigging. He was bursting to tell me a "big secret" Cronks used to work for us before his drinking got the best of him Drunk as he was, he seemed to earnestly want to make it up to me by telling me about a small and uncharted island out in the Sinnar that he happened across on his way back west He claims that it is volcanic and that there is a bounty of peridot and onyx just lying about the place. I admit the samples he showed me were indeed fine He says that he and five of his sailors put ashore to look for fresh water. He said the sour stink of the place quickly changed his mind about looking for water, but that he found dozens of the stones just lying about on the beach. Finally, he told me that when he and his crew started to hack and cough because of the smell, they thought it best to bugger off I let him mark the spot on my chart but told him that it sounded like a fools quest The old sot remained insistent that what he was telling me was true And, while certainly a drunk, I have to admit that I never knew Cronks to be a liar. It still seems a fools errand to chase to some fanciful island off the known charts But as I felt bad for him and was more than a little intrigued by this story of a treasure-filled island, I decided to hire him back I made no promises about diverting to this fanciful island, but he was thrilled at the prospect of being at sea again.

Yule 10th

The past two days have been busy with selling our Bridgeport cotton and produce and buying grain and ore to sell in San Casco. We have done very well indeed! I was able to get better prices than I had hoped for Weighing on my mind is this island that the old soak Cronks spoke of "Crocodile Island" indeed How could a croc survive out in the middle of the ocean? Madness But if I am being honest with myself, I am excited about the very thought of a fortune like that just lying about It could take our business to a completely different level. We could live like kings! I must think on this longer

Yule 11th

Now that our business in Warsley is behind us this idea of a short side trip south to this little island is sounding like a better and better idea. We are already ahead of schedule, so a couple of weeks at most spent finding the place followed by a few days of filling chests with precious gems will not only not cost us any time but will make us the richest family in the region. Cronk is confident that he can navigate us to this island. The crew is behind me on this, so I would never forgive myself if I did not take advantage of this opportunity. It is what father would do. Fortune favors the bold!

Oeros 17th

Damned rudder is broken. Here we are in the middle of the Sinnar and have to undertake a rudder repair while at sea! That is not easy under the best of conditions. But I have a good crew and my carpenters are the best there are. We will get this done. Well we really don't have any choice, do we?

Foeros 3rd

That was a damned tricky fix. It took three separate tries to lower the repaired rudder into place as the damned waves would not give us a moment's respite! But now we are ready to go. We are quite a bit off course, having been blown south and west due to our lack of a rudder. The winds are favorable, so now onward to this mysterious island!

Freyrmond 16th

What a fortunate day! Both Quell and Belon were with us this day as we sighted the Discovery, a ship known to me, as is its captain, Captain Quindal. I had a chance to have dinner with Captain Quindal on his fine ship. It was good to see him again. I told him of our recent travails concerning our rudder. He graciously provided us some extra timber to replace that which was used in the repairs.

Because he has worked for us before and did more to train me in the seafaring life than any other, I trusted him with the details of our trip to the treasure-laden island. In fact, I shared the map coordinates Cronk gave me and encouraged Captain Quindal to trek there and explore it for himself. He pointedly asked after my father. I got the none-too-subtle hint. I assured him that I would hire a wizard in San Caseo to send an arcane message to father. That is our SOP in any event. Father always wants to hear that his ships and crew are well and on schedule. He will be in for quite a surprise when he learns of the vast fortune that I will have secured for the family!

Eostre 4th

Belon has been with us, for we have found the island! It is not very big and is clearly volcanic. Cronk was not exaggerating about the smell. Despite the nasty fumes, the place seems to flourish with life. We have anchored for the night. In the morning, I will lead an away team of two boats onto the island to claim our riches!

Handout 5: Kzanto's Map

Handout 6: Aquan Liturgy

PLAYER MAPS
THE GRISK PINEAPPLE PLANTATION

1 Square = 5 Feet

CROCODILE ISLAND
N
W
E
S
0 2 4 6 8 10
MILES

Tzar'Grandula — Part 1

Tzar'Grandula
200 Feet
8 Squares
The Tooth
Tunnel
Section Through

Craniform Colony

The Tooth — Side View

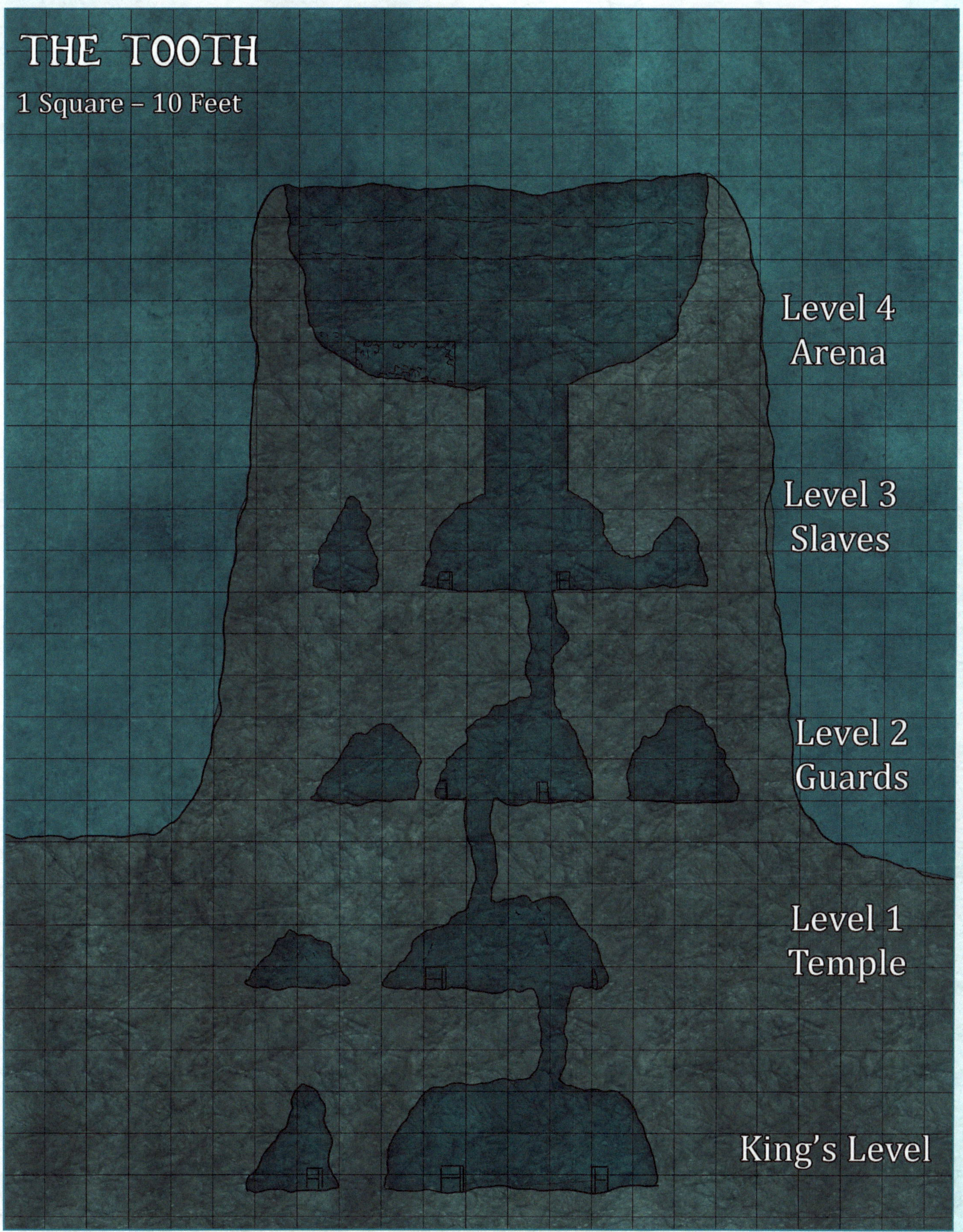

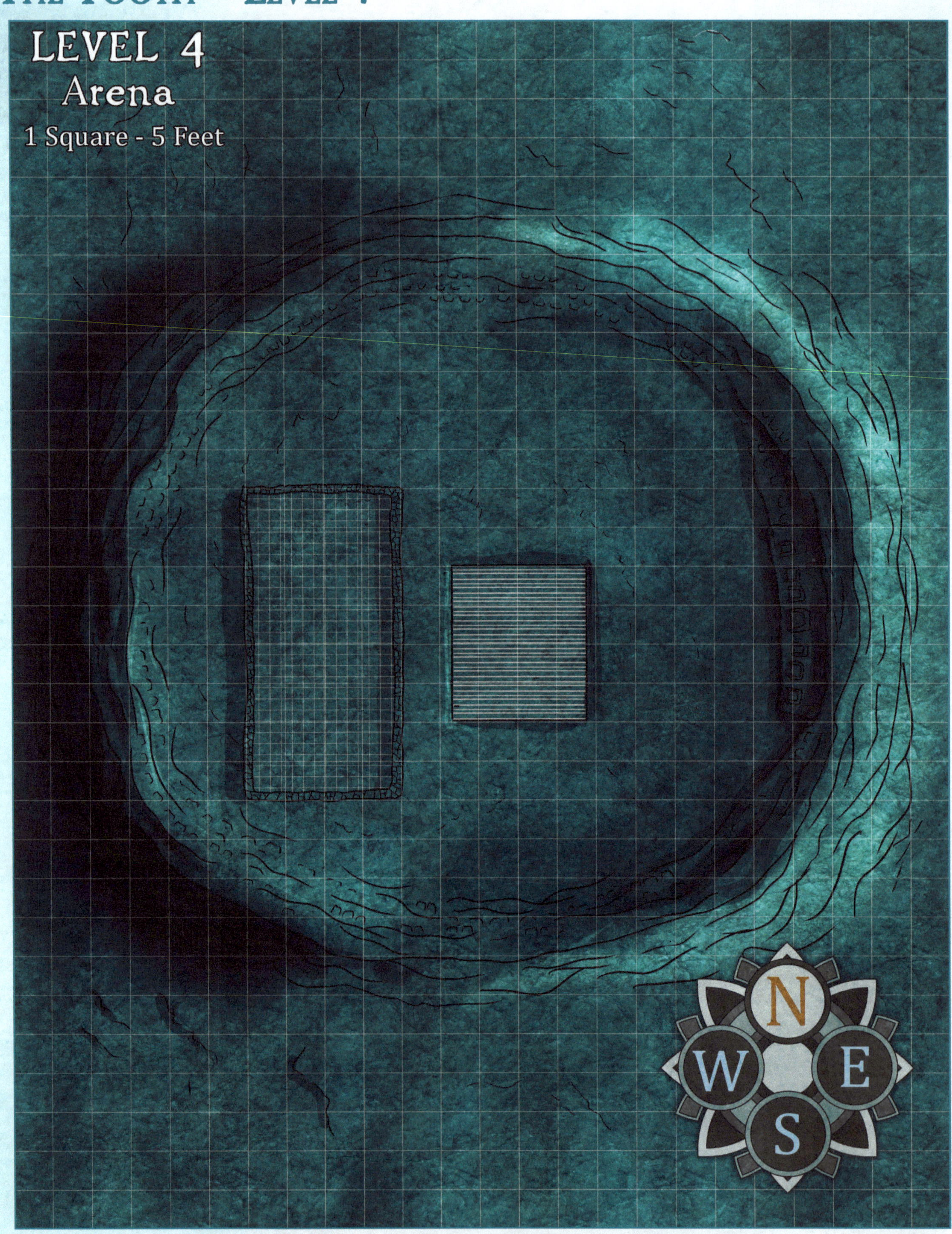

LEVEL 4
Arena
1 Square - 5 Feet
N
W
E
S

The Tooth — Level 3

The Tooth – Level 2

The Tooth — Level 1

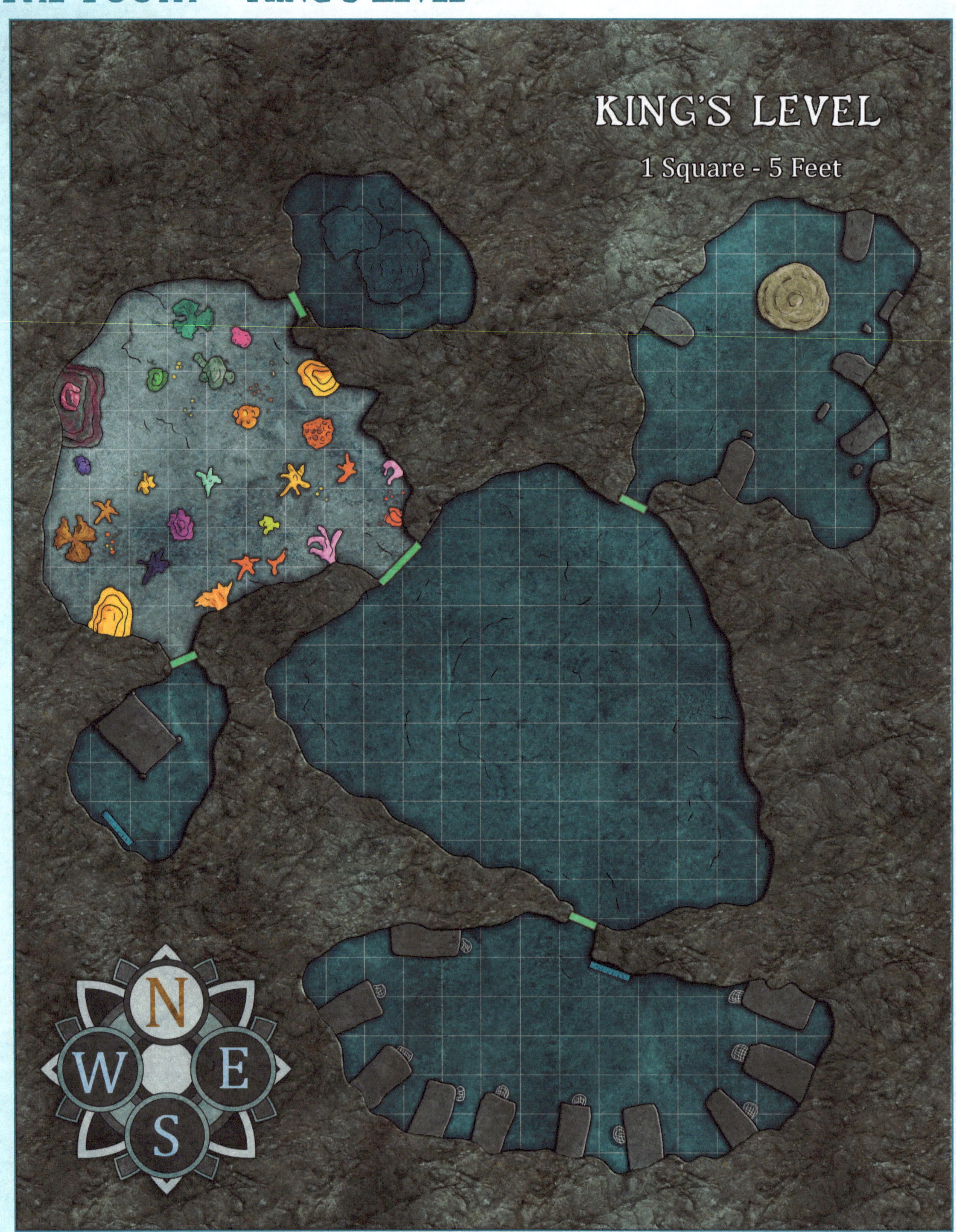
KING'S LEVEL
1 Square - 5 Feet
N
W
E
S

The Bounty

THE DISCOVERY